TRAPPED

The lunacy of the last few moments hit Candice hard. Was she actually in her transparently wet silk pajamas, in her swimming pool, with a determined ferret and a naked handyman, at six o'clock in the morning?

She was.

And no question about it, Austin Hyde was naked.

Lord, was he naked. Amazingly naked. Disturbingly naked.

And Candice realized his intent too late. In one smooth lunge his arms were on either side of her, her back against the pool wall.

There was no escape.

With agonizing slowness, Austin pressed his body against hers from toe to chest. The shock of it numbed her for an instant . . .

. . . before a riptide of sensation rocked her world. . . .

Mr. Hyde's Assets

Sheridon Smythe

LOVE SPELL BOOKS NEW YORK CITY

LOVE SPELL®

January 2000

Published by

Dorchester Publishing Co., Inc.
276 Fifth Avenue
New York, NY 10001

ISBN 0-505-52356-6

Printed in the United States of America.

To my wonderful big sister, Pat Diamond, for her loving support throughout the years. When I hear your warm, infectious laugh, I'm reminded of your big heart and sweet nature. Thanks for believing in me. I love you!

—Sherrie Eddington

If you ever doubt that there is a God in Heaven, watch the miracle of birth.

Sadly many babies are born into abusive or neglectful situations. Yet there are a like number of potential parents out there who would give anything to love and cherish the little one someone else doesn't want.

I'd like to dedicate this book to all those wonderful people like my friend Misty Sanders, with hearts full of love to give to a child. The ones who keep trying no matter the odds, whether it's in vitro, artificial insemination, or adoption. Don't give up. It will happen. Also, for little Anna Marie and her parents, Brad and Tina. A few of the really lucky ones.

—Donna Smith

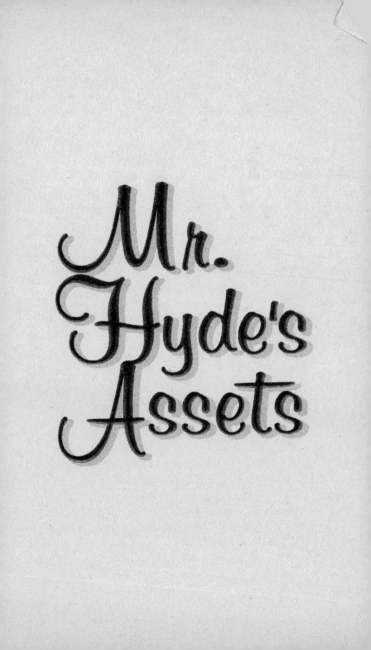

Mr. Hyde's Assets

Chapter One

"Test tube babies," Austin Hyde muttered, wiping at his forehead.

Damn Jack Cruise anyway for running such an embarrassing place as this clinic for in vitro fertilization and artificial insemination, he thought.

With one last sweep of the brush, he finished painting the rosy red mouth on the smiling baby, then carefully descended the ladder several steps so that he could study the sign that read, LITTLE MIRACLES, GENETIC REPRODUCTION.

Austin frowned, dangling the brush from his fingertips as he ran his gaze slowly over his creation, a lifelike image of a chubby infant wearing nothing more than an old-fashioned triangle diaper and a smile. Not bad—although he had no intention of telling Jack how many days he'd spent sneaking peeks into strollers to impress the image in his mind.

Below the ladder, two elderly women slowed to admire the little cherub, shading their eyes against the bright April sunshine as they grinned up at Austin. He grinned back, and they tittered like teenagers before moving on.

Still smiling, he climbed down and removed his shirt, using it to wipe the sweat from his chest and neck. After he painted the rattle in the baby's hand, he'd be finished. Jack had been very specific about the rattle. Blue—with yellow stripes.

Crazy guy.

Of course, Austin had recognized the weirdness of his half brother's mind a long time ago, and it amazed him that Jack Cruise had settled for a Ph.D. in biochemistry and managing this clinic rather than finishing medical school, which might have enabled him to personally experiment on hapless victims.

Thank God he hadn't!

Yet was this really preferable—Jack working at a sperm bank? Did he do these things just to torture Austin? When they were kids, Austin had had to bloody a few noses over Jack's nerdy appearance; he now had to defend Jack's crazy profession much the same way. Given how different they were, sometimes it was hard to believe they'd shared the same mother.

Austin shuddered, flinging his damp shirt across a ladder rung and turning in time to see a white BMW purr up to the curb on the opposite side of the street. With casual interest, he watched as the door opened. Tanned, narrow feet encased in delicate leather sandals stepped onto the pavement.

Attached to the feet were a pair of long, slim legs.

His interest sharpened. Slowly, he lowered his sunglasses down his nose, an appreciative smile curving his mouth. Maybe his day wasn't wasted after all, he thought.

The woman stood and adjusted the short white sundress that definitely complemented her golden skin, then shut the car door. A warm breeze ruffled her blond, shoulder-length hair and played havoc with the flared skirt of her dress.

She looked elegant, sassy, and sexy all rolled into one heart-hammering package.

Austin wished she'd remove her oversized shades. With a body that perfect, there had to be a flaw somewhere. Bushy eyebrows at the very least. Mesmerized, he watched her cross the street and head in his direction. She walked like a dream, and as she came closer, he realized her legs were bare of anything but her tan.

But wait, surely she wasn't coming *here*, to the artificial babymaker.

She was. Heading straight for the clinic. Austin felt a pang of disappointment; without a doubt most of the clinic's clients were *couples*. Ah, hell, he should have known a woman that gorgeous would be taken.

Still, he wouldn't mind getting a look at her eyes, just to satisfy his curiosity. He was thinking of a logical excuse to stop her when a white van bearing the logo *Sacramento Star* screeched to a halt at the curb.

At the sight of the news van, the woman faltered in the middle of the street. Frantically, she swung her head around as if considering making a run back to her car.

Austin frowned, checking the traffic the blonde might have to brave to avoid the guy getting out of the van. What was going on? Was she a celebrity? If so, Austin didn't recognize her. But then, he spent most nights painting canvases, not watching television.

"Mrs. Vanausdale! Can I ask you a few questions?"

The strident voice came from the young man stepping out of the van. His newsprint tie clashed with the light blue crumpled summer suit he wore, as did his worn tennis shoes. He looked as if he'd rummaged through a yard sale for the ensemble.

Austin took in the heavy Nikon camera swinging from the man's neck, the lens reflecting the sunlight as it swayed to and fro. The reporter paused a moment to push a thick lock of brown hair from his eyes before slamming the van door and darting out into the street and into the woman's path.

She squared her shoulders and moved around him, but the persistent reporter followed, clicking away with his camera and circling her like a hungry vulture.

"Mrs. Vanausdale, is it true that you once worked in a Burger Barn, making less than minimum wage?"

She walked faster, high heels clicking on the pavement. Austin felt a pang of sympathy for the blonde, figuring he should do the proper Boy Scout thing and help her out. He tensed, ready to step in if the reporter didn't back off before she reached the building.

"How about your alcoholic stepfather? Is he still around? Will you go back to working at the burger joint if you lose your inheritance? Mrs. Vanausdale, will you have the baby if you lose the case?"

Austin saw her lips tighten. When she reached the door, he stepped up to block the reporter's progress. He placed a firm but gentle

13

hand in the middle of the guy's chest to halt his headlong rush after Mrs. Vanausdale. "Get lost," he ordered.

"I just want to ask Mrs. Vanausdale a question before—"

"You asked, and she didn't answer. Take a hint."

"But—"

"Get lost. The lady doesn't want to talk to you."

"Look, mister—"

Austin dropped his hand but took a threatening step forward. The man backed away, stumbling over the curb and falling on his butt. Keeping a wary eye on Austin, he scrambled up and crawled into the van, muttering beneath his breath.

"Thank you."

The soft, grateful voice reminded Austin of tanning oil left out in the sun—hot and sensual.

The blonde had taken off her sunglasses, Austin saw when he turned around. Her eyes were green—no, gold. Golden-green. Beautiful cat's eyes, he thought with a groan. Now why did she have to go and be beautiful all over? She was supposed to have a big nose or crossed eyes. Damn. There should be a law against being that pretty.

"Do you do this often?"

Austin blinked, suddenly aware of how he must look, bare-chested, arms akimbo. He moved to the ladder and grabbed his shirt, curiously embarrassed. "Do what often?" Drool? Pant? Get aroused over the sight of pink toenails? She was married—and rich, by the looks of it. Two strikes against her. Damn, why did she have to be rich? The marriage part he might have forgiven, but not the wealth. He'd had his fill of that type. Then again, maybe she'd be willing to give it all up and live simply, as he did. *And have you forgotten what the reporter said? She's pregnant, you fool.*

No, he hadn't forgotten. It was just hard to imagine. His gaze dipped to the shadowy cleavage revealed by her dress, then moved on down to those smooth, wonderful legs. Thank God for shades; they allowed him to look his fill without coming off as an ogler.

She brushed a golden strand of windswept hair from her cheek and nodded at the news van still parked at the curb. "Rescue women in distress."

Rescue women in distress? Ha! If only she could read his mind. On second thought, he didn't have the money for bail. "Only when they're being chased by obnoxious reporters."

She smiled, and this time Austin was ready for her—he thought. He shifted, distracting himself by shrugging into his shirt. Hell, he needed *something* to distract him, before she figured out what was on his mind from the tight stretch of his jeans over a certain area.

"Thanks again."

"Any time," he muttered, watching her push through the clinic door and disappear behind the tinted glass. Rattled more than he cared to admit, he got back to business. He spent the next several minutes reminding himself that she wasn't his type—and married, to boot—trying to erase her from his mind.

Thirty minutes later, he finished the sign, wondering when the blonde would reappear. Maybe he should go inside and find something cool to drink. Perhaps take a casual look around. He couldn't be blamed for being thirsty, could he?

He stopped short just inside the door when he caught sight of the reporter arguing with Jack. How . . . ? He glanced outside to the news van still parked at the curb, then back at the reporter. Jack sounded annoyed, which made Austin grin despite his irritation.

Something, apparently, had finally ruffled his unflappable little brother.

"How many times do I have to repeat myself? I will not, cannot, release confidential information on *any* of our clients."

Good for him, Austin thought. Now, how in hell had the reporter gotten inside?

"I'll pay you twenty thousand dollars for Candice Vanausdale's records," the reporter announced outrageously.

Austin whistled between his teeth. Twenty thousand wasn't something to snicker about. Would Jack . . . ? Nah. Austin shook his head. Jack was crazy, but he *did* have ethics.

"I don't care if you offer me fifty thousand, I still—"

"Okay, fifty thousand. But for that amount, I want a sample of—"

"You're sick, you know that? I'd be ashamed to leave my house if I were you. For the last time, our records are not for sale."

"If you'll just let me take a peek, I won't reveal my sources," the reporter persisted.

Austin took a lazy step away from the wall and crossed his arms. Jack might just need his help on this one.

"Get out before I call the cops!"

Whoa, Nelly! Jack sounded hopping mad. Austin couldn't keep a silly grin from his face. Maybe nerdy, mad-scientist Jack, who as a child had scared him more times than he could remember with his hare-brained experiments, deserved to be hassled. Still, he thought with a sigh, Jack was his little brother, and nobody pushed his little brother around.

With a fatalistic shrug, Austin sauntered over and inserted himself between the two men. The reporter outweighed his miniature brother by fifty pounds, which still left him about half the size of Austin.

The reporter's eyes widened in recognition, but this time he'd made it *into* the clinic and obviously wasn't going to give up easily. He made a halfhearted effort at curling his lip.

Jack snickered.

Austin narrowed his eyes.

"You again," the reporter quavered. "Excuse us, we're having a conversation here. I believe the bathroom's that way."

Austin smiled pleasantly. He preferred to handle things with the minimum amount of damage. "I believe the *door* is *that* way."

"This is none of your business, mister. Why don't you go back to cleaning the toilets or whatever it is you do and let me do *my* job?"

"I'm an artist, not a plumber. Although I do dabble in metal pipes on the side—weight-lifting." Deliberately, Austin ran an assessing eye up and down the reporter's thin frame, as if judging his meager poundage.

The reporter missed the subtle warning. He craned his neck around Austin's broad shoulders. "Mr. Cruise, I—"

Austin shifted casually, blocking his access to Jack. "Actually, you should call him Dr. Jekyll— and *I'm* Mr. Hyde."

This time, the reporter caught Austin's implication. His eyes widened in alarm, and he let out a squeak as Austin picked him up and slung him over his shoulder like a sack of grain.

"Hey, put me down, you—"

Austin did, gently—right on his backside in the middle of the hot sidewalk outside the building.

When Austin glanced toward the spot where the BMW had been parked, he saw that it was gone. He experienced a curious letdown, knowing he wouldn't see the blonde again. She must have left by the side entrance while Jack stalled the reporter. Who must have sneaked in earlier by that same side entrance.

Just as well the woman was gone, Austin told himself firmly. Her kind would be nothing but trouble to a guy like him.

Dusting off his hands, he strode back inside, whistling a jaunty tune to drown out the reporter's inventive curses. Jack waited for him, grinning that sheepish smile that always made Austin want to ruffle his thick, dark hair. He resisted the urge.

Clapping him on the back, Jack asked, "What would I do without you? Did you see the look on the guy's face when you told him you were an artist? Of course, that's the same look everyone gets—no one believes a bruiser like you could be hiding the soul of a sensitive, creative type. Let's go to my office and I'll get you a Coke."

Austin didn't protest; painting, not to mention throwing reporters out on their butts, was thirsty work. He chose to ignore Jack's laughing reference to his insensitive-looking body. Who the hell said an artist had to have a certain look, anyway?

"Thanks for the help, Aussy."

"Don't call me that," Austin warned. "And you owe me five hundred bucks for the sign."

"And I'll pay you, I'll pay you. Of course, you'd be doing me a favor by waiting until the fifteenth. I'm expecting a large check by then." Jack closed his office door and motioned Austin to take a seat, loosening his tie as he made for his own comfortable chair behind the desk. "Whew! I can't believe the nerve of those guys. Vultures, every one of them."

Austin lifted an eyebrow as Jack paused for breath. "That Coke you mentioned?"

"Yes?"

"Where is it?"

Jack slapped his forehead and jumped up, removing two frosty cans from a compact refrigerator. He opened them and handed one to Austin before flopping back into his chair with a noisy sigh. "As I was saying, she came to sign a few papers, and that reporter followed her right into the clinic!"

Austin eyed his brother over the soda. So the reporter was right. If the blonde had come to sign papers, then she must have "purchased" a baby, either through in vitro or artificial insemination. "Who is this Candice Vanausdale, anyway?" he asked.

"Don't tell me you've never heard of her. Rich tycoon's wife? Howard Vanausdale? Third richest man in the state of California? He owned every Howard Clothing store in the United States." Jack shook his head as if he couldn't comprehend Austin's ignorance. "His wife has made the headlines several times in the past year."

"What's so special about her?" Austin tried to sound uninterested, but every nerve ending seemed to stand at attention as he waited for the answer. He should forget about her. Hadn't Jack just told him how wealthy she was? How married?

"I'm glad you asked that question. She *is* special, and I've been waiting for the right time to talk to you about her."

Uh-oh. Austin didn't like the sound of that. Maybe he didn't want to know about the infamous Mrs. Vanausdale after all. Jack was acting even more strangely than usual, and Austin's instincts regarding his brother rarely failed him. Jack grinned, but Austin detected the telltale tic in his left cheek.

Frissons of alarm lifted the hair on his arms. It reminded him of why he'd nicknamed Jack Dr. Jekyll in the first place. Jack, injecting the nanny's food with his own brand of Spanish fly, just to see if anything would happen . . . For years afterward Austin had forced Jack to sample his food before he would touch it. And that was only one of many such incidents. Austin knew Jack didn't do his experiments out of spite, yet sometimes he still felt like wringing his scrawny neck.

"Well, it's really sad what happened to Mrs. Vanausdale. Sad, sad story." Jack shook his head.

Austin slowly lowered the Coke to his knee, his gaze on Jack's face. He couldn't shake his bad feeling, and when Jack became redundant, it increased the feeling. Hell. "Go on."

Jack fiddled with his tie, twisting it around and around. "She and her husband were planning to have a baby, in vitro, which you know is the fertilization of the egg in a lab—"

"I know. Go on." Austin gritted his teeth, remembering the last time he'd wanted to beat the holy crap out of Jack. He was sixteen and suffering from incredible itching on the soles of his feet. It didn't take him long to tie the affliction to Jack. Buckling under torture, Jack finally confessed to planting homemade itch powder in Austin's socks—just to see if his recipe would work, of course.

Given the kind of experimenting Jack had grown up to do, Austin feared this might be something a bit more serious.

"Remember, this information is strictly confidential." Jack frowned. "I shouldn't even be telling you." When Austin remained silent, he went on. "Anyway, they had begun the process, and we were about to check the potency of Mr. Vanausdale's sperm—"

Austin cleared his throat, never comfortable when Jack began rattling on about such things.

"—when Howard's plane went down over the Atlantic Ocean."

What a nasty break, Austin thought, ashamed of the relief he felt on hearing the news. She wasn't married. Of course, she was still rich. And still pregnant. Shrugging, he said, "She looks young. She could remarry someday. Have babies with her next husband."

"She could." Jack propped his feet on the desk and studied his shoes. "But she doesn't have to. In fact, she told me she doesn't intend to ever remarry. Howard's been dead almost a year, but she went ahead with the in vitro three months ago. It was a successful venture."

"Using her husband's . . . ?" Of course she had. What a stupid question. Austin frowned as Jack began to twist his tie again.

"Not exactly." Jack laughed a little too heartily.

Austin didn't like the sound of that laugh. Not one bit. "What do you mean, not exactly?"

Jack jumped up from the chair as if his pants had caught fire. With a nervous smile, he removed a newspaper from the neat stack on the corner of his desk and thrust it into Austin's hands. "Look at that." He tapped the front page for emphasis. "Ain't she a beauty? Reminds me of an angel. Now, could you say no to a face like that?"

Reluctant to tell Jack he'd met her in the flesh—and what flesh—Austin glanced at the black-and-white photo, scanning the caption. *Candice Vanausdale, wealthy widow of deceased tycoon Howard Vanausdale, uses husband's frozen sperm to keep inheritance.*

By the time he finished reading the article below the picture of the solemn-faced blonde, he discovered a very nasty taste in his mouth. He took a swig of the Coke and tossed the paper onto the desk.

"She did it for the money?" Saying the words felt ugly. Austin didn't care how beautiful Candice Vanausdale was, he couldn't respect someone who brought a child into the world for the sake of money. Just as he couldn't respect people who believed money could take the place of affection and good old-fashioned love.

Jack felt that way, too. So why . . .

"She'd planned to have a child anyway, Austin." Jack replaced the newspaper in the pile and carefully realigned the edges. His gaze flitted nervously from Austin to the papers, then back to Austin. "You read the article. Howard's family—his two greedy sons, in cahoots with an estranged uncle—is trying to take everything just because Candice didn't produce an heir."

"Not enough reason to have a child," Austin growled. "Hell, the father's dead!"

"Uh, no, he's not."

Dumbfounded, Austin stood and leaned over the desk. Jack edged back in his seat, his face paling. Now Austin *knew* something was up. "I know you're going to tell me where this is leading, little brother. I also know I'm not going to like it." He lowered his voice another octave, signaling danger. "Am I?"

Jack stared at the bulging muscles in Austin's exposed forearms and visibly swallowed.

That did it.

Austin grabbed the lapels of Jack's lab coat

and lifted him out of the chair, bringing them nose to nose across the desk. "It's been a long time since I beat the crap out of you."

"We're grown men—"

"*One* of us is," Austin hissed. *"What is it?"* He shook Jack lightly, consciously leashing his strength despite his growing agitation. Adrenaline rushed into his veins, triggering his panic button. Jack—Jack Cruise was the only person in the world whose antics could make him afraid. "What did you do this time, Jack?"

Jack's voice came out in a croaking whisper, but Austin felt no compulsion to loosen his grip. "When I tested the old man's specimen a few days before the first scheduled procedure—just before he died—the count wasn't only low, it was nonexistent."

Austin frowned. Something wasn't clicking, although he sensed it should be. He'd never paid much attention to the medical terms Jack spouted like poetry. Now he wished he had. "But you just said the operation was successful."

"It . . . it was." Jack licked his lips. "She wanted a baby so desperately, you see, and I just couldn't tell her the truth."

"The truth." Austin knew he wasn't making sense, but he seemed helpless to complete a sentence.

Jack managed to nod. "Right."

Abruptly, Austin let go. Jack fell into the chair, gasping for breath. Overplaying it, Austin thought, refusing to feel guilty. He took a deep breath himself. "I hope you didn't do what I think you did, Dr. Jekyll."

Jack shrugged helplessly. "I couldn't help myself. I figured it wouldn't do any harm, and who's to know? As soon as I found out the in vitro was a success, I disposed of the evidence." A note of desperation crept into his voice. "If you had been me, you wouldn't have been able to look into those gorgeous, tragic—"

"Cut the crap, Bozo," Austin snapped, edgily running his fingers through his hair. "You could go to prison for this, you know. Have you thought of that? If anyone finds out you used another man's *specimen* in place of Howard Vanausdale's, *you could go to jail.*"

How many times had he repeated this scare tactic to Jack since he'd began messing with his first chemistry set at the age of seven? He'd lost count. He blew out an exasperated breath that made Jack jump.

"I know I should have thought it through. I'm sorry, Austin."

And how many times had that same pitiful response echoed back to him? An equal number of times. Austin glared at his brother, weary to the bone. "What if the baby doesn't look anything like her husband and she gets suspicious? It scares the hell out of me to think I helped you with the freezing experiments when you first got this job at this godforsaken cloning clinic—"

Jack whimpered. *Whimpered.*

Austin froze in the act of pitching his empty Coke into the wastebasket. His incredulous gaze pinned Jack to the chair. "You didn't."

Jack whimpered again.

"You didn't. Say you didn't. Tell me *now!*" The can fell to the floor with a clatter. "Tell me I'm wrong, tell me I'm crazy for thinking what I'm thinking."

He waited. Frozen, petrified, and almost positive he was going to have to kill Jack. When his half brother tried to shrink into the chair, he knew he was doomed.

"I—I'm sorry, Austin. I—I doubt the baby *will* look anything like Mrs. Vanausdale's late husband, because *you* don't look anything like her husband."

Blood pounded in Austin's ears until he thought it would deafen him.

But no, it wasn't his blood pounding; it was someone knocking on the door of Jack's office. With angry, jerky steps, Austin stalked to the door. He didn't care if it turned out to be the President; he'd get rid of whoever it was because he didn't want anyone to witness the bloody scene that was about to occur.

He yanked it open. "You'll have to come—" he began.

His stomach bottomed out in a sickening rush.

He'd recognize those gorgeous cat's eyes anywhere.

Chapter Two

It was her!

Standing there with her hand poised to knock again was Candice Vanausdale, the rich widow of tycoon Howard Vanausdale—and, according to Jack, *the mother of Austin's baby*.

Austin thought he would croak. He was certain his heart actually stopped beating for the number of seconds it took her to speak. A quick glance behind him told him Jack had turned white, as if he had seen a ghost. And he—he probably looked like a man on the imminent verge of a heart attack, with a red, sweating face and round, terror-stricken eyes. No wonder she looked puzzled.

The silence in the room drowned out the pounding in his ears.

"Am I interrupting something?"

Same soft, husky voice, smooth as aged whisky—and just as deceptive. Austin stared, noticing a dimple in her chin and wondering— due to shock, he was certain—if their baby would inherit the trademark. It sure as hell wouldn't inherit anything from Howard Vanausdale!

Jack recovered first, jumping to his feet and racing around the desk, his nervousness seeming to vanish as his professional manner took over. Austin wished it was that simple for him. All he could do was gawk at her cat's eyes and try to imagine her rocking a colicky baby in the middle of the night. Or, even less imaginable, changing a dirty diaper. Come to think of it, he couldn't imagine *himself* doing any such thing, either.

But wasn't a mother supposed to, rather than hire a tight-lipped nanny who smiled when parents were around and pinched when they weren't? He swallowed hard and gripped the doorknob until he was certain he left marks in the galvanized steel.

"Mrs. Vanausdale! What brings you back?" Jack cried, coming forward to take her hand.

When Jack passed him, Austin stopped himself from snarling out loud. Instead, he nearly twisted the doorknob off in an effort to keep his hands from circling Jack's neck.

"I can't find my purse, and—"

"Your purse!" Jack opened his mouth in mock horror.

Austin wanted to shove his fist into it.

"Of course! I found it right after you left and put it in a safe place. I was going to call, but a little something came up." He risked another glance at Austin, openly pleading.

Austin swallowed a snort. Oh, something came up all right, but it was hardly little. And it was going to get bigger. Much bigger. Like the knot he was going to put on Jack's head.

Mrs. Vanausdale swiped a nervous tongue over her bottom lip, looking distinctly uneasy, Austin thought. But then, a person would have to be both deaf and blind to miss the tension in the room. And if she hung around very long, she'd get a complimentary ticket to a violent wrestling match.

When she settled her gaze on Jack again, a warm, spontaneous smile curved her full lips, causing a startling kick in Austin's gut. He wanted her to smile at *him* that way.

Well, hell, did he like her or not?

He couldn't decide, because he didn't know the *real* Mrs. Vanausdale. Would the real Mrs. Vanausdale send a nanny to the hospital with her child for a tonsillectomy, just so she wouldn't miss the first day of her cruise to the Bahamas? Would the real Mrs. Vanausdale hire an entire circus to host her son's birthday party in the hopes he wouldn't notice that she wasn't there?

That soft, enticing voice broke into his unpleasant memories.

"The purse?" she reminded Jack hesitantly.

Jack slapped his forehead and raced around his desk, jerking drawers open until he came to the last one. He pulled a white beaded bag out and, with a triumphant smile, brought it to her. "There you go! If you need anything else, just let me know."

She flashed him a grateful smile and took the purse. "Remember, if you think of anyone—"

"I will, I will. Keep in touch, and don't forget to call when the little miracle gets here!"

"Yes, yes, I will, Dr. Jack." She smiled again, darting a quick, shy glance at Austin.

Jack shut the door on the retreating woman and hastily scurried to his chair behind the desk.

Austin wondered if he was stupid enough to believe the sizable hunk of wood would protect him. Dr. Jack, indeed. Dr. Jekyll was more like it. This time, Jack had gone too far. "You can't do this. It's not only unethical, it's illegal!"

"It's done." Jack shrugged helplessly. "This

isn't like going to the store for a refund, Austin. Candice Vanausdale is pregnant, and she's going to have the baby."

"My baby." Austin returned to his chair and sat down abruptly, bending his head forward between his knees. He'd kill Jack, as soon as he was certain he wouldn't pass out. This was impossible, wasn't it? He was going to be a father, and he hadn't even had sex with the woman!

"Are you okay?" Concern made Jack momentarily forget his fear. "Austin . . . I'm sorry, I really am. I didn't know you would get this upset, and—"

Austin's head shot up, stopping Jack's words. Spots danced before his eyes. He took a deep, slow breath. In, out. Carefully. There, his head began to clear. At least he was spared the humiliation—and danger—of fainting in front of Jack. God knew what parts of his body might be missing when he came to.

"This is insane," he muttered, glaring at his brother. "I can't believe you did this to me."

"I couldn't help it, Aussy. She was so eager to have her baby, and I—I just did it. I replaced her husband's specimen with yours before our doctor did the procedure."

"Without thinking it through."

"Without thinking it through. I should be shot, I know, but if you had been there—"

"I would have said no," Austin cut in harshly. "I would have told her the truth, just like you're going to do."

Eyes wide, Jack began to shake his head. "No, no. I can't tell her. As you said, I could go to prison, and—"

"So?" Austin carefully rose from the chair. "You deserve it, you little weasel. We'll give her time to get home, then you're going to pick up the phone and call her."

"And tell her what? That she's going to have my half brother's baby? A *stranger's* baby?" Jack laughed shakily. "She'd have my butt in jail so fast, my head would spin."

Good, Austin thought, because his *was* spinning. He felt no sympathy. True, he was a stranger to Mrs. Vanausdale; he didn't think their brief encounter conferred familiarity—or warranted sharing a baby, as much as he admired her physically. But he couldn't forget the things she might do for money. And he would not—*would not*—have his child raised in that environment. "You're going to tell her."

"Austin, I—"

"Jack." He took a threatening step forward, and Jack hastily nodded.

"Okay, okay, I'll tell her."

Austin turned away, forcing his shaky legs to move in the direction of the door.

"Where are you going?"

"To the john. When I come back, you'd better have your story rehearsed." Stalking out, Austin headed for the bathroom and some cold, reviving water.

Dear Lord, how could this have happened? He felt hot all over, mostly from embarrassment. To think, that drop-dead gorgeous woman was at this moment carrying *his* child, and she didn't even know it! Would she be disgusted to learn the father wasn't a rich tycoon with Mayflower ancestors but an unemployed aspiring artist? Of course, he could always reassure her by showing her his bank account.

But no, he wasn't touching the ill-gotten money left to him by his father, not for her or anyone. It could sit in the bank and rot, for all he cared.

He made it to the bathroom and stoppered the sink drain, letting the basin fill with cold water before he quickly doused his face and neck.

She was rich, and he knew what rich women did with their children. They paid a nanny to take care of them, tuck them into bed, and soothe their aches and pains. Later, when they were old enough, they sent them to expensive boarding schools in Switzerland and promptly forgot about them.

Austin knew. Hell, Jack knew it, too. As children, they had both sworn never to do the same to their own offspring. He grabbed a towel and mopped the water from his face. Jack knew how he felt, yet he had done this anyway. Well, he could just *un*do it.

Wishing it were that simple, he returned to the office. Jack offered him a wavering smile. Austin scowled, doubting he'd ever forgive his brother for this latest stunt. "Well?"

Jack evidently found the wall very interesting. "I'll call her . . . and make an appointment, tell her we've got something important to talk to her about. I think you should be the one to tell her. Gently." A quick glance at Austin's clenched fists rushed him on. "This is going to be a shock, and—"

"Oh, really?" Austin snarled sarcastically.

"—and it could be harmful in her condition."

Austin hadn't thought of that. Hell, he hadn't thought of a single practical thing since Jack told him the alarming news. What, exactly, did he plan to do about the child.

Damn Jack for getting him into this mess in the first place!

In the safe haven of her designated workroom on the second floor of the Vanausdale mansion, Candice blew the dust from the miniature ottoman and set the sandpaper aside. A little varnish, she mused, and it would be finished. With a nervous mixture of guilt and pride, she placed the carved oak ottoman inside the doll-house in front of the matching chair she'd made last week. She ran a finger over the upholstery on the chair and along the smooth varnished wood the ottoman would soon match.

A fifty-fifty chance she'd have a girl. And if she didn't . . . Candice shrugged. No reason a boy couldn't enjoy a dollhouse. The sex of her child mattered little to her; a healthy baby was all she wanted.

Staring at the two-story dollhouse she'd painstakingly created over the past year, she struggled to forget Howard's reaction to her artistic efforts.

It was no use.

Each time she completed a new piece of furniture, Howard's scornful laughter would mock her. *Why waste your time on this silly handmade stuff when we can buy the best? Our baby will have everything money can buy.*

Ugly, relentless memories time had not faded. She wanted to forget, tried to, but she couldn't shake the fear that at any moment her condescending late husband would pop up and ridicule her heartfelt handiwork.

Steeped in her dark thoughts, Candice jumped as the housekeeper slid a tray onto the desk. She hadn't heard Mrs. Merryweather approach, although she'd left the door open, comfortable with the fact that she and the other woman were alone in the enormous house.

"Here's your lunch. Just what you've been cravin', spinach salad with crumbled bacon and chopped egg."

Candice rubbed her hands in appreciation. "Thank you, Mrs. Merryweather. I'm starved."

"Well, you're lucky. I couldn't keep anything down for the first six months with all three of my young'uns." She gave a rueful shake of her head. "Guess that should've been a warning of how much trouble they were going to be."

"I do get queasy when I smell coffee."

"Yes, you do."

"And certain perfumes or colognes."

"Nothing strange about that. Now, when you start cravin' dirt, we'll worry." The housekeeper laughed and moved to the window to pull aside the curtains.

Candice hadn't realized the noonday sun had passed over and the room had grown dark, she'd been so engrossed in her work. She stretched and rubbed the grit from her eyes. "Aren't you going to join me for lunch?"

Mrs. Merryweather plopped her hands on her ample hips and shook her head, her admiring eyes on the gleaming white dollhouse trimmed in bright red. "Already eaten, thank you. I've made lemonade and a fresh batch of cookies, in case those men are hungry." She peered into the house, exclaiming over a tiny braided rug in front of the fireplace. "Ooh, look at that!"

Candice followed her pointing finger, flushing at her admiring tone. She couldn't get used to hearing praise instead of scorn. "I made it yesterday."

"Why, it looks so real!"

Candice ducked her head to hide the silly tears that sprang to her eyes. She cried at the drop of a hat these days. "Thanks. What time is it?"

Mrs. Merryweather straightened the rug and carefully dusted the furniture with a single feather she had pulled from the duster in her hand, a comical look of concentration on her face. Candice smiled, thinking she wouldn't have to worry about dust in the dollhouse as long as the housekeeper lived and breathed.

"Time for the applicants to start arriving. Are you sure you don't want to sit in on the interviews?" Her light brown eyes regarded Candice through the miniature kitchen as she rehung a tiny copper pot that had fallen from its hook.

Folding her napkin in her lap, Candice picked up her fork and speared a piece of egg. "I'm sure. I'm especially sure you know more about hiring a handyman than I do. Howard . . . Howard always took care of those things." She frowned into her salad, adding a piece of fresh spinach to the fork. It didn't mean that she wasn't capable, of course, just that she wasn't *comfortable*.

"We've got to be careful who we hire, you know. They could be spies for *them*, or from the tabloids."

Just what she needed—one of the enemy in her camp. Candice shuddered at the thought of her ruthless in-laws succeeding in getting someone inside, the bite of food in danger of sticking in her throat. She swallowed hard. "Maybe we should have the FBI run a check on anyone we consider for the job."

Tiny copper pots clanged together as Mrs. Merryweather removed her hand and looked at her sharply over the roof. "I'm serious. And it wouldn't hurt to ask if they've had any experience in bodyguarding, either."

"That would be a bonus," Candice said wryly. Although she couldn't imagine anyone *that* versatile. What she really needed was a handyman who knew something about everything and was also talented enough to help her finish the nursery. Really, Mrs. Merryweather wasn't thinking rationally. Such a man, at a price they could afford, likely didn't even exist.

Although the sign painter she'd seen at the clinic might have come close, she mused. He'd certainly *looked* very capable, and he was a tal-

ented painter, as well. Maybe she should ask
Dr. Jack about him.

The housekeeper ran her feather duster
lightly over the dollhouse roof, pausing to pat a
tiny shingle into place. "I'll look for brawn *and*
brains—and I'll make sure he can look me in
the eye. A man who can't do that has something to hide." Mrs. Merryweather cocked her
head. "How on earth did you make these tiny
bricks for the chimney?"

"With clay," Candice answered absently. She
crunched on a bread stick, thinking about the
sign painter. *He'd* had no trouble looking her in
the eye—and other places, as well. Howard had
sometimes looked at her with that kind of
intensity, but only when scanning for flaws in
her makeup, a loose button, anything that
hinted at imperfection. The painter had looked
at her as if . . . as if he *liked* what he saw. Her
face warmed at the memory.

Sharply, she reminded herself of the lawsuit
pending against her. Howard's relatives, determined to take every dime, were slandering her
name, digging into her past. And they seemed
to have a way of knowing her every move practically before she made it. Scandal was something she must avoid at all costs.

So she had to stop thinking of the painter,
she decided firmly. She wasn't an innocent

young girl any longer, dazzled by wealth and social standing; nor was she so naive a handsome flirt could turn her head. She was a mother-to-be with the hounds of hell—the media and Howard's relatives—at her heels.

"Lady, you're gonna have my baby."

Austin frowned at the closed door and shook his head. No, that wasn't it. "Mrs. Vanausdale, I know this will come as a shock to you—maybe you should sit down."

He chewed his inner lip. Hell. "Lady, Jack Cruise has done something very foolish. . . ."

Damn.

"But I think we should have him committed, rather than sent to prison. . . ."

No, that wouldn't work either, because he couldn't—wouldn't—place more innocent people, even institutionalized ones, in Jack's path.

He lifted a fist to pound on the door, but it opened before his knuckles connected. A brawny, wide-shouldered man who stood a good three inches taller than his own six feet faced him. Austin's jaw dropped as he stared at the close-cropped hair and dangling earring. His eyebrows collided. What the hell?

The man nodded curtly and shouldered past him, striding down the walk. Austin turned his head to follow the lumbering form, his imagination soaring. Well, Mr. Vanausdale might be dead, but it was for certain *Mrs.* Vanausdale wasn't!

As if he wasn't shocked enough, he turned back just in time to nearly collide with another macho man, this one sporting a garish orange muscle shirt and tattoos on both arms. Austin stepped out of his way. At least this one wasn't wearing an earring, he thought with a grumble.

Well, none of this was any of his business.

Wait. Yes, it was. She was carrying his child, dammit. Hadn't he read somewhere that too much athletic sex wasn't healthy for the baby? Yes, he was positive—

"If you'll come right this way, we'll get started."

Austin snapped his head around, staring down at the short, gray-haired woman in the doorway with absolute amazement. Her face was pleasantly seamed with laugh lines, and she looked him over in a way that made Austin think of the time Jack had sat for days using a magnifying glass to watch mold grow on a piece of bread.

Who was this? The maid? With a house this size, Austin figured there had to be a maid. Probably several. His own mother had employed so many he was constantly tripping over them.

And Mrs. Vanausdale might be a looker, but with her kind of money, he doubted she even had to flush a toilet.

Shaking his head, Austin focused on the older woman's interested gaze. When might she finish her inspection? And just what qualities did she inspect Mrs. Vanausdale's male visitors for? He didn't know what was going on, but, by God, he was going to put a stop to it. For now, though, he would play it cool to ensure he got inside.

"I'm here to see Mrs. Vanausdale." There, he didn't actually growl. Under the circumstances, she was lucky he wasn't shouting.

The door opened wider. "Well, you have to please me first, young man. I'm holding the interviews in the den."

Austin choked, fearing his eyes would pop from his head. "I—I'm here to see Mrs. Vanausdale," he repeated hoarsely. But he wasn't sure he *wanted* to meet her any longer. Hell, maybe he should just forget about it, pretend Jack hadn't told him what he had, and—

"Do you have a prison record?"

"No!" Austin answered before he could catch himself. What the hell kind of question was that, anyway? He frowned, but the woman didn't appear intimidated in the least. In fact, she beamed at him.

"Well, then, your chances are good, because

you're the first man today who *doesn't* have a record. Follow me, and I'll get you something cool to drink while we talk." She turned and led the way down the hall.

He followed, wondering if there was the slightest possibility he could be dreaming all this.

The gray-haired woman waved her arm to the right. "Go on in there—I'll be along with a nice glass of lemonade."

Austin hesitated, glancing at the door. Should he simply leave? Pretend none of this had ever happened?

She returned before he could decide, thrusting a tall glass into his hand. Ice clinked, and lemonade sloshed precariously to the rim. "There you go. You look thirsty. I'll bet you're a hard worker, aren't you?" She winked at him.. "I can tell—you're sweating. And hard workers are thirsty people. There, have a seat, and let's get down to business."

Austin moved into the spacious den, his gaze quickly assessing the furnishings. Not bad, not too flashy. But then, maybe Mrs. Vanausdale had decorated with sweaty, muscular bodies in mind. . . . He avoided the sofa and sat in a chair, finding his thoughts too wild to contemplate and his legs too shaky to support him. He'd stay for a moment, just long enough to confirm what he thought was going on. Then he'd leave and forget about this having-his-baby business.

In about six months he'd place an anonymous call to Social Services so they could check on the newborn's home environment.

The gray-haired woman settled into a chair across from his and sighed. "I'm Mrs. Merryweather, the housekeeper. We're looking for someone who's got stamina and ain't afraid of hard work. We're willing to pay well but not outrageously, you understand. You're welcome to use the apartment over the garage, but you'll have to feed yourself. No benefits, standard holidays, two weeks vacation unless she needs you to—"

"Excuse me."

Mrs. Merryweather blinked. "Yes?"

"Could I speak with Mrs. Vanausdale? I've have something to discuss with her." He was amazed at his pleasant tone; it was in direct contradiction to the nasty taste in his mouth.

Mrs. Merryweather blinked again, this time in rapid succession. "So you're not interested in the handyman job?" Her expression fell. "And I was hoping . . . you look intelligent, and she might be needing a bodyguard, too. I know it's a bit much to ask of one man, but she's easy to work for, and—"

"Bodyguard?" Austin leaned forward, instantly alert. Swiftly, he sorted through her earlier words. Obviously he was way off the mark about what those brutes were doing here. The housekeeper was interviewing for a handyman—and a *bodyguard?* "Has Mrs. Vanausdale been threatened?" he asked sharply. The possibility alarmed him, which in turn surprised him. But, hell, she *was* carrying his child. *His child* might be in danger!

He thought he detected a gleam in the housekeeper's eyes. Just what he needed, another insane do-gooder like Jack.

"Well, not exactly, but there have been a few calls—" When Austin opened his mouth, she rushed on in a hushed whisper, "I haven't mentioned them to her because of her condition, you know. Mrs. Dale—that's what the staff calls her—is expecting." Her face screwed together in genuine concern. "I don't like to worry her."

Austin rubbed his jaw, stifling the urge to laugh at all the ironies of his situation. If he released the laughter, this woman would surely detect the madness in the sound and send him on his way.

Carefully, he set his glass down on the coffee table and prepared his answer. He hoped he wouldn't regret his decision.

But he suspected he would.

Chapter Three

It was him!

Candice stood at the patio doors leading from her bedroom to the pool area, a tiny corner of the heavy drapes pushed aside so she could watch the man cleaning the pool. She'd done these little spying missions a hundred times over the past three days since she first saw the new handyman Mrs. Merryweather had hired.

No doubt about it, he was the sign painter from the clinic, the very one she had wondered about when considering the perfect handyman. He had gallantly saved her from that pesky reporter, and he certainly painted a good sign. Still, her reaction had been alarm. What was he doing here? Why would a painter apply for the job of handyman? It chilled her to think he might have followed her home. . . .

But he had to have seen the ad in the paper, or he wouldn't have known about the job, she reasoned. Yet, it was still a strange coincidence. He was either legitimately looking for work, or he was up to something.

Candice intended to find out which, but without tipping her hand. Thus the surreptitious spying.

She chewed her lower lip, watching his muscles ripple and bulge as he clumsily swung the net into the water and raked it across the surface. Sweat gleamed on his bronze skin—a lot of skin revealed by cutoff jeans, frayed and worn in several disturbing places, and no shirt.

Didn't the man own any shirts? she wondered, frowning. Howard would not have allowed an employee to stalk around half-naked, no matter how hot the weather. Especially if he thought *she* might bump into him.

Howard would . . . Candice tightened her fingers on the curtain, clenching her teeth and squeezing her eyes tightly shut. No, she wouldn't go there, wouldn't think about Howard.

Gradually, the tension eased. She took a deep, relieved breath—and felt ashamed, as always. Howard wasn't here, would never be again. She needn't worry what he would say or think or do. Her life was finally her own—or it would be when this nasty business over the will was finished.

Lifting her chin, Candice continued her "stakeout," as she called it in her mind. She would find out what the painter was up to sooner or later. Too bad she wasn't confident enough to approach him and just ask him why he'd applied for the job.

Not yet, anyway. In the year since Howard's death, she'd managed to break many old habits—habits he'd drilled into her—but talking to strangers wasn't one of them.

"Nice-looking young man, don't you think?"

Candice gasped and whirled, the curtain fluttering from her fingers. She met Mrs. Merryweather's knowing gaze with acute dismay. What must the housekeeper think? To catch her *watching* the handyman . . . "I was just—just checking on his progress," she breathed, doubting the shrewd housekeeper would swallow her lame excuse.

Mrs. Merryweather bustled to the king-size Queen Anne bed in the center of the master bedroom and set a stack of freshly laundered sheets on the chair next to it. She brushed the wrinkles from her apron and nodded at the window. "He doesn't know much about cleaning the pool."

"Or trimming hedges," Candice added dryly,

relaxing as she realized the housekeeper didn't intend to comment on her unseemly behavior. She pictured the poor mangled hedges that graced the circular drive, biting back a smile. Well, it *was* funny, when she thought about it.

At the beginning of the attack on Howard's will by his relatives, the judge had frozen Howard's assets until the matter was settled. Left with no choice, Candice had reluctantly released the household staff, with the exception of Mrs. Merryweather.

But, the two women had soon come to the dismal conclusion that they couldn't do everything themselves—they would have to hire *someone*. They had put their heads together and come up with the brilliant plan of hiring a handyman, someone who knew a little about everything.

So far, their plan had backfired.

Mrs. Merryweather shook her head of graying, tightly permed curls and began stripping Candice's bed. "I have to agree with you there. Did you see those hedges when he finished? Looked like something straight out of *The Shining*. I swear, I think I saw an elephant and an ostrich. He might not know how to trim, but he knows how to shape."

"That's because he's a painter." Candice could have kicked herself the moment the words were out. She hadn't meant to spill the beans because she didn't want to answer questions. Too late.

Mrs. Merryweather shook a pillow into a clean pillowcase and propped it on the bed, her sharp gaze on her. "You know him?"

Candice sighed inwardly and resigned herself. "I met him, sort of, last week at the clinic. He was outside—painting a sign. He stopped a pesky reporter from following me inside the building."

The housekeeper looked alarmed by this news. "Do you think he followed you here? Should we have the police run a check on him?"

"No, I—"

"I think we should. I'm tellin' you, Mrs. Dale, I don't trust Mr. Howard's deadbeat family. I don't trust them at all."

"They wouldn't dare do anything to hurt the baby. Besides, I think Dr. Jack knows this guy personally." Candice hated the way her voice trembled. She wasn't as confident as she wanted the housekeeper to believe, and she couldn't forget the sound of shouting she'd heard when she'd returned for her purse. It had not been Jack Cruise's voice she'd heard, but the painter's. Rough and angry. Very angry.

Mrs. Merryweather gathered the stripped bedclothes and crossed the room to stand before Candice, wearing a familiar stern frown.

"Don't brush off the danger, Mrs. Dale. With you out of the way, those Vanausdales would get all of Mr. Howard's money, and they wouldn't have to wait for a judge to decide."

Candice attempted to reassure her. "I'm not brushing it off, really. But I'm not going to jump at every shadow, either."

With a sharp jerk of her head in the direction of the window, Mrs. Merryweather said, "You've seen for yourself—he's no shadow. A big, brawny man like that could snap a woman in two. If I'd known about this, I wouldn't have hired him."

Candice felt compelled to defend him, since she'd sowed the seed of suspicion. "He seems harmless. . . ."

"We're all alone here."

"We've got neighbors—"

"You think they'd hear us? Two acres of woods surround this house!"

Candice was beginning to get spooked. Before long, she would become as paranoid as the housekeeper. Then they would both go insane. Firmly, she said, "We can't fire him on such flimsy suspicions. It wouldn't be fair."

The housekeeper rounded her eyes. "Who cares what's fair if we're dead in our beds?"

A mighty splash interrupted their heated conversation. Both women froze. Candice stared in question at the housekeeper, who stared back, equally puzzled.

"Do you think he . . . ?" Candice turned in the direction of the patio doors that led to the pool area, Mrs. Merryweather on her heels. "Do you suppose he fell in?" she whispered, pulling the curtain aside to take a look.

"I wouldn't be surprised." The older woman pressed her nose to the glass and squinted.

They gasped simultaneously. The handyman floundered in the deep end of the pool, splashing frantically. His head went under, then he bounced up again to claw the air.

"Help!"

His muffled, gurgled shout made Candice jump. "Dear God, he can't swim!"

Mrs. Merryweather pressed a hand to her chest. "Oh, Lord, neither can I! But what if this is just a trick to lure you into the pool so he can drown—"

But Candice wasn't listening. She scrabbled at the door latch, yanking the sliding glass open so hard it bounced back into Mrs. Merryweather as she followed. A man was drowning; there wasn't time to worry about hidden agendas.

She hurried to the far side of the pool where the handyman had been working, her heart in her throat, vaguely aware the plump housekeeper followed. Looking around, she searched for something—anything—she could use as a lifeline as the man continued to thrash in the water. She spotted the utility pole and grabbed it up. Leaning over as far as she dared, she stretched the net across the water.

"Grab the pole!" she shouted, her voice raspy with panic.

His answer was a gurgle as he dropped once again below the surface. Candice moaned in fear. Was it the third time? There was no time left—no time to wonder if she would be strong enough to save him. She had to try.

Quickly, she shed her pumps and jumped in, gasping as the sun-warmed water rushed over her, soaking her expensive linen slacks and white silk shirt. She kicked to the surface and swam for the drowning man. When she reached him, she slid her hands beneath his arms and lifted him up until his head broke the surface.

He struggled, but, thankfully, he wasn't struggling *against* her. As he sputtered and gasped for air, she felt the roughness of his jean shorts as the waves slapped his lower body against her thighs. The thin material of her pants was now plastered to her like a second skin, leaving little to protect her from the oddly intimate contact. Unnerved, she quickly moved her legs out of reach, still holding on to him.

She began to backpedal, dragging him along. When she reached the edge of the pool, she leaned against it to catch her breath, supporting his weight with the help of the water.

He rolled in the water, and she gasped when his hand flattened against her stomach as if he were searching for something to brace himself. Candice froze, telling herself it was an accident, that there was nothing personal about his touch. And of course he was dazed—that was why he was taking so long to *remove* his hand. She lifted his arms and encouraged him to hang on to the side until he caught his breath— so she could catch hers.

He obeyed sluggishly, as if still dazed by what had happened. Finally, she noticed his breathing begin to even out. Candice continued to watch him closely, working at stabilizing her own breathing. He'd given her quite a scare.

"Mrs. Dale, are you all right?" From the side of the pool, Mrs. Merryweather crouched down and studied Candice with a worried frown. "You know you shouldn't be lifting."

"He wasn't heavy, Mrs. Merryweather. The water . . ." She wiped her streaming hair out of her eyes, watching the handyman do the same. Yes, he was coming around. His eyes no longer looked wild, and he'd stopped choking on the water he'd swallowed.

"I'll get some towels." Mrs. Merryweather

57

caught Candice's eye and gave her a meaningful look before she added loudly, "I'll be right
back—I won't be out of sight. Just over here at
the pool house."

Candice covered a giggle with a wet hand,
pretending to cough as the housekeeper hurried after the towels. The man was half-
drowned, and Mrs. Merryweather still thought
they were about to be murdered!

"What's so funny?" a slightly raspy voice
asked.

She jerked her head around, losing her grip
on the side of the pool and treading water as
her startled gaze collided with the handyman's.
Spiky black lashes framed vivid blue eyes, eyes
that were regarding her with unmistakable
curiosity and—was that a hint of censure?

The latter confused Candice.

Whatever happened to a simple thank-you?
she wondered. Reestablishing her grip on the
coping, she slicked her hair away from her face
and glanced toward the pool house and Mrs.
Merryweather. "It's—it's a private joke." She
tried to cross an arm over her chest and still
hang on to the pool side, conscious of how
transparent the wet silk of her blouse was. At
any moment, he might look down and see . . .
She cleared her throat nervously, wishing the
housekeeper would hurry with the towels. This

was nerve-wracking. "Are you okay now?" she asked.

"I'm fine. Thanks." With a mighty lunge that nearly launched a shriek from her throat, he lifted himself up and out of the pool in one graceful motion.

He shook himself like a wet dog, slicking his gold-streaked hair away from his tanned face. "Give me your hand," he commanded softly, staring down at her.

Candice swallowed and obeyed, gasping when he lifted her out of the water as if she weighed nothing. When she stood, he held her steady with big hands encircling her waist. Candice knew it was nothing more than a courtesy, but she trembled regardless, remembering the housekeeper's comment: *A big, brawny man like that could snap a woman in two.*

She pushed the terrifying thought away and attempted something she hadn't in a long time—normal conversation with someone other than the housekeeper, Jack Cruise, and her lawyer. "I—I guess this means we're even."

He didn't pretend not to understand. A faint smile of remembrance curved his mouth. "I don't know about that. I'd call the trade a little uneven—my life versus your privacy?"

"I—Mrs. Merryweather didn't tell me your name," she ventured, moving away a bit as she changed the subject. He dropped his hands without hesitation, and Candice let her breath out slowly. She was also wrong about his ogling her. He kept his eyes on her face with a searching intensity that popped a question into her mind: What was he looking for? After a moment, he gave a faint nod, as if he found his inspection satisfying.

When he finally took his eyes from her face, it was to glance briefly in the direction of the pool house. Before she could relax, he pinned his gaze on her again and thrust out his right hand.

"I'm Austin Hyde." His voice was deep, low, just as she remembered it.

Hesitantly, she placed her hand in his. He gave her fingers a gentle squeeze. At his touch, a tremor ran up her arm, straight into her chest, and her heart began to beat swiftly.

The frightening reaction brought her back to reality. Caution returned. He was a man—a powerful man. Maybe not rich powerful but strong powerful and also, she suspected, controlling powerful. The straight, square set of his jaw told her that. She pulled her hand free and crossed her arms over her chest. Strong-willed. Demanding. Commanding. Those were qualities she had to avoid.

To their left, they heard the slamming of a door. Mrs. Merryweather emerged from the pool house wearing a thunderous expression and carrying two small towels. "Well, I don't feel so guilty anymore about having to let that lazy Misty go," she complained. "I always said, 'Misty, make sure there are plenty of towels in the pool house,' but did she listen? No, she didn't. Never gave it a thought, I'll wager."

Candice took one of the towels from her hand and began to dry her hair, avoiding Mr. Hyde's amused gaze.

"So, you don't know how to swim?" Mrs. Merryweather looked disapproving, although Candice knew the housekeeper feared water nearly as much as she feared snakes.

He answered her, but his gaze remained fixed on Candice. She shivered and pressed the towel against her chest.

"Can't seem to get the knack of it. Maybe I haven't had the right teacher."

Was he implying—? Candice jerked her gaze away, mentally shaking her head. Of course he wasn't hinting she should teach him to swim! Years of isolation had turned her into a silly fool. She didn't know how to act or react to men, and she didn't have a clue how to guess what was on their minds. But then, she firmly reminded herself, she didn't want to know. Ever again.

Mrs. Merryweather continued to glare at him. "Well, I guess you should stay away from the pool until you learn. Mrs. Dale ain't in no condition to be hauling giants like you out of the water."

Instead of being offended by her tone, he seemed to be amused. He reached behind him and plucked a faded tank top from a lounge chair and casually slipped it over his head. "Pregnancy doesn't necessarily make a woman an invalid."

The housekeeper bristled. Candice hid a smile behind her towel, trying not to gawk at the sight of his rippling muscles. Mr. Hyde obviously had no idea what he was getting into by challenging Mrs. Merryweather, mother of three.

"Oh?" Mrs. Merryweather queried archly. "You know a lot about pregnancy, do you? Married with kids of your own? I don't remember you mentioning that on your application."

Candice held her breath, telling herself it didn't matter, it was none of her concern, and she certainly wasn't interested.

"No, but I've researched the subject some."

Candice's breath whistled quietly between her teeth. So, he wasn't married. She didn't really care, and it wasn't relief she felt, not really. Or maybe simply relief that he could devote more time to the multitudinous tasks requiring his attention.

Like the unfinished nursery.

Before she could lose her nerve, she asked, "Mr. Hyde, would you like to come in for a glass of lemonade? There's something I'd like to discuss with you."

"But, Mrs. Dale! You can't—"

"We're not out of lemonade, are we?" Candice lifted an eyebrow, trying to convey a silent message to the housekeeper: She wanted to find out why Mr. Hyde was here, why he'd applied for the job, and she was tired of spying. "I'm sure Mr. Hyde could use some refreshment after his ordeal." She shifted her gaze to his for a brief moment. "Couldn't you, Mr. Hyde?" Secretly, her courage surprised her. But there was something about the man that inspired trust. And he *had* saved her from the reporter.

His eyes twinkled as he swiped the small towel across his neck and face before tucking it into the waistband of his low-slung shorts.

"After all the chlorinated water I swallowed, lemonade sounds good."

Mrs. Merryweather seemed to realize she wasn't going to win the argument. But her expression spoke volumes, and Candice knew she would be in for a lecture later about welcoming this relative stranger into the house with her.

"Well, I guess I can take time to whip up a sandwich or two to go with it," the housekeeper said reluctantly. "I'll just go on ahead and get that laundry from your room, Mrs. Dale, and close your doors. You get out of those wet clothes now, you hear?"

"Yes, ma'am." She flashed the housekeeper a cheeky smile. "We'll be right along."

When the housekeeper left, Candice's courage went with her. She was alone with a man other than Howard for the first time in years. Nervous now, she retrieved her pumps and returned to Mr. Hyde, clutching the shoes and the towel against her chest. He stood at ease, thumbs hooked into his waistband. Sunlight glinted off the highlights in his hair and sparkled on the water drops splattering his shoulders.

Candice tried not to stare but found it impossible, just as she had found it impossible the past three days. Howard had been slim, with soft muscles. Mr. Hyde was firm—hard. When he shrugged or moved, it created a rippling wave of muscle, tempting her to follow it with her fingertips.

She licked her dry lips and forced herself to meet his gaze. *He knows,* she thought suddenly. *He knows what I'm about to ask him.*

Well, there wasn't any delicate way of putting it, she decided. She couldn't relax without knowing. She took a deep breath and blurted it out. "Why are you here?"

Mr. Hyde's Assets

* * *

Austin had been asking himself that same question over and over since Mrs. Merryweather had mistaken him for a job applicant. Taking the position had been an impulsive response, something like Jack would have done—and that thought scared the hell out of him.

What *was* he doing here? Spying on the future mother of his baby? Waiting for the right moment to come out with the truth? *Mrs. Vanausdale, I hate to give you the bad news, but I'm the father of your baby.* Ha! She'd dial 911 so fast, he'd never know what hit him until the cuffs—or the straitjacket—was on.

He'd hoped by taking the job he would get to know more about her, and that maybe this would give him some idea of what to do about their unbelievable situation. That hadn't worked out, though, for she'd kept to herself, enclosed in that big, sterile mansion probably making God-knew-what kind of plans for *his* child.

Oh, he'd noticed her watching him and had thought curiosity would eventually drive her out to ask questions. But when the third day came and she hadn't, he had to go to Plan B: pretend to drown.

And now she was here, in the flesh—wet flesh—and all he could concentrate on was controlling his libido. Mrs. Vanausdale was all woman, right down to the faint curve of her stomach. Austin gritted his teeth, remembering how she'd stiffened when he'd placed his hand there, over their baby. Was she repulsed by him? After all, he wasn't the suave, sophisticated, rich dude her husband had been.

So, what was he doing here? Very good question. Only he didn't have the answer. Not today.

He shrugged, deciding a half truth was better than an outright lie. "I can use the money." She frowned; evidently his answer wasn't satisfying enough. What did she think? That he had followed her home from Little Miracles like a panting puppy? Or that he was working undercover for the enemy, the other Vanausdales? He suspected the housekeeper thought so.

Man, would they be surprised to discover how wrong they were.

And suddenly, inspiration struck Austin as he remembered what the housekeeper had said about Candice's possibly needing a bodyguard. What better way to get to know the real Candice Vanausdale than to convince her he cared about her welfare and could prove perfectly protective?

Taking the initiative, he began walking in the direction of the house. "Better get going before Mrs. Merryweather comes looking for us." He smiled, hoping to ease her tension. She was jumpy on her own, and bashful, to boot. Unusual qualities in a woman of wealth and uncommon beauty.

She played right into his hands, moving into place beside him. "She's concerned about me."

Bingo. "So am I."

She stopped dead in her tracks, a look of such surprise on her face, Austin *had* to believe it was real. "You are? Why?"

Now came the tricky part. He schooled his expression into what he hoped was a look of bewilderment. "I'm not sure. When I saw you at Little Miracles, I just got this feeling you needed somebody you could trust. Then Jack mentioned you were looking to hire help and showed me the ad in the paper, and since I was looking for work . . ." He let her draw her own conclusions, secure in the knowledge he'd already coached Jack on what to say and what not to say.

She continued walking, and so did he. After a moment, she asked so softly he had to strain to hear her, "*Are* you someone I can trust?"

Austin waited for the rush of victory but was disappointed. She sounded lost, hopeful yet afraid. And he felt like a heel.

He was saved from answering by the buzzing drone of an approaching helicopter. Simultaneously, they tilted their heads and shaded their eyes to look at the sky.

He recognized the distinct blue and white stripes of the Channel Four news helicopter just as Candice grabbed his hand and began to run the last few yards to the back door, pulling him along with amazing strength.

Sheer panic vibrated in her voice. "Hurry, they can't see us together!"

"Why the hell not?" Austin shouted back, wishing he had a high-powered fire hose handy.

"Scandal!"

Austin frowned at her answer as he followed her through the door Mrs. Merryweather held open. Of course. How could he have forgotten?

The money. It was all about the money.

Chapter Four

"Miserable vultures! Mrs. Dale never hurt anyone, so why can't they leave her alone? She can't even walk in her own backyard for fear of those newspeople pouncing out of the bushes and snapping pictures, and now this! A helicopter!"

Staring at the housekeeper's rigid back as she chopped viciously at something on the counter in front of her, Austin had to agree the helicopter was a bit much. Still, where there's smoke there's usually fire, as the old saying went.

The notorious widow had gone to change, leaving him in his wet shorts and damp shirt, alone with a very angry housekeeper. Well, he could handle Mrs. Merryweather.

He'd just keep his mouth shut and listen.

"Gettin' pale from being cooped up in this house all day! She needs fresh air and sunshine, but she can't go outside."

Pale? No fresh air and sunshine? Austin didn't like the sound of that. It wasn't healthy. And all because she was afraid of the media. Which explained why she hadn't ventured out since he'd been here. Who could blame her, when—

"No harm in her wantin' a baby, is there?" Mrs. Merryweather snapped without turning around. "And so what if Mr. Howard ain't alive? I raised my own three after Jim died, and so can Mrs. Dale. Between the two of us, that young'un won't want for anything."

Uh-oh. Between the two of them? Austin didn't like the sound of that, either. He cringed to imagine his child being raised by a recluse and a drill sergeant. In this palace. Surrounded by lurking media and crazed, money-hungry relatives.

Austin's emotions warred between pity and disgust. Well, did he feel sorry for Candice Vanausdale or not? Was she the victim, or had she smoothed the sheets of her own bed?

"Why doesn't she remarry?"

He hadn't realized he'd translated the thought into words until Mrs. Merryweather swung around and pinned him with a glare cold enough to freeze his shorts. Too late, he now remembered that Jack had said the widow didn't want to remarry. Ever. But . . . why not? He eyed the knife in Mrs. Merryweather's hand and declined to repeat his question. *She* didn't know that it *was* his business.

And just where was the infamous Mrs. Vanausdale? She was taking a long time to change, he thought, returning the house-keeper's unblinking glare with an innocent look. Hopefully, she would decide he was just another dumb jock and forget he'd asked such a personal question about his employer.

She continued to stare, as if deciding his fate.

Funny, during the interview the old battle-ax had fluttered her eyelids like a teenager in love. Now she stared at him as if he bore a thief's brand on his forehead. In fact, maybe he should ask where the bathroom was, so he could check.

Or, rather, one of the many bathrooms. At least his child would have no trouble making it to the potty. That is, if he or she didn't trip over a maid or two along the way. Poor mite. Of course, that was if the poor mite didn't slip and fall on a highly polished marble floor on his way to the potty. Or stick himself with a twenty-four-carat gold diaper pin.

Dammit, a forbiddingly formal mansion was

no place for a child to grow and play. He should know. *Jack* should know. What had Jack been thinking? Oh, he'd forgotten. Jack didn't *have* a brain to think with—at least not a normal one, anyway.

Still, that was no excuse. The miserable, lowlife mutt!

Austin caught his frown before it formed, shaping his lips into a pleasant smile instead. He would charm this old battle-ax if it killed him, and get to know the mother of his child so that he could make a decision.

Which would be . . . ? Damned if he knew. But before his baby was born, he *would* know. Even if it killed him.

He jumped as Mrs. Merryweather slammed a plate of sandwiches down in the center of the table, quickly following it with two tall glasses of lemonade.

The sight of the sandwiches reminded Austin that he hadn't eaten lunch. On cue, his stomach growled.

"Well, for heaven's sake, would you go ahead and eat? I can hear your stomach makin' a racket!"

Austin grinned at the housekeeper's mockexasperated tone. She'd forgiven his blunder. "Thanks, but I'll wait on Mrs. Vanausdale."

"Mrs. Dale." Mrs. Merryweather folded the dishtowel she'd been using to wipe the spotless cabinets and turned to face him squarely. "Mrs. Dale is what the hired help calls her. Vanausdale's too much of a mouthful for most folks."

Meaning? Austin suspected the housekeeper had just delivered a not-so-subtle put down, but if he were going to get along with the old busybody, he'd have to swallow his pride. "Mrs. Dale, then."

Actually, he'd prefer Candice. His grin widened as he imagined the shock on the housekeeper's face should he dare. Oh, what fun!

But, no, if he were to make progress, he had to be good and charm not only "Mrs. Dale" but Mrs. Merryweather, as well. What a double-daunting challenge.

"I'm sorry to keep you waiting," a honey-warm voice said from behind him.

Austin tensed, a ripple of awareness skirting down his spine. God, her voice would make a monk hard, he thought, slowly turning around. Not to mention the rest of her.

His gaze started at her sandled feet and moved up the immaculate slacks with their razor-sharp creases to the silk blouse almost exactly the same colorless shade as the one she'd worn earlier. For a brief instant, his hot gaze lingered on the pull of fabric, with one slightly strained buttonhole, across her breasts.

Somehow that tiny flaw breached her perfect, untouchable image and made him think of satin sheets and naked limbs.

Hers.

His.

Hot and sweaty and tangled.

Not for the first time, Austin sensed a hidden fire in the widow—something she probably wasn't aware of. Oh, but he was.

She'd dried her hair and clasped it with a barrette at the nape of her neck, leaving a fringe of soft blond bangs tangling in her eyelashes and the rest hanging down her back in a silken sway. More erotic, forbidden images flashed through his mind at the thought of her hair unbound, wild and soft.

Abruptly, Austin shifted his eyes to her flushed face, surprised to find her watching him with anxiety and fear—and not a trace of the self-assurance he expected to find.

What the hell was going on? She was a beautiful woman, surely accustomed to appreciation from the opposite sex.

"Mr. Hyde, I—"

"Austin," he nearly growled, still trying to unravel the mystery of her reaction to him.

She took the chair opposite him at the table, looking everywhere but in his direction. Shy, apprehensive. But her voice was impressively firm—and ridiculously prim—when she began again, "I'm more comfortable calling you Mr. Hyde."

Austin stared at her bent head for a long moment, fighting the urge to reach across the table and rip open the top three buttons of her blouse and jerk the barrette from her hair. This lady needed a lesson in relaxing, letting her hair down, he decided. After all, if she was going to raise *his* child—

"How did you know I was pregnant?"

As she asked the question, she jerked her gaze to his, as if expecting to have caught him off guard. Well, she might be rich, and she might be beautiful, but she wasn't yet up to matching wits with him.

Austin kept his own expression innocent as he reached for a sandwich. "First of all, I heard what the *Sacramento Star* reporter said to you outside the clinic." Which wasn't a lie. Only everything that followed was. "And Mrs. Merryweather herself confirmed it during our interview."

He sank his teeth into the sandwich and bit into something crunchy. Chewing cautiously, he opened the bread and peered inside.

"Cucumbers," Mrs. Merryweather said smugly. "Mrs. Dale needs her veggies."

Austin shrugged and swallowed. He hated

cucumbers, but he'd be damned if he'd give Mrs. Merryweather the satisfaction of knowing it. Catching Candice's eye, he winked. She blushed and almost smiled.

There. She was limbering up. He knew she could do it. A few weeks and he might have that top button undone. After swallowing another bite of sandwich, he said, "Aren't you going to eat?" She needed to eat. She looked too thin, and with the baby coming . . . Hadn't he read that an expectant mother should eat enough for two?

She shook her head, a slight frown of confusion marring her brow. "I've already eaten, thank you."

What, a few carrot sticks and a stalk of celery? This lady needed looking after, and he might be just the man to do it. After all, he didn't want his baby underfed, did he? Austin pushed the plate across the table, but she pushed it back, and the sudden flare of anger in her eyes stopped him from pressing his point. He guessed grilling steaks on the patio was out of the question.

For now.

"So you don't read the papers?" She sounded skeptical.

"No. I don't have time." He didn't much. They depressed him, anyway. Especially after reading about her.

A small silence followed before her next words. "How long have you known Dr. Jack?"

Austin choked on his sandwich. He grabbed the lemonade and took a healthy gulp. Dr. Jekyll was more like it, as this lady would agree if only she knew what Jack had had done to her.

When he decided he wasn't dying, he said, "Most of our lives. He and I . . . attended the same school." Well, they *had*. The same private school in Switzerland. But somehow he didn't think Mrs. Dale *or* the formidable Mrs. Merryweather would swallow that information easily.

He caught the meaningful glance Candice shot at Mrs. Merryweather, who stood at the kitchen counter with no obvious intentions of moving. The housekeeper made a noise that sounded like a snort of disbelief.

Damned drill sergeant probably didn't believe man had walked on the moon, either. "You can check with Jack, if you'd feel more comfortable," he added, receiving a narrowed glare from Mrs. Merryweather. He'd written everything down for Jack, and so help him, if Jack screwed up, he'd really kill him this time.

Candice looked embarrassed. "That's not necessary, Mr. Hyde. I'm sure you're perfectly harmless."

Another snort from Mrs. Merryweather.

Austin couldn't resist. "Right. After all, I had the perfect opportunity to drown you in the pool."

This time Mrs. Merryweather gasped, and to Austin's curious delight, Candice laughed.

Her rich, husky laughter shot a strange sensation right to his groin. *Down boy. It's just a laugh, and you've heard a million of them.* But not like this one. "Did I say something funny?"

"Well—"

Candice cut in on Mrs. Merryweather, still chuckling. "It's a private joke. Someday I'll tell you."

"You will not!" Mrs. Merryweather whisked the plate from the table just as Austin was reaching for another sandwich. He missed.

Hell, a man had to eat.

"It's time for you to get back to work, Mr. Hyde. Best you start by fixing that leak under the sink. You *can* do that, can't you? And you . . ." The housekeeper whirled on Candice, who tried to look repentant and failed miserably. "It's nap time for you, Mrs. Dale. I think you've had enough excitement for one day, and you need your rest. You should use the east guest room upstairs so this big lug won't disturb you with his clumsy crashing around."

Austin reached around the stocky woman and snatched a sandwich off the plate, winking at Candice, who hastily got to her feet and fled the room.

But not before Austin caught sight of her smile. He couldn't suppress a grin in return, although Mrs. Merryweather stood glaring at him. Yes, "Mrs. Dale" was warming up nicely. There might be hope for her yet.

"Stop gawking, and get to work!"

Austin popped the stolen sandwich into his mouth and dusted his hands on his wet shorts. "Yes, ma'am. Just show me the pipe, and I'll fix it. You *do* have superglue, don't you?"

Mrs. Merryweather nearly dropped the plate. Her mouth rounded, and just before she blasted him, Austin held up a hand. "Just kidding."

And he was. Sort of. Surely he could fix a little leak, couldn't he? How hard could it be?

Sleep? Ha! Not with Austin Hyde downstairs, still clad in those clinging wet shorts that outlined his . . . everything! Candice giggled, then quickly shushed herself at the sound of soft footsteps coming down the hall.

Mrs. Merryweather, she presumed, checking to see if she was indeed taking a nap as ordered. Candice closed her eyes and forced herself to breathe evenly—no small feat, considering her surprisingly wicked thoughts.

The door creaked open and after a few seconds clicked shut again. Candice waited a good five minutes before getting up and crossing to the window. Quietly she eased the blinds up and made herself comfortable on the cushioned window seat.

Her gaze went immediately to the hedges lining the drive. She smiled, deciding Mrs. Merryweather was right: The hedges *did* resemble animals. That one *was* an ostrich! Her gaze studied the next one. Yes, an elephant, and beside it the distinct shape of a rhino. If Mr. Hyde stayed on and kept creating these odd ornamental topiaries, her child could enjoy the whimsical shapes just as she was enjoying them now.

Mr. Hyde, who was definitely no handyman, and who didn't know how to swim. But he could make her laugh. And although Mrs. Merryweather wasn't aware of it, Candice suspected she, too, was softening toward their new help.

Why was he here, really? Was it for the money, as he claimed, or was there some truth in his declaration that he thought she needed someone? A friend, a true, trustworthy friend.

A wonderful kind of pain squeezed her heart as she considered this possibility. To have someone protective around who actually cared about *her*, someone other than Mrs. Merry-weather, sounded like . . . Heaven.

It also sounded like an illusion, she reminded herself. And she had learned the hard way that illusions a person was fool enough to believe could hurt.

Candice forced herself to face the facts, to list the reasons someone like Austin Hyde couldn't sincerely be concerned about her. For starters, he didn't even know her. And she was pregnant with another man's child. Also, people accused her of having this baby just to get Howard's money, and although it wasn't true, she knew many people believed it. Would Austin Hyde be one of them?

They were all so wrong. Candice wanted this baby more than anything—had wanted a baby desperately even before Howard died. Howard had promised, and when conventional methods hadn't worked, he'd agreed to try Little Miracles. Well, Candice wasn't letting him off the hook just because he got himself killed. He owed her this baby, and she had damned well earned it. And the money, too.

It had been Hell on Earth living with an obsessive like Howard Vanausdale. She should have left him, but . . .

Candice sighed and propped her chin on one palm, staring out the window. Why had she kept punishing herself? The plain fact was that she hadn't had the heart to leave him when it came right down to it. How could she leave a man who was down on his knees, begging her to give him another chance? She'd always felt she owed it to him to give their marriage another try.

Again and again.

Obligation was a powerful force, one Candice had learned at an early age, when she'd promised her dying mother she would take care of her stepfather. And she had, despite his mental abuse and cold silences.

Was it any wonder that wealthy, sophisticated Howard Vanausdale had turned her head? When she was nineteen, he had waltzed into her dreary life and thrown stars into her eyes. He had promised to love, cherish, and give her the world.

And in return she had promised to love him and never leave him. She should have questioned why he so often demanded reassurance on that latter point—or at least wondered why she was wife number three.

Lord, but she'd been so green and stupid and desperate to escape her horrible life. How could she have known?

But that was over now. Now she would have a child of her own to cherish and nurture, and with Howard's money—their child's money—

she would never have to suffer the heartache
and misery of marriage again. Besides, she
would never put her child through what she
had gone through with her stepfather.
Evidently a man could not love another man's
child.

And even if Howard's relatives won the case
against her, she would simply get a job and
support herself and the baby. At least it would
be raised in a loving environment. The money
wasn't important to Candice other than as
security for her child—Howard's child. She
was fighting the other Vanausdales for her
baby's inheritance, and she didn't care what the
rest of the world believed.

Her thoughts drifted back to the funny,
endearing Mr. Hyde.

Maybe Mr. Hyde's presence here was Dr.
Jack's doing. Candice smiled at the thought.
Generous, tenderhearted Dr. Jack. It sounded
just like something he would do, send her
someone like Austin Hyde to help out and
make her laugh and feel secure. Someone she
could call a friend, without any pressure or
fear or suspicions.

Someone to watch over her until the baby
was born and—

A shadow loomed in the window with a sud-
denness that took her breath away. Candice
scrambled out of the window seat, landing

harmlessly on the carpet. Something—some-one—was looking in the window at her! One moment she was looking out, and the next a face had appeared. How could that be? Lord, she was two stories up!

Cautiously, she rose to her knees and peered at the sill, her heart clamoring in her chest. Maybe she'd imagined it, because surely it was impossible to—

The face suddenly lunged against the pane and pressed tight, smashing its nose into a grotesque mask.

Candice screamed.

Another turn and he'd have the pipe loose. Austin grunted and muttered a curse beneath his breath, not caring if the hovering, suspicious housekeeper heard him. He tightened his grip on the wrench and squeezed. One more twist and—

Candice's scream echoed through the house. Startled, Austin jumped, bumping his head on the sink. The pipe came loose, spewing water onto his already damp shorts, the floor, and Mrs. Merryweather's shoes.

Austin jumped to his feet, ignoring the gushing water. "What the hell was that?" he demanded, staring at the housekeeper's wide-eyed expression.

For the first time, Mrs. Merryweather looked flustered—downright scared, in fact. She clutched her bosom. "Why, I think it's Mrs. Dale!"

She spun and headed for the stairs, Austin at her heels. She didn't move fast enough for him, and as he raced past her, he shouted over his shoulder, "Which way?" Dammit, he had no idea where he was going. The housekeeper had said east, but he wasn't certain which room. Raw terror urged him on. That scream had chilled his blood and nearly stopped his heart. Visions of murderous in-laws filled his mind.

"End of the hall, to your right!" Mrs. Merryweather puffed from behind him.

Austin stretched his legs in an all-out run, reaching the room and skidding to a stop in the doorway. His heart did the same when he say Candice lying on the floor, still as death.

Mrs. Merryweather nearly ran into him. "Dear God, what happened?"

Austin knelt beside Candice, frantic at the sight of her pale face. "I think she's fainted."

Mrs. Merryweather hovered over them. "Should I call the doctor?"

Austin felt for a pulse, sighing in relief to find it steady and strong. "Yes, call the doctor! Now! What are you waiting for?" He'd never felt so helpless in his life. Why had she fainted? Was she going to be all right? Was something wrong with the baby? Did this have anything to *do* with the baby? Oh, why hadn't he finished that damned book Jack had given him?

Mrs. Merryweather dropped the phone, scrambled to pick it up again, and began dialing, mumbling beneath her breath. Her forehead was a mass of concerned wrinkles as she kept darting glances at Candice, then back at the phone.

Austin gently lifted Candice in his arms. Why, she was as light as a feather! No wonder she had fainted; she was starving herself. And she looked so damned pale. Fear clawed his gut, and he didn't stop to wonder how he had become so concerned for this woman so soon. At this moment all he could think about was how badly he wanted her to open her eyes.

He lay her gently on top of the satin goosedown comforter before checking to see if Mrs. Merryweather had managed to dial the phone.

She had, thank God.

"Dr. Robinson? Mrs. Merryweather here. Mrs. Dale has fainted or something. She screamed, and then we found her lying on the floor. . . . Yes, we've got her on the bed now. Yes, Mr. Hyde checked her pulse." There was a long pause, then Mrs. Merryweather said impatiently, "He's the handyman. No, he wasn't with her at the time. No one was. No, there wasn't any excitement that I know of. Yes, she had lunch. . . ."

Austin rounded the bed, his mouth set with grim determination. He wanted answers, and he wanted them now. "Give me the phone." Mrs. Merryweather didn't argue. Instead, she took over his vigil by the bed, smoothing Candice's brow and patting her limp hand.

Gripping the phone, Austin snapped into the receiver, "This is Austin Hyde. I want to know why Mrs. Vanausdale fainted!"

After a startled pause, the doctor reminded Austin of her condition, which escalated Austin's blood pressure. "I know she's pregnant, but what does that have to do with fainting?"

Mrs. Merryweather spoke up. "Maybe she's been working too hard."

She flinched when Austin swung a fierce gaze her way. "Working? What the hell is she doing working? Isn't that what you're getting paid for? Where are the other maids? Where's the rest of the household staff? There must be more maids in a house this size." He glanced around, noticing for the first time how quiet the house was. And no sign of anyone other than Candice and Mrs. Merryweather.

Mrs. Merryweather huffed. "I do my job,

mister, and I can't keep on her every second of the day. She sneaks around and—"

The doctor temporarily forgotten, Austin burned with an irrational anger. "You should have—"

"Don't you go blaming me, young man! As for what happened to the staff, that's none of your business, and Mrs. Dale would tell you so herself if she could, the poor dear. In fact, she's likely worn out from saving your useless butt from drowning!"

That accusation stopped Austin cold. Guilt swamped him. Maybe it *was* his fault. God, what if her impromptu rescue had really hurt her or the baby? He'd never forgive himself!

An indistinguishable noise from the bed interrupted their spat. In unison, they turned to look at Candice, who was now stirring on the comforter. Austin moved closer, his relief so great, he thought he'd have to sit down. The bed looked good. Hell, right now the floor looked inviting.

Her voice sounded weak but clear. "It's not your fault, Mr. Hyde. Someone was looking through my window." She tried to sit up, and the housekeeper jumped to arrange the pillows behind her. "He pressed his face against the windowpane and it scared the daylights out of me. I guess that's when I fainted."

It took a moment for her words to sink in. When they did, Austin dropped the phone and headed for the window. "Mrs. Merryweather, get rid of the doctor and call the police," he ordered.

Chapter Five

"No!"

Austin's bare feet came to a halt at Candice's startled exclamation. He turned with a frown, his mind on catching the intruder. "What? *Don't* call the police? Why in hell—"

"Watch your mouth, young man!"

They both ignored Mrs. Merryweather.

Candice said, "Because if you call them, it will be all over the papers tomorrow. I don't want the publicity."

"I know someone who . . ." Austin trailed off as Candice adamantly shook her head. Damn, but she was hardheaded. He tried again. "This guy is a friend who—"

"No, Mr. Hyde. No police. I'm fine, and whoever it was is long gone by now."

The stubborn tilt of her chin convinced Austin she wouldn't change her mind. Okay, so willfulness was a good trait, wasn't it? Maybe their child would inherit—

Wait a minute! The safety of his child was at stake here. "Maybe you need a little time to think about this."

Mrs. Merryweather stepped forward as if to intervene, but Austin stopped her with a warning look. He was tired of her bullying. "Mrs. Merryweather, I'm sure Mrs. Dale would like a cold glass of something after her ordeal."

Beneath his burning gaze, Candice nodded. The housekeeper huffed and stomped from the room. After she was gone, Austin moved to the bed and gazed down at Candice. She looked fragile and lovely, this woman who carried his child. Yet she had to be strong to fight her late husband's family and bring a child into the world alone.

A lump formed in his throat. He thought about Jack, and how lucky his brother was to be alive. It was Jack's fault he was here, worrying himself to a frazzle over a wealthy widow who could hire ten burly guards but obviously didn't have the common sense to do it.

Damn Jack.

He sat on the edge of the bed and held her gaze for a long moment. The lump in his throat got bigger, for she returned his unwavering stare with big eyes filled with both strength and vulnerability. Softly, he asked, "What's the real reason you don't want the police involved? Did you recognize the man?"

"No, I didn't know him." She hesitated, dropping her gaze as if to gather her strength. When she lifted it again, there was a hard glint in her eyes. "This kind of thing has happened before, someone on the property peeking and the police never find out who it is."

"But there's a story the next day? In the papers?" Austin was beginning to see what she was getting at. "So you think it's a plan of some kind, just to get your name bounced around in the tabloids?" He watched her swallow. Damned if it didn't make him hungry. What *was* it about this woman? Rich women *never* appealed to him, yet this one . . .

"It seems that way. And now, with you here . . ."

Ah, he got it. "With me here, they'd really have a field day, huh?" She was a fast thinker. He liked that. Rubbing his chin, he mimicked, "Lonely Heiress Hires Love Slave!" She laughed, and it seemed natural that his hand found hers. A small, fragile hand that held hidden strength. "Hey, you're pretty sharp for a—" He stopped, thinking she probably wouldn't appreciate that brand of male humor. He had to remember who she was.

Rich, pregnant, and a confirmed widow.

"Woman?" she supplied with a shy but teasing smile. "Should I take that as a compliment?"

"Well, of course." He laughed with her, deciding he liked this side of Candice Vanausdale. Maybe she should faint more often. No! He took that thought back. He *never* wanted to go through that hell again.

Knowing Mrs. Merryweather would charge into the room at any moment, Austin asked a question that had been nagging at the back of his mind. "Don't you have any family that could stay with you until . . . ?"

A shadow crossed her face, making Austin regret his stupid question. He hadn't meant to make her sad or distress her in any way. Hadn't he read in that damned book that stress was bad for pregnant women?

"My mother died when I was eight. I've got a stepfather, but we don't communicate often."

Austin sensed she really didn't want to talk about it. Fine by him. He just wanted to know a little of her history, since she was going to have his baby. Speaking of which, he couldn't seem to get that fact out of his mind for longer than a few seconds. Was he, then, actually warming to the idea? Impossible!

Crazy.

Damn Jack!

"Thank you for coming to my rescue once again."

Well, hell, why did she have to go and sound so sincere? Austin knew he was about to overstep his bounds then, but he couldn't stop himself. Yes, he was probably moving too fast, but how else was he to get to know her? Certainly not with Mrs. Merryweather breathing down his neck. "You need to relax more, you know. All this stress is bad for the baby."

"Oh? And what would you know about that?"

His lips twitched at the sparkle in her eyes. He sobered fast. Indeed, what did he know? More importantly, *why* would he know? *Think fast, Hyde!* "Well, I've done some research."

"So you said earlier. Why?"

Was there a hint of suspicion in her voice? Nah, probably just his paranoia. Still, he'd better make it good to make it believable.

Of course! Jack.

"Actually, I sometimes helped Jack study when he was in pre-med. You know, for finals and term papers and all. He had planned to become a doctor."

"I'm not surprised. He's a very intelligent

man, and very knowledgeable about many aspects of medicine."

That pucker between her brows made him want to kiss it away. God, she was gorgeous. He cleared his throat and tried to jerk his mind back to the subject at hand. What was it? Oh, why he knew what he knew about pregnancy and babies. "Anyway, I guess a lot of it stuck in my head. Like the fact that you should laugh more."

"Really?"

"Yes. And not worry." He tried to look his most serious as he dropped what he was pretty certain was an outright lie. "And eat a wide variety foods. In fact, I think you and I should have pizza tonight. My treat. My place—uh, your place—over the garage."

His heart thumped loudly as he waited for her reaction to his bold invitation. Gently, he reached up and closed her mouth. She tortured him by licking her lips.

"Mrs. Merryweather would—"

"Doesn't the woman sleep at all?" He was whispering now, his eyes on her mouth. No need for lipstick. She had a curvy mouth, a kissable mouth. "Can't you sneak out?" Just the two of them, coconspirators. What a dirty dog he was.

Well, hell, his motives were pure, weren't

they? He wanted to get to know the mother of his child, and he wanted to keep her healthy. She looked too strung out, and no wonder. Anyone with her problems would suffer stress. He was just trying to help. Nothing wrong with that, right? Then why was he whispering and watching the door?

"Okay."

Austin's eyes widened. "Okay? You will?"

She smiled slowly. It was a beautiful, winsome smile, and Austin's heart lurched in response. Damn Jack.

"Why not? I can trust you, can't I?"

What a rotten, lowlife—

"Mr. Hyde?" A tiny note of uncertainty crept into her voice. "Can't I?"

"Yes, of course." His own smile felt painful and fraudulent. "I'm harmless, aren't I?"

About as harmless as Jack with his specimens.

Hoping he didn't look as guilty as he felt, Austin stood. "I'm going outside to check things out—after I shut the water off under the sink." At her puzzled look, Austin started to explain, but at that moment Mrs. Merryweather's angry muttering reached their ears. Her voice grew in volume as she drew nearer.

". . . water everywhere! Take me hours to mop it up! Handyman, ha! If he's a handyman,

96

I'm Cindy Crawford."

Candice glanced at the door in total bewilderment. "What—"

Austin shushed her. "I'll explain later. I'd better go while the going's good."

Her hand shook as she applied a light shade of lipstick.

Mr. Hyde had stared at her lips.

Candice leaned forward and studied her reflection in the mirror, wondering if he'd found some flaw. Howard had never complained about her mouth—one of the few things he *hadn't* complained about—other than to lecture her about making certain her lipstick was fresh and never smeared.

No. Not thoughts of Howard, not now.

Candice pulled a tissue from the box and wiped the lipstick from her lips. She then set them in a determined line and mentally reminded herself that she didn't care what anyone thought about her lips or any other part of her. It was what *she* thought that counted, right? Besides, wearing lipstick would draw attention to her mouth, and if Mr. Hyde had found something wrong . . .

As she stared into the mirror, her expression suddenly crumpled. What was she doing? Sneaking around, waiting for Mrs. Merryweather to go to her room upstairs, wondering what Mr.

Hyde thought of her mouth. Anticipating seeing him again.

The handyman.

So? She wasn't a snob, had never been a snob. She came from a poor family, had even worked hard for a living herself. Howard had been the snob, and his years of brainwashing were trying to take hold now.

But Howard was dead, and Candice reminded herself that his beliefs had never been her own. Now she could think for herself again, and she *liked* her way of thinking. Watching the mirror, she squared her shoulders and softened her mouth. There. Now, that was more like the old Candice. Before Howard. Before her mother had died. Before she realized that her stepfather hated her.

Mr. Hyde was nice, and funny, and he seemed to be harmless. Yes, he was handsome, very much so, in a shivery, dangerous sort of way. And was *big*. And tawny. Like a lion.

But harmless. Gentle. She was sure of it. She suspected he sensed her loneliness, but she felt secure that as long as she kept things on a platonic level, so would Mr. Hyde.

Just as a self-reminder, she would continue to call him Mr. Hyde. That should do the trick.

Satisfied with her rationale, Candice smoothed a nonexistent wrinkle from her white silk shirt and tugged on the split skirt in a boring shade of gray. She really should go shopping now that she could pick her own clothes. But she still hated to go out. Invariably, she was recognized and harassed. Maybe she should try ordering from a catalog. She frowned. And get more of the same elegant, boring clothes she wore now?

Not a chance!

Flicking off the bathroom light in case Mrs. Merryweather happened to look in, Candice moved silently to the sliding doors and let herself out onto the dimly lit patio.

She was nervous. Extremely so. What if she were wrong about Mr. Hyde? She should have called Dr. Jack and asked some questions. She should have confessed to Mrs. Merryweather so someone would at least know where she was. This was the most reckless thing she had ever done, and—

Stop being paranoid! Candice stopped at the edge of the back drive leading to the garage and took a deep breath. It was just a friendly get-together for pizza. That was all it was and ever would be. They came from two different worlds, and—

No. That didn't matter, and it wasn't true anyway. Mr. Hyde possessed plenty of admirable assets; they just weren't monetary. He had a beautiful smile, wit, whimsy, and a mischievous nature that made her feel warm and giggly, more like her old self again.

But Mr. Hyde *was* a stranger. Yet did that matter? They were only having pizza, not getting married. She wasn't ever going to marry again, so why even think about it? She patted her stomach fondly. No wicked stepfather for this child.

But she couldn't resist the lure of companionship, the promise of friendship. Besides, he made her laugh. Her sandals crunched on the gravel as she forced herself to move on. He'd said ten o'clock, for an early "midnight" snack—an hour after Mrs. Merryweather generally retired for the night. According to her watch, she was exactly on time.

The steps leading to the apartment over the garage loomed ahead. At the top of the landing, a small light glowed. Butterflies danced in her stomach. Her palms began to sweat. *Friendship, friendship,* she recited beneath her breath as she climbed the wooden steps. Nothing to it. *All* there was to it.

She was just out of practice. Howard had been jealous and critical of the few friends she'd tried to cultivate during their marriage.

No Howard tonight. Nada. None. Zip.

Candice closed her eyes, took a deep breath, and knocked quietly on the door. Mrs. Merryweather had ears like a hawk, and sound

100

carried on the warm, still night air.

Mr. Hyde answered the door quickly, a blur of golden hair and fierce blue eyes. Candice had little time to do more than gasp as he grabbed her arm and pulled her inside. They landed against the wall next to the door, his body almost touching hers, his breath warm against her ear as he whispered in a deep, mock-sinister voice, "Were you followed?"

A scream had locked in her throat. Now her body went limp as a noodle, then instantly rigid again when she realized going limp caused her to press against him. They were already too close—so close she could smell the mint toothpaste on his breath and feel his belt buckle against her belly.

The man was hopelessly insane.

Breathlessly, she inched along the wall until her body was free. Her laugh came out all shaky, revealing. "You scared the dickens out of me!"

"Well, we can't have that, can we? Especially when you're here to relax." But he smiled wolfishly, his eyes dancing with the devil. His hair was still damp from a recent shower, and he wore a faded striped cotton shirt open nearly to the waist of his low-slung jeans, almost as if he had forgotten to button it.

And he was barefoot.

Candice swallowed, jerking her gaze up, only to collide with the disturbing sight of his bared chest. She looked away, anywhere but at him. The man obviously needed tutoring in etiquette. To say the least, shoes were expected when inviting a woman—

"Take off your shoes."

Candice gawked at him. "What?"

He leaned a casual arm against the wall, smiling mysteriously as he repeated, "Take off your shoes. And let your hair down. In fact, it wouldn't hurt to unbutton the first few buttons of your shirt as well."

She gasped. "I beg your—"

"Lady, you don't have to beg me for anything. Just crook your little finger, and I'll come running."

His drawling words shivered over her, alarming and arousing at the same time. She never should have come; she should have known her friendly, harmless version of Mr. Hyde was too good to be true. Drawing herself up, she pressed her unpainted lips together, hoping the hurt didn't show. "I think coming here was a mistake. You obviously have the wrong impression of me, Mr. Hyde."

"Nope." He was smiling again, a secret, coaxing smile. "Just showing you how to loosen up, relax, have some fun."

Candice tried to swallow, but her throat felt

too dry. Tears threatened, adding to her humiliation. How had she misread him so totally? Considered him a potential friend? "I think your idea of fun is very different than mine, Mr. Hyde."

"Nope. We have the same ideas. You just don't know it yet. Let me show you."

His arrogance amazed her. Adding to her outrage, he reached for her shirt collar, as if to unbutton it. She slapped at his hand, then made a clumsy dive for the door. It wasn't easy, with all six feet of him in the way. "Let me out of here, you barbarian!"

"Nope."

"And stop saying that!" She wiped a strand of hair out of her eyes and glared at him. So what if her lips trembled and he knew she was about to cry? She didn't owe him anything, and she didn't care what he thought. In fact, first thing in the morning she would have Mrs. Merryweather fire him!

He grabbed her gently by the shoulders, holding her effortlessly as she struggled. Finally, she released an exasperated breath. She wasn't frightened . . . yet. Which was absurd, considering she was being held hostage by a brawny, golden-skinned handyman who could easily snap her in two, as Mrs. Merryweather had warned.

That reminder should have scared her, but it

didn't. Instinct told her she was safe. It had to be instinct, or maybe sheer stupidity, but something about that smiling mouth and those dark blue, twinkling eyes clobbered any fear she might have felt.

"Mrs. Dale, relax."

Well, that was comforting—he was mauling her but still addressing her with respect. "How?" she snapped, glaring up at him. She blew harshly at that irritating strand of hair that had worked loose from her barrette, wishing she could fix it so he wouldn't think her slovenly.

Dear God, what was she thinking? She shouldn't care about such a thing. Besides, Mr. Hyde wouldn't care if her hair was mussed, or her lipstick smudged, or if anything else was out of place. Why would he?

"That's what I'm trying to teach you here," he said with a smile. She drew a sharp breath. And realization belatedly began to dawn. What had he been trying to tell her for the last ten minutes . . . before she had twisted his meaning so? How could she be so dense? All she had to do was take a good look at his eyes and see the gentle, merry light dancing there. Not insanity, not arrogance, not lust, but fun-loving, caring human emotion. And somehow—amazingly— understanding.

The resistance left Candice like a rush of air

104

from a balloon. She sagged against him, her head falling to his shoulder. She couldn't look at him, not after that embarrassing display. "I'm sorry. I . . . I guess I misunderstood you." His chest jerked a bit, and she realized he was laughing and trying to hide it. Heat flushed her cheeks, but she wasn't angry. She deserved to be laughed at.

"I'll say. Woman, you are one uptight person," he teased. "Good thing I'm here to give you some lessons in relaxing."

"I know," she mumbled, glad for the concealing shelter of his shoulder. He smelled like soap, a clean, manly scent, reminding her of a commercial she'd seen long ago for Irish Spring. And he smelled faintly of paint, a not unpleasant smell. Just as she was about to pull away, she felt his hand on her hair. She stilled, wondering, fearing.

Hoping?

A few seconds later there was a slight pressure against her neck; then she heard the distinct click of her barrette snapping open. Her hair tumbled free. She rarely wore it loose. Howard . . .

Mr. Hyde's voice sounded slightly rough. "That's better. Now, how about those shoes."

Candice leaned away, shaking her hair out a little self-consciously. It felt strange but good. And she felt shy and reckless, a confusing combination. But then, this man had a way of doing that to her.

When he took her by the hand and led her to a chair, she didn't resist, even though now he would see her feet and likely poke fun at her. She had such ugly—

"You have beautiful feet. Elegant, so slim and . . . sexy."

Sexy? Candice's mouth fell open in shock. "I—my feet are big and ugly and—"

"Nope. They're beautiful." As if to prove his point, he lifted her leg and admired her foot from every angle. "See that curve? High arches—a sign of nobility. Long, slim toes. Smooth heels. I even admired them the first time I saw you."

The first time he'd seen her, that day at the clinic, she had indeed been wearing sandals, she remembered, to complement a rather daring dress she'd bought long ago. One Howard had forbidden her to wear. Donning it that day had been a tentative step toward independence, and an attempt to camouflage herself from the media.

"In fact, your feet were the first thing I noticed about you."

"They were?" she squeaked, trying to draw her foot away. He held fast. A pulse pounded where his thumb pressed into the arch, and his skin felt hot. It had to be, because everywhere his hand touched, she burned.

Finally letting go of her foot, he rose and placed her shoes by the door, then came back, kneeling before her. Candice held her breath. He'd said something about unbuttoning her shirt, but surely he wouldn't—

He would. He did. One button at a time. But with all the emotion he might exhibit while undressing a child. Candice was shocked at the disappointment she felt, berating herself for her shameless thoughts. Friends, that's what they were. And that was all she wanted or needed. She was his employer, and now they were striking up a tentative friendship.

Her breath hitched in shock as his knuckles grazed the top of her breasts.

An accident. A pure and innocent accident, she was certain, even as a startling, unfamiliar warmth flooded her stomach and thighs.

Just as she was about to panic over her own reaction, he suddenly backtracked and refastened a button, not looking at her as he mumbled, "Just the first two will suffice."

He settled back on his heels and finally met her gaze, his eyes clear, his gaze direct. The teasing light had faded, replaced with an elusive emotion Candice would have given her eyeteeth to decipher. She experienced a burning need to know Mr. Hyde, inside and out.

"Now you look the way a mother-to-be ought to."

She blinked, startled. She wasn't certain *what* she'd expected him to say, but it wasn't that. Her curiosity got the better of her. "And what did I look like before?"

His gaze drifted slowly over her, still unreadable, serious. "My mother," he stated quietly.

Chapter Six

Candice resisted the urge to slap her hands over her ears. Surely he hadn't said . . . "I don't understand."

"No, you wouldn't." He sighed, looking uncomfortable. "It's a long story. Forget it. I'm sorry I ever brought it up."

Candice wasn't one to push. Even when he'd pried into her personal life earlier, he'd had the grace to back off. She would do the same. But some day she hoped he'd trust her enough to confide in her. Because she sensed he needed to, wanted to, she told herself. And because she was curious, which, she also told herself, was natural.

The timer on the oven began to buzz, breaking the queer silence. They both turned to look in the direction of the tiny kitchen adjoining the small living area. Candice knew the apartment also boasted a bedroom and a bath. Furnished with cast-offs from the big house, it was actually a homey, comfortable place. She recognized the mauve-and-blue striped sofa and chair; she'd ordered them for the den, and Howard had hated them.

That's in the past, Candice. All in the past.

"You *made* a pizza?" she registered. Then she flushed, realizing her surprise might sound rude. Lots of men cooked these days, didn't they? "I mean . . ."

With a grin, Austin let her off the hook. "No, I sent out earlier so the deliveryman wouldn't wake the dragon. I put the pie in the oven to reheat a few minutes before ten. Come on, let's eat."

She placed her hand in his outstretched one, and he gallantly helped her rise. Much more of this and she might want to move in. He made her feel . . . like a person instead of an object. Like a woman, instead of just a dutiful, obedient wife. Feminine, yet strong.

Weak-kneed with desire.

Candice covered her gasp with a cough. Lord, what was wrong with her? She was a widowed, moral, pregnant woman who . . .

Who possessed normal desires.

Desires? Well, maybe it was a hormonal thing, because she'd never really experienced desire this way before.

In a daze, she accompanied Mr. Hyde to the table, where he politely pulled out her chair.

When she was seated, she watched him turn to take the pizza from the oven. She smiled at the sight of the smoking box, relaxing a bit as she realized that at least the man lacked expertise in the culinary department. Another few moments and the cardboard would have burst into flames.

While he shoveled pizza onto paper plates, Candice dug her toes into the carpet, trying to remember the last time she'd eaten a meal barefoot. Maybe as a child. Never with Howard.

Candice sighed and hooked her hair behind her ears. A breeze from the ceiling fan above the table caressed the skin exposed by her now open collar, making her a bit uneasy again. Then she reminded herself that loosening her collar had been an innocent act, a lesson in relaxing. Oddly, though, it was working the opposite way. It made her more conscious of her femininity.

Mr. Hyde turned to bring the filled plates to the table and set one before her. Broad-shoul-

111

dered and barefoot? He looked every inch the confident, comfortable male.

A moment later, he sat across from her and scooted a can of ice-cold Coke her way.

She noticed it was decaffeinated, and she smiled. Then she scanned the table, puzzled. "No forks?"

"Nope." The grin was back, the strange shadows gone from his expression. "It's illegal to eat pizza with a fork."

"Another . . . lesson?"

"Yes, ma'am."

She watched him pick up a slice of pizza and take a huge bite. How many years had it been since she'd eaten pizza? Way too many. Just looking at the greasy pepperoni sitting atop a thick layer of gooey cheese made her mouth water. After a surreptitious glance to make sure he wasn't watching, she lifted the hot slice and took the plunge.

It was delicious, every fattening, cholesterol-laden bite of it, and probably worth the heartburn Howard always told her would come after eating such plebian fare.

Howard was probably turning over in his grave.

"You've got tomato sauce on your chin," Austin pointed out matter-of-factly.

Candice automatically grabbed for her napkin and dabbed her chin—before catching sight of his mischievous expression.

"Gotcha. Lesson number two: don't take everything and everyone so seriously." He started on his third slice of pizza. She was still working on the first. "By the way, are you going to breast-feed?"

Candice jerked in shock, and the pizza in her hand did a somersault, landing pepperoni side down on her silk blouse.

Austin kept right on eating, his look way too innocent to be believable. He shrugged his big shoulders. "Pizza now, baby puke later—one way or the other, that shirt had to go."

Lesson number three? Candice wondered. She peeled the pizza from her shirt, grimacing at the stain left behind. Yuck.

Austin pushed back his chair. "I've got a T-shirt you can throw on."

"No, I—that's okay." The possibility of wearing his shirt sounded so . . . intimate.

He kept on going as if she hadn't protested, returning with a black and gold football jersey. "It's my favorite shirt."

"You played football?" Why was she surprised? With those shoulders and muscled thighs, was it any wonder?

Nodding he rolled the shirt into a ball and threw it, football style. She caught it, fingering the material. Silly tears stung her eyes. She must be tired, to cry just because he'd offered her his favorite shirt.

"Tight end. You know where the bathroom is?"

Tight end. Referring to the position he played in football conjured up an image of him cleaning the pool in those indecently short shorts. Oh, boy, was it ever. Another admirable asset of Mr. Hyde.

Candice scrambled to her feet and headed for the bathroom to change before he could notice her flaming face and guess her illicit thoughts. She shut and locked the door, unfastening her blouse with shaking fingers. He *did* have a tight butt, and was it really all that horrible of her to notice?

Slipping the jersey over her shoulders, she moved to stand in front of the mirror over the sink. There was a dab of pizza sauce at the corner of her mouth, and Coke fizzling on her upper lip. The shoulder seams of the jersey hung nearly to her elbows, the hem to her knees, covering her skirt and making it appear as if she had nothing on beneath.

Austin had created the perfect disguise, she thought, looking at her wide-eyed expression. Nobody would recognize this teenager wannabe. Including Mrs. Merryweather.

Including herself.

"You okay in there?" He rapped on the door.

Her heart leaped against her ribs. "Y—Yes, I'm fine. I'll be out in a moment." Darn and double darn! Even her voice sounded like a teenager's, all fluttery and silly. Maybe Mr. Hyde *wasn't* such a good influence. She had to agree she was a little uptight, but this was a rocket blast in the opposite direction.

Maybe she shouldn't open that door and let him see her like this.

"I don't own a camera, you know."

Candice wiped at her mouth with a piece of toilet tissue and eyed her messy blouse, deliberating on whether she should wear it anyway. Although the jersey covered more, she felt more exposed emotionally. Nearly naked. This was too much, too soon.

He tapped on the door again. "However, there is a hidden video recorder in there. Can't be too careful these days—most people don't consider it stealing to take toilet paper."

Despite herself, Candice nervously scanned the tiny enclosure, calling herself nine kinds of silly. She found nothing, of course. If only he'd go away, let her compose herself.

"I can't believe you can stand up to a clan of money-hungry in-laws, but you can't face *me*."

Candice froze. Anger wiped out her shyness in the space of a heartbeat. She jerked open the door, surprising Austin. "I thought you said you didn't read the newspapers!" she flung at him with unmistakable accusation and a big dose of hurt.

He'd lied. And if he'd lied about that, then how could she trust him at all?

Austin tried to think of the best word to describe his stupidity. He'd committed a major blunder, and just when he was making so much progress. Still, his mouth watered as he took in the sight of Candice standing, so furious, in the bathroom doorway. She was one beautiful bundle of sexy mama, with her hair all tousled and wearing his jersey in a way he never could. Gone was Miss Chilly, and in her place was Ms. Hot Tamale.

Yet, he still couldn't picture her burping a baby. No, a baby wasn't in this picture at all. But *he* was, and the things he wanted to do to her, a baby should never be exposed to.

Maybe it wasn't such a good idea to embark on this quest to loosen her up. It might be interfering with his objectivity just a tad. He had to remind himself, sternly, that Candice Vanausdale was everything he *didn't* like in a woman. Yeah, so maybe there was a chance she might make a good mother, with his help, but she'd always be Mrs. Howard Vanausdale. Rich. Spoiled. Sophisticated. Uptight.

And not for you.

That inner warning seemed to bounce in one ear and out the other into oblivion.

When he finally managed to swallow and force his gaze to her eyes, he immediately realized just how seriously he'd blundered. In more ways than one. He said the first thing that came to his dazed mind, which just happened to be the truth.

"When Jack told me about the job, he filled me in on a few things he thought I should know." He swallowed again, but it didn't ease the dryness in his throat any more than it had the first time. "For safety's sake, he told me he'd read about the trouble you've been having with Mr. Vanausdale's relatives."

Was she believing him? He couldn't really tell. She just stood there, looking like the first arrival for a teen slumber party. Maybe he should have left well enough alone. Maybe if he had, he wouldn't be entertaining the very naughty thoughts he was thinking right now. Like, hauling her against him and kissing the hell out of those extremely kissable lips. Or lifting his jersey and finding out if her breasts were a perfect fit for his hands, as he suspected they were.

She curled her fingers around the doorjamb, and Austin noticed with a jolt of surprise that her nails were short and unpainted. Obviously, this lady had not been spending her time at a beauty salon getting manicures.

But then, she didn't get out much because of the media, who must know something he didn't. Otherwise they wouldn't be going to the trouble they were, right?

Right. Austin felt better. Justified. His chest swelled with relief. He was back on track. In focus without a camera.

He smiled at the pun.

She knocked the smile right off his face with the low, vibrant timbre of her fury. "You've been making fun of me, haven't you? All of this"— she plucked at his jersey and swung her honey-gold hair—"was just a game to you, wasn't it?" Her hands came down on her hips, outlining her waist.

Austin helplessly dropped his gaze for a quick look before jerking it back to her angry cat's eyes. Whew! Nothing wimpy about *this* woman! She was burning—burning to punch his lights out.

"You thought it would be funny to dress me down, bring the rich widow to her knees."

"Now, hold on a damned minute—"

"What was the next *lesson*, Mr. Hyde? Skinny-dipping in the pool?"

Well, now that she mentioned it . . .

"Would that loosen me up, do you think? Make me look more like a mother-to-be? And if I got *really* lucky, a reporter would get a nice big glossy for the paper. Now that would be something for the scrapbook—something to save for my child!" She took a step forward, and he took a step backward, colliding with the hall wall.

To Austin's pleasure, she kept coming at him until her body was shoved up against his. But her blistering glare told him this wasn't his lucky day; she just didn't realize what she was doing, she was so spitting mad.

And hurt, he now saw. And that bothered him. Not that she was mad—that proved she had backbone. But the hurt was something else. He wasn't into inflicting pain. In fact, he'd wanted to make certain his child would be okay, wouldn't suffer as he and Jack had. But maybe he'd gotten carried away.

She grabbed his chin and stood on tiptoe to try to achieve his eye level. And her voice sank to a contemptuous whisper, making Austin wonder just exactly what his efforts had unleashed. He never would have imagined this tiger inside Candice Vanausdale's petite kitten's body.

"To think I was feeling sorry for you earlier with your sad, puppy-dog eyes and unhappy hints about your mother. When all the time you were inwardly laughing at me, trying to humiliate me."

That did it. Austin did the only thing he could think of to snap her out of her hurt and convince her otherwise; he moved his hands to her waist and leaned to cover her mouth with his.

She stiffened in shock, but at least she wasn't fighting him. Still, she wasn't responding yet, either.

He ran the tip of his tongue across her tightly closed lips, conscious of her rigidity beneath his hands. All she needed was a little more coaxing to relax and let him kiss the hurt away, he decided. In the meantime, he wouldn't think about the hard points of her breasts poking his chest, or her belly pressed against his. Neither would he give a thought to the delicious feeling of her pelvic bone pressing against the straining hardness in his jeans.

Lord Almighty, but she was a taste of Heaven. She fit him in all the right places, and the heat between them should definitely be labeled a fire hazard. If only she would realize it.

He continued to coax her lips apart in tiny, gratifying degrees. Finally, he sighed as her mouth opened to his. She tasted of pizza and the sweet, sweet honey of desire, and he moaned from the sheer pleasure of it.

The second moan was not his, however, and the instant he realized this, Austin's control dropped a few yards shy of a goal. A touchdown wasn't far away, but, hell, he couldn't take advantage of her like this. She might be tough, but he knew—*knew*—that she was also breakable.

Oh, and don't forget pregnant. Austin eased his hold on her and slowly, ever so reluctantly, pulled his lips away and settled them on her cheek. Her warm breath came in tiny, rapid puffs against his face. He wasn't a bit surprised to find his voice thick. "I swear I wasn't making fun of you." He felt her lashes sweep his cheek as she slowly opened her eyes. A butterfly kiss, he remembered from a long time ago. What nanny had told him that?

At the moment, it didn't matter. Nothing mattered but that she believe him.

When she moved her head to his shoulder, she unintentionally buried his face in her hair. Austin inhaled the smell of green apples, then released his breath on a ragged sigh. His knees felt ridiculously weak, reminding him of his younger days and necking in the backseat at drive-ins. "You—you didn't finish eating."

Sheridon Smythe

"No. I didn't." She lifted her head to look at him before she stepped away.

Austin envied her resilience. She was flushed, and there was an odd, dazed expression on her face, he thought smugly, but damned if she didn't walk straight, which *he* couldn't do. He felt drunk on desire and antsy at the same time.

Hell, why didn't he just admit it? The lady turned him on, rich or not, pregnant or not! Pregnant . . . with *his* baby. Austin paused to steady himself against the wall, the enormity of that fact hitting him squarely in the belly.

He wanted her, but he had never made love to her, and she was already carrying his child. Fire spread quickly, racing to his groin. The thought, the simple, irrefutable fact that she carried his child, *turned him on?*

The realization staggered him, nearly buckled his desire-weakened knees. He leaned against the wall, glad Candice appeared too bashful to look at him.

Well, I never. One of his nannies used to say that, usually in response to some prank he or Jack had instigated.

A nanny. Something he was determined his child would never have to suffer. Okay, so they hadn't *all* been bad, but the statistics had not been good.

Six months. He had six months to work on

122

this wealthy woman, to convince her how wonderful raising a baby could be. To make her understand that a child absolutely needed a mother who cared and proved it. To show her how to have fun and enjoy life, so she could better be that healthy, happy mother.

And he had to do all of this without taking the mother of his child to bed and making wild, never-ending love to her?

Austin began to chuckle. The chuckles grew into belly laughs, the more he thought about his predicament. Through laughter-induced tears, he saw Candice staring at him. He tried to imagine how she would look if he blurted out the truth right now, and the image sent him into harder laughter.

She couldn't have known what he was laughing about, but something in his expression must have reassured her, for she smiled. Then giggled. Finally she laughed along with him.

Somehow, he made it to the table and fell into the chair opposite hers. Wiping his streaming eyes, he finally managed to contain his hilarity. She was a good sport about it, handing him a napkin and chuckling as if she knew exactly what he was laughing about.

And this thought nearly set him off again. To bring himself under control, he forced himself to think of more serious things. Okay, so this *was* serious, but he needed something that would take his mind off the fact that the woman sitting across from him was going to have his baby and didn't know it.

Wouldn't believe it, most likely. Hell, no *most* about it. She would not believe it. She would think it an absurd lie designed to get her into the sack. Fact was, if Austin believed it would work, he'd be tempted to tell her.

But then, he reminded himself, he'd been the one to stop what had started happening, and he'd best remember why. She'd been through a lot, what with losing her husband and now having to deal with his obnoxious relatives, and with a baby on the way, to boot. He was no pregnancy expert—he hadn't even finished the book *From Discovery to Delivery*—but he was smart enough to realize she didn't need the added stress a new sexual relationship would bring.

Oh, sure, there were definite pluses, but Austin thought they were mostly to *his* advantage. This lady was manna to the media, and they would eat her alive if they ever found out. And so would her husband's relatives. Between them, they would break her into a million pieces and sweep what was left of her under the rug.

Well, he would do what he could to keep her safe from all that. Jack had done enough damage.

Speaking of Jack . . . damn him. Now things had become even more tangled.

"I'm sorry," they both said at once, finally daring to look at each other.

Candice blushed, and Austin thought it was the most endearing thing he'd ever seen. He couldn't fathom how she'd kept such innocence, and he didn't know why it mattered to him.

"I shouldn't have—"

"I didn't mean to—"

They both halted again and eyed each other as if for the first time. She had crossed her arms and now looked quite at ease with her hair down and wearing his football jersey. But gazing at her mussed hair reminded *him* of how it had gotten that way, leaving him anything *but* at ease.

Seeking a distraction, he went to the desk in a corner of the room and retrieved the object he'd found beneath her window after the trespasser had frightened her into fainting. He wished he'd gotten his hands on the bastard, but at least they now had a clue.

She unfolded her arms and sat up, tension returning to her face as she stared at the diamond-studded gold wristwatch he placed on the table. "Where did you find this?" Picking it up, she turned it over, studying it with a puzzled frown.

Austin watched her face intently, hating to be the one who'd put the frown there. "On the ground below the east guest bedroom window, after you saw the intruder. It must have come off while he was climbing on the trellis."

"So that's how he got up there." She set down the timepiece, looking disgusted and weary.

Austin resisted the urge to cuddle her against his shoulder. It wouldn't be wise, no matter how much she looked as if she needed it. "Ever seen it before?"

"No. But it's expensive."

"I gathered that," he said dryly. She'd never suspect how much he knew about diamonds and gold. His mother had loved jewelry—more than she'd loved her own kids. "And I can't imagine a reporter wearing this, can you? So that leaves . . . ?" He had his suspicions, but he wanted to see if she agreed with him.

Her gaze met his, somber and heart-tugging. "My in-laws. They must be getting desperate to get some mud on me. Luke says they don't stand a chance of winning, but—"

"Luke?" Austin growled. "Who's Luke?" He had assumed she was all alone in the world, except for Mrs. Merryweather, of course. The thought of another man in her life cut through his gut like a scythe. Which was stupid, because he knew he didn't own her just because she carried his baby. Right?

Well . . .

"Luke McVey. He's my lawyer."

He didn't like that winsome smile. And this Luke guy? Probably a stuck-up, suit-wearing, slick-haired—

"He's also a friend."

Hell. Austin decided not to hound her about the *friend* part. She didn't need the stress, he reminded himself. He'd just have to find out on his own in due time. Because of the unusual circumstances of her carrying his baby, of course.

Taking his seat, he crossed his arms and tried not to stare at the way her hair shimmered in the light. Expensive shampoo could do that, he told himself. Probably wasn't her natural color anyway. The moment he thought it, he cursed to himself, because it reminded him of how he could find out. He just managed to contain an anguished groan.

Damn Jack.

Double damn Jack.

He cleared his throat, hoping that would somehow clear his mind. Get it good and clean. "Just how far do you think these people would go to get at you?" At his question, her frown returned, and so did the shadows in her eyes. He liked them better when they were blazing with fire, or dazed with desire.

"I don't know. I really don't. Mrs. Merry-

127

weather . . . thinks I'm not serious enough about the danger."

"That settles it then." Austin tightened his jaw. He could do it—for the baby. And yes, for Candice. Mrs. Dale. Maybe it would be a good idea to keep calling her that, just as a self-reminder. "I'm moving into the big house," he announced.

Chapter Seven

Believing he was teasing her again, Candice waited for laughter, a smile, that tiny glimmer of wicked amusement she was becoming accustomed to seeing in his handsome features.

His jaw remained hard and square, his eyes dead serious. What an excellent poker face—if it *was* a bluff.

Finally, she broke the tension with a little laugh, which came out as a squeak. "You're kidding, right?"

He shook his head slowly.

"But why? What would your staying in the . . . house achieve?"

"Your safety. My peace of mind. Probably Mrs. Merryweather's, too."

Well, Candice wasn't too sure about that, considering Mrs. Merryweather's suspicions about Mr. Hyde himself. Also, there was this . . . attraction to consider. Just the thought of Austin Hyde sleeping under the same roof with her made her warm and achy in unmentionable places. Hormones, of course. She made a mental note to ask Dr. Robinson about this phenomenon during her next visit. And to find out what she could do about it.

His soft voice commanded her attention. "Unless you don't trust me?"

Instinctively, Candice sensed her answer was important to him. She didn't know or understand why, but it added to the warmth building within her by slow degrees.

Knowing this, experiencing this strange, aching reaction, how could she even consider his suggestion? It wasn't only Austin she didn't trust. After what had happened here tonight, she didn't have much faith in her own self-control, either. She had enjoyed his touch, his kiss, his closeness, and the wondrous desire he'd stirred inside her.

Deciding the watch on the table needed her undivided attention, she cast her gaze down and mumbled, "Do you think it's wise?" He knew what she meant, didn't he? A quick peek up showed that he did. His lips had curved into a rueful smile, and she watched him shrug.

"If I promise to be good?"

Candice crossed her legs at his low, husky entreaty. She had to. Something was certainly out of whack with her body, because her inner thighs were quivering. So was her voice, she discovered. "You weren't being bad . . . it's just that this is the worst possible time for me to . . . get involved with anyone." *And I'm pregnant with another man's child*. The silent reminder jolted her down to her bare toes. Austin Hyde actually *desired* her, even knowing this? She didn't know much about these things, but it somehow seemed odd.

Or maybe Mr. Hyde had forgotten about her condition during those few heated, wonderful moments.

"I understand." He rubbed a hand over the back of his neck and grimaced. "I . . . I was out of line tonight. It won't happen again unless you want it to."

He sounded sincere, which, perversely, hurt Candice's feelings.

Then he added something that wiped out her recent theory about his forgetting about her condition.

"However, I think you should consider the baby. His or her safety."

Slowly but surely he was tumbling her

excuses, weaving a spell of enchantment and longing with his low-voiced logic. Candice had to admit the prospect of his presence in the house held appeal. And maybe he wouldn't mind spending a few evenings painting and working on the nursery. After all, he *was* the handyman, and he'd be right there. Her mind latched on to the thought like a lifeline.

Her conscience snorted sarcastically, reminding her that he was only about forty-five seconds away living over the garage.

To the dismay of her conscience, though, she heard herself agreeing. "Maybe it's *not* such a bad idea. Maybe I'd sleep better, knowing—" No, she wouldn't. She licked her lips. "Mrs. Merryweather would sleep better, knowing you were in the house. But what about the media? If they found out a man was—"

"They won't. And if they do, then we'll say I'm your bodyguard, which won't be a lie."

She fingered the hem of the football jersey, then uncrossed her legs. The way he looked at her made her fidget like a schoolgirl in study hall. "Why are you doing all this?"

Austin chuckled, his white teeth flashing in his suntanned face. Candice swallowed. Lord, but his smile held the kick of a 110 volts.

"Would you believe me if I said it was for the money?"

Before she could think, she shook her head.

He inclined his own, as if he weren't surprised. "Then I'd have to say that I like your company. It's a little lonely living out here. Besides, I really do worry about you and the baby, especially after today."

Candice tensed. "You didn't live alone before?" Was there a woman? Was he divorced? Tomorrow, she would make that call to Jack Cruise before she went stark raving mad with curiosity! And then the rest of his words caught up with her. He worried about her *and the baby*.

Before she could delve into the questions his statement aroused, he answered her first query momentarily confusing her.

"Roommate." He let a few seconds pass before he added, "Male. Another good-for-nothing artist."

Her objection was spontaneous. "I happen to admire artists." What would he say if she told him *she* had artistic aspirations herself? Well, technically woodcarving was probably a craft. But, either way, she wasn't ready to reveal that part of herself, to risk ridicule, even though he didn't seem the type who would. Another thing she had noticed about Mr. Hyde was that he wasn't judgmental.

Yet, even knowing this, the thought of blurting out the truth terrified her. Howard's scathing comments about her "foolish little hobby" still haunted her. And old habits were hard to break.

But suddenly that last realization deepened the appeal of letting this funny, sensitive man have the run of her house. He was fast becoming the light at the end of a dark and difficult tunnel. With him, she felt safe, she felt cared for, she felt alive again. And if Mr. Hyde had a hidden agenda for wanting to move in, then she would deal with it when the time came.

If she wanted to. And if she didn't . . . then she was certain to have the experience of her life. Either way, it was her choice.

Her choice. She actually had a choice.

A rush of renewed relief enveloped her. She was strong. Resilient. In control of her own life now. Nobody would tell her what to do ever again. She had made this decision, and she felt good about it, knowing it was the best thing for her and her baby, and maybe even for Mrs. Merryweather. With Mr. Hyde around, maybe Mrs. Merryweather could take a little time for herself instead of spending every waking hour making sure Candice wasn't bothered, or hungry, or just plain alone.

She took such a deep breath, it left her giddy. Or was it the promise of an adventure? "Give me time to prepare Mrs. Merryweather."

Austin cut his gaze to the ceiling, rubbing his shadowed jaw. "That might take a while," he muttered. Then he stuck out his hand. "Meanwhile, let's shake on the deal."

Candice stared at his big hand. Her mouth went curiously dry, and her toes curled into the carpet as if they sought mooring. She hadn't forgotten how that hand had felt clamped to her waist as he held her against the hard length of his body. Lord, how *could* she forget? The man must have soaked up a lot of sun today to hold that kind of heat!

Finally, she placed her hand in his, her eyes flying wide when instead of shaking it, he turned her palm up and began to explore her fingers with the intensity of a fortune-teller.

"What's with these callouses?"

Trapped in the powerful beam of his gaze, Candice stammered, "I—We had to let the maids go." It wasn't the entire truth, but it wasn't a lie, either. She couldn't bear the possibility of his laughing should she tell him that she'd earned the callouses mostly through hours of carving and sanding, painting and varnishing.

In an effort to distract him, she blurted out more than he had a right to know. "The court froze Howard's assets until it reaches a decision, and the amount I'm allowed isn't enough to support a household staff." That was an understatement. Oh, why was she telling him this anyway? Chances were he already knew, despite his assurance that he didn't read the papers. Since Howard's death, Candice had discovered that nothing was confidential, nothing was sacred, and everyone could be bought.

Jack, Luke, and Mrs. Merryweather were about the only people she trusted these days.

And now . . . maybe Mr. Hyde.

She tugged at her hand. He let her go, but his mouth was set grimly. When he spoke, his tone was flat, accusing. "So you've been scrubbing floors."

She fidgeted in her chair, tearing her gaze away. "Mrs. Merryweather would never let me scrub floors, silly." If he didn't stop looking so concerned, he might convince her he really did care. And then she would really feel like a fool. Because nobody could care that much about someone he had only just met—and about an unborn child that was not his own.

And who would care about a rich widow the tabloids proclaimed to be conniving and so immoral she would impregnate herself using her dead husband's frozen sperm just to keep her fortune?

Mr. Hyde couldn't know this wasn't true, yet he hadn't questioned her about it. And if he didn't yet know all the sordid details, then he was the only person on earth who didn't. She admitted she was naive, but she wasn't *that* naive.

Maybe Dr. Jack could shed some light on this strange situation. Yes, if anyone could help her unravel the mystery of Mr. Hyde, it would be Dr. Jack. Austin had revealed their lifelong friendship, and—

No. Not Austin, but Mr. Hyde. When he stopped being Mr. Hyde, she was in deep trouble.

She stood, relieved to find her legs steady. "I think I should go home."

"I'll walk you to the house."

"No, I—"

"Yes." His voice deepened, sending a shiver down her spine. "You shouldn't be out walking alone, especially at night."

Candice started to remind him that she had walked over by herself but decided it wasn't worth the argument. Besides, she liked the idea of lingering in his company a few moments longer. Despite their differences tonight, and despite the upheaval he had caused in mind and body, she had had a good time.

They made the trek downstairs and onto the garage drive, through the narrow path behind the house to the sliding doors leading into her bedroom before another word was spoken.

Austin broke the silence. "I'm going into town tomorrow to pick up a few things from my apartment. Do you need anything?"

Candice curled her fingers around the latch

of the door before turning to look at him. The faint glow of the pool lights failed to reveal his expression. But then, she had no business wondering if he might want to kiss her one more time.

She tried to sound brisk as she said, "Mrs. Merryweather does our shopping."

He shrugged his big shoulders. "Need any baby things?" he suggested. "We could go together, and I'd be there for you in case you got nabbed by a reporter."

She narrowed her eyes, wishing she could see *his* eyes. Why in the world did he keep bringing up the baby? She started to ask him outright, then hesitated. Maybe another day. Right now she didn't want to ruin a lovely— well, *almost* lovely—night. "Thanks for the offer, but I don't think—"

He sidled close, cutting off her words with the simple motion of placing his hand over hers where she grasped the door latch. Candice jumped at the instant heat, the strange electric charge that raced up her arm. Now she *could* see his expression, the slow, heated way his eyes traveled over her. The man could do indecent things with those eyes.

"You could wear my shirt," he drawled softly. "I guarantee you nobody would recognize the formal Mrs. Howard Vanausdale in that get-up."

Candice sensed a subtle insult behind his smooth words, yet she couldn't manage a spark of anger. He was right. Nobody *would* recognize her. "I'll—I'll think about it." He couldn't know that the thought of spending an entire day in his company made her feel giddy.

"Good enough." He sent the door sliding open, frowning down at her. "You left it unlocked?"

Flushing at his censorious tone, Candice quipped, "Taking your bodyguard duties seriously, aren't you?"

"Someone needs to."

He moved her gently aside and strode into her bedroom, flicking on the lights as he went. Frozen in surprise, Candice waited dutifully by the door until he searched her closet, the bathroom, and the small sitting room she planned to convert into a nursery. By the time he returned to her, she was having a hard time keeping a smile at bay. It just felt so darned strange having someone care so much. It felt good. Great, in fact.

But why *would* he care? She couldn't banish the question from her mind. She trusted so little and so few that it was next to impossible not to question his kindness and the possible motives behind it.

"Okay, it's all clear."

Candice stepped into the room with a silent

139

sigh and turned to let him pass her. "Thank you for—"

His arms closed around her from behind, pulling her gently against him. She felt fire on her neck as he whispered, "Hold still. I just want to feel you against me again."

She was helpless to say no to something she wanted just as much, so she did as he asked, taking shallow breaths and hoping he'd let the strength return to her legs before he let her go.

He made no move to release her. Instead, he shifted his arms, splaying one hand beneath her breasts as the other settled over the slight swell of her stomach. Candice felt the room whirl. Every ridge, every muscle of his pressed along her entire length.

He held her this way for long, delicious moments. Candice had never felt so cherished, so desirable. And when he trembled, her body thrummed in answer.

She tried not to think about his hand on her stomach and what it meant as she basked in the glorious sensations ricocheting through her body.

It was no use. Her baby was too much a part of her to forget, even in an unforgettable moment like this.

Was there a significance in the gesture? Had *he* forgotten about the baby—Howard's baby?

The question flew from her mind as he pulled her hair aside and placed a hot kiss on her neck.

Then he released her.

Thank God he did so slowly, Candice thought with a shaky inward laugh. Otherwise, she was certain she would have fallen to the carpet in a helpless heap of quivering desire.

As his hands fell away, she turned around, fully intending to seek his kiss.

But he was gone, the whisper of the door sliding shut the only evidence he'd been there at all.

Candice placed a trembling hand over the spot on her neck he had kissed and closed her eyes. It was just as well, because she was terribly afraid she would have begged him for more than just a kiss.

Tomorrow, she would call Dr. Jack—before she placed her complete trust in this stranger and invited him into her home.

And very possibly into her bed.

After that, she would call Dr. Robinson. Unfortunately, Candice feared that no prenatal vitamin he might offer her would cure what ailed her.

The next day, going on ten o'clock, Austin came to collect Candice. When Mrs. Merryweather opened the door to his knock, she glared at him for a full thirty seconds before waving him inside.

"She shouldn't be going out, you know," she grumbled, slamming pans around on the counter with unnecessary vigor. "Those bloodhounds will recognize her, mark my words. They always do."

Austin's heart did a funny flip-flop. "She's going, then?" He didn't realize until now how much he'd been looking forward to the outing, or how afraid he'd been that she wouldn't go.

Mrs. Merryweather continued to glare as if he'd invited Candice to join him in a bank robbery instead of an ordinary trip into town. "Oh, sure. You're happy as a lark, aren't you? What do *you* care if she gets hounded by reporters? It won't be *you* who lies awake all night wondering what kind of sludge they're going to print the next day."

A good portion of Austin's happy anticipation faded. Mrs. Merryweather was right; he was taking a big risk inviting Candice out.

But he wasn't ready to change his mind.

"I'll take good care of her," he promised, meaning it.

The housekeeper raked him with a scornful glance. "I'm sure you will. But even you, with all your brawn and bluster, can't stop those vultures from making up their own pack of lies about Mrs. Dale." She sent a metal colander clattering into the sink. "Have you considered what they'll think if they see her with you?" she demanded.

He hadn't, he realized. Hadn't thought about anything much beyond spending time with the intriguing Mrs. Dale, of getting her away from this museum and showing her how to have some fun. Hell. "Maybe you're right, Mrs.—" Austin began.

"No, she's wrong," Candice interrupted, startling him.

He turned to find her staring at Mrs. Merryweather with something akin to defiance. He felt a surge of pride at her show of spunk, and in a way that was fast becoming familiar, his heart kicked into overdrive at the sight of her.

She wore her hair in a youthful ponytail, but she was clad in a pair of expensive khaki trousers and a familiar looking neutral silk blouse, not his football jersey. How many of those damned boring silk shirts did she own, anyway? Austin wondered.

"It isn't fair that I'm forced to hide from the world," Candice continued.

Mrs. Merryweather plopped her hands on her hips and seemed to make an effort to temper her stridency. "It's just until after the hearing."

"Which could take months," Candice retorted, her saucy ponytail bouncing with life.

Austin wanted to grab it and tug her forward for a big sloppy kiss. Wouldn't Mrs. Merryweather be shocked?

"I'm sick of hiding, I'm sick of this house, and I'm sick of these clothes." She lifted her chin. "I'm going out, and whatever happens is not Mr. Hyde's fault, is that clear?"

Mrs. Merryweather opened her mouth as if to protest, then apparently changed her mind. She presented her back and began scrubbing the sink with a vengeance. Austin heard a pathetic little sniff and actually found himself feeling sorry for her.

"You're old enough to know your own mind, I suppose," she mumbled.

It was their cue to leave. Austin surprised Candice by grabbing her hand and leading her to the back door. Just as he opened it, Mrs. Merryweather spoke again. The anger was gone, but the worry remained.

"If you're gonna be out anyway, would you mind picking up a dozen eggs?"

Candice broke free and crossed the room, hugging the plump housekeeper. "Of course I will. And don't worry, I'll be fine. What's the worst thing that could happen?"

"I don't want to imagine," Mrs. Merryweather grumbled, hugging her in return. Then she pushed her toward the door. "Go, and have a good time. Make it worth your while."

When the door closed behind them, Candice cast him a shy glance. "She's a bit like a mother to me."

"I noticed," Austin said with a quirk of his brow.

Their gazes met. He smiled and chucked her beneath the chin, gaining an answering smile in return.

Austin led the way to the garage, where he kept his truck parked out of sight at the insistence of Mrs. Merryweather. As they entered the cool, shadowy interior of the building, he said, "We'll take my truck so we don't attract unwanted attention." He pointed to the rusty old Dodge pickup parked between the Rolls Royce and the Cadillac.

Candice stopped abruptly. "You call *that* inconspicuous?" she squeaked, then clamped a hand over her mouth. She looked immediately contrite. "I mean, I'm sure it's safe, but—"

"It is." Austin knew it was ridiculous to feel offended by her obvious distaste, but he did. Embarrassed, too. Of course she'd be more comfortable in her BMW, or the Rolls Royce her husband had driven when he was alive, or even the Cadillac Mrs. Merryweather used for errands, but she would also be *noticed*.

145

"Austin . . . I didn't mean to offend you."

"Forget it," he said briskly. The fact that she had called him by his first name softened the offense. A lot. He just wished she would do it more often.

As he opened the passenger door, he stepped back in dismay. Where had all the junk come from? Funny, he'd never noticed the tool kit sitting on the front seat, or the old box of paintbrushes on the floorboard. And where in hell had all the newspapers come from? He seldom even *read* the newspaper!

Glancing at Candice across the hood of the truck, he tried to sound casual. "I need to clear out a few things before you get in. Would you mind grabbing a trash bag from my apartment? They're beneath the coffee machine, I believe."

"Of course," Candice agreed readily.

When she had disappeared from sight, Austin went into a frenzy of cleaning. He shoveled the newspapers into the back seat of the Cadillac, cursing when he noticed the dates. He should have thrown them out years ago. If Candice saw them, she would probably never believe he no longer read the paper. And he didn't, and hadn't since the day he'd opened the paper and found an ugly, detailed article about his father.

What would she say if she knew that her baby's grandfather had once been a drug smuggler? Oh, Drummond Hyde had owned legitimate money-making companies as well, but those properties had only been a front to hide the real business of selling illegal drugs. And though the government would have loved to seize his illegal gains, he'd managed to launder enough to leave a sizable amount behind.

His inheritance. As if he could ever touch it without feeling sick.

Austin slammed the Cadillac door and got back to work, never willing to dwell for long on something he'd rather forget. He made himself a mental note to retrieve the papers later, before Mrs. Merryweather found them.

He pitched the tool kit into the back along with the other odds and ends already rattling around in the truck bed and hefted the box of paintbrushes into his arms. Turning, he surveyed the garage, looking for a place to temporarily stash the box.

Ah, a nice dark corner. Striding quickly to the spot, he dumped the load onto the floor and returned to the truck. The seat was relatively clear, but the floorboards remained knee-deep in crumpled fast-food sacks, paper cups, and a few objects Austin didn't care to try to identify.

147

"Here you go. The bags weren't where you said, but I rummaged around until I found them. I hope you don't mind."

Austin swung around, deciding she could rummage all she wanted if it meant he'd get to see her smile. With the elusive, sexy scent of her perfume lingering pleasantly in his nostrils, he took the bag and began stuffing trash into it. Finally, he could see the black rubber floor mats. Maybe she wouldn't notice the sticky remains of a Coke he'd spilled yesterday.

With a flourish he hoped disguised his embarrassment, he stood aside and waved an arm. "Your carriage awaits you," he drawled, dropping the bag of trash behind her.

Candice hesitated, glancing inside. "Seat belts?"

Austin gave his head a mental slap and began to dig around in the seat in search of the safety belts. He wasn't entirely confident the truck *possessed* seat belts, but he held on to hope for as long as he could.

His fingers bumped against something. With a triumphant grin, he pulled it out, only to mutter a disgusted curse when he realized he held a petrified hamburger, and not the end of a seat belt. How in hell—?

"Find it?" Candice queried at his back, sounding amused.

"Ah, no, not yet." Blocking her view with his

body, Austin searched for a suitable hiding place for the burger. The sack of trash sat behind Candice on the garage floor, so that was out of the question, unless he wanted her to see just how big a slob he was.

And for some insane reason, he didn't.

Growing desperate, he opened the glove compartment, then quickly slammed it shut on the horrors that greeted him there. Obviously, the glove compartment wasn't a good place to stash chocolate doughnuts, especially in warm weather.

There was only one solution, he decided.

He stuffed the hamburger into his shirt and backed out of the truck. "Give me a moment to change shirts. I've gotten something on this one."

"Did you—"

He didn't stay to hear her question, rushing upstairs to his apartment and changing in record time. By the time he returned, Candice had found a seat belt on the passenger side, and one for him as well. She looked so pleased, Austin had to resist the urge to kiss her sweetly smiling mouth.

On second thought, why should he resist?

She gasped as his mouth touched hers for an all-too-brief instant. With a saucy wink, Austin moved around the truck and slid into the driver's seat. He slanted her an apologetic look, yet made it clear he wasn't really sorry for kissing her. "Didn't mean to keep you waiting."

"I'm fine."

She sounded as if she meant it, which pleased him. He started the engine and maneuvered the Dodge carefully between the Cadillac and the Rolls Royce. Soon, they were heading down the long drive to the main street. Austin cracked a window, welcoming the cool air. He wasn't about to let a cloudy day mar his good mood.

"So, where are we going?"

"You mean, first?" Austin glanced in the rearview mirror, relaxing as the house grew smaller and smaller. He didn't realize how cooped up *he'd* begun to feel until now; he could scarcely imagine how Candice felt. "Our first stop is Kmart."

"Kmart?"

He turned his face to hide a grin. "Yes, Kmart. It's a discount store that—"

"I know what Kmart is," Candice said stiffly. "I've shopped there before."

Not in a long while, Austin thought to himself. But then, her husband had owned a chain of expensive clothing stores; he supposed there wasn't any need to shop elsewhere.

They rode in silence until he swung the rattling truck into the Kmart parking lot. "Stay here," he instructed. "I'll be back in a flash."

"But—"

"It'll only take a moment."

It took longer than a moment for Austin to choose the neon pink over the lime green. After a quick glance into his wallet, he added plain white tennis shoes and a pair of socks to the ensemble. He couldn't keep from grinning as he imagined the look on her face.

Today, he vowed, Candice Vanausdale wouldn't be recognized.

Chapter Eight

Candice tried to keep a straight face when she pulled the lightweight, bright pink sweats from the plastic Kmart sack.

She tried hard, in fact, conscious of Austin watching her with a solemn intensity that made her want to squirm and blush. The last thing she wanted to do was to hurt this endearing man's feelings.

But in the end, a betraying giggle escaped. Then another. She smothered the first one with a cough, but not the second or the third or the fourth. Finally, she slumped in the seat and covered her face with her hands, overcome with helpless laughter.

"Something funny?" he demanded, sounding ridiculously hurt.

Candice sobered instantly. "You—you really want me to wear this?"

"Do you want to have fun?" he countered. A twinkle crept into his eyes, followed by a slow curving of his lips.

It was at that moment that Candice realized she'd been had. She sat upright in the seat. "You! You had me thinking that I—that you—oh!" She reached into the bag, withdrew a tennis shoe, and threw it at him. It bounced harmlessly against the window and landed in his lap.

Austin gave a low, husky laugh that sent shivers down her spine. He kept on laughing as he started the truck and steered the vehicle out of the parking lot. "Get changed, will ya? We've only got about fifteen minutes before we get to Clyde's."

"Who's Clyde, and—" Candice broke off, shocked as the rest of his words sank in. "Get changed?" she asked faintly. Certainly she had heard him incorrectly.

"That's what I said." White teeth flashed in a wicked grin. "I'll be driving, so you don't have to worry about my looking. Don't tell me you've never changed in a vehicle before?"

No, she had not! Well, not that she could

remember. Candice sputtered, "But—but what about everyone else?"

They pulled onto the freeway, blending into the heavy lunch-hour traffic. She glanced around at the cars surrounding them on all sides and shook her head. He had to be joking.

Didn't he?

She looked at him but detected no sign of teasing in the square cut of his jaw; he stared straight ahead with an air of intense concentration. Could she? Should she? She jerked her gaze back to the bug-spattered windshield in front of her, worrying her bottom lip between her teeth.

He was daring her, of course.

"Ten minutes left," he said without looking at her. "You finished?"

Candice wet her lips. "I—I haven't started."

"You *are* wearing a bra, aren't you?"

Heat swept into her face at his bold question. "Of course."

"Well, think of it as your bathing suit top."

"I can't."

"Why not?"

"Because it *isn't* my bathing suit top."

Austin rested his right arm across the top of the steering wheel, rubbing his jaw with his free hand. "Most of the bathing suit tops I've seen cover *less* than a bra."

Candice thought about the demure one-piece suits Howard had insisted she wear and decided against commenting. It would only lead to questions she didn't want to answer.

Slowly, she withdrew the garish pink outfit from the sack and set the rest aside. Was she actually considering doing something this outrageous? She was well past the age of giving in to a dare . . . wasn't she? Fingering the soft material, she thought about how much more comfortable it would feel around her thickening middle. Not only more comfortable, but totally unlike anything Mrs. Howard Vanausdale would wear.

No one would look twice at her. Her lips twitched. Well, maybe they'd look twice because of the outfit's color, but not because they recognized the person within.

Howard would have—

Candice drew in a sharp, angry breath at the unwelcome thought. That did it! With trembling fingers, she unfastened the buttons of her blouse. She didn't dare look at Austin; her skin already felt flushed and hot just thinking of his eyes on her as she undressed. If he watched her, she didn't want to know.

She was struggling into the top when a car horn sounded loudly beside her window. Too mortified to look, she froze, her face buried in the neck of the shirt.

"Don't worry," Austin assured her, his voice shaking with laughter, "he's honking at the car ahead of us. Some kid is giving him the bird."

With a swift jerk, Candice lowered the top over her flaming face and pushed the sleeves up. She didn't believe him for a moment. "So why are you laughing?" she demanded through gritted teeth.

"Because the kid looked about three years old."

Candice didn't share his humor. "Someone should teach him better manners."

"Someone," Austin drawled, unaffected by her stern tone, "must have taught him how to use his middle finger."

He did have a point, Candice reluctantly conceded, struggling out of her pants and into the sweat bottoms. A pleasurable sigh slipped between her lips as the waistband stretched comfortably around her waist.

"Better?"

"Yes." Candice rolled the window down a notch to cool her flaming cheeks, adding, "But I still think your idea of fun differs greatly from mine, Mr. Hyde."

"So you've said," he grumbled. "Don't you think you should start calling me Austin?" He clicked on the blinker and began to inch the truck into the next lane.

Feeling unaccountably edgy, Candice folded her arms and stared out the window. "Give me one good reason I should."

He steered the truck onto the exit ramp before delivering his outrageous answer. "Because you just took off your clothes for me."

Candice kept her face turned away from him so he couldn't see her blush. The man was incorrigible!

Sometime later, at Clyde's Rib Ranch, Austin eyed Candice over a meaty, messy rib with a feeling of satisfaction. Neon pink wasn't exactly her color, but then, neither was the barbecue sauce on her chin and nose. Still, he couldn't have been more aroused if she'd been sitting across from him naked and covered in barbecue sauce. "How do you like the ribs?" he asked abruptly, wisely dispelling the beginnings of a wonderful fantasy.

"Mmm," she mumbled, dropping a rib bone and diving for another. She forked baked beans into her mouth and took another bite of rib as if she hadn't eaten in a week.

Austin chuckled. He couldn't resist teasing her. "Let's hope they don't charge me extra for the sauce."

With a bewildered glance at the cluttered table, Candice swallowed and asked, "What sauce?"

"The sauce you're wearing on your face."

She started to reach for a napkin but drew

her hand back at the last moment. Her eyes narrowed in suspicion. "I don't believe you this time."

Austin shrugged. "Suit yourself. I mean, it doesn't bother me, and it *is* a good camouflage."

"I still don't believe you."

"It's true."

The waitress interrupted their playful argument to give them their check. "Everything all right?" she asked, ripping the ticket from the book and laying it beside Austin's plate. She glanced from Austin to Candice, her gaze widening. "Good Lord! I'll get you a towel for your face, Mrs. Vanausdale. The ribs are good, but they sure are messy!"

Austin tried to keep a straight face as Candice turned fiery red, nearly matching the sauce. "I did warn you," he pointed out.

"You *knew* I didn't believe you!" she hissed furiously. Snatching a napkin and nearly upending the holder, she began scrubbing at her face.

Suddenly, she froze. Austin caught sight of her horrified expression, and at the same instant he realized what the waitress had said. *Mrs. Vanausdale.* The waitress had called Candice by her name, and worst of all, without the slightest hesitation.

The shredded napkin fell from Candice's nerveless fingers, barbecue sauce still high-lighting her suddenly pale skin. She looked like a little girl who had just lost her favorite Barbie doll. A *messy* little girl.

Austin muttered an oath and shoved his plate aside. "How the hell did she recognize you?"

"We . . . we should go," she said, her voice growing stronger. The crushed look faded from her eyes; resignation, then determination, took its place.

Still cursing, Austin flung more than enough money onto the table and took her arm, guiding her through the lunchtime crowd. They passed their waitress along the way, and Austin snatched the wet towel from her hands without pausing.

"Wait! You can't take that!"

"Watch me," Austin muttered, shoving the door to the diner open. Ahead in the parking lot, their worst nightmare awaited them; he was tall, blond, and carried a camera. The waitress must have called him the moment they'd stepped into the restaurant and she recognized Candice, Austin thought. He'd heard some members of the press often offered enticing rewards for tips.

The reporter caught sight of them and pushed away from the van he'd been leaning against. He began to walk eagerly to meet them.

"Austin," Candice warned needlessly.

"I see him." An image of Mrs. Merryweather's knowing, accusing face loomed larger than life in Austin's mind. He had to think of something, and he had to think of something fast. He refused to end this memorable day with egg on his face.

As the reporter came closer, Austin slowed his pace. A germ of an idea began to take shape. It was outrageous, preposterous . . . but what else could he do? Decking the bastard wouldn't work; it would only generate more unwanted attention.

"Mrs. Vanausdale, may I ask you a few questions?"

Why did they bother to ask if they could ask? Austin wondered viciously. If she said no, they'd ask anyway. Stupid jerks.

Throwing himself into the role he'd quickly created, Austin stopped in the middle of the parking lot and propped a hand on his hip. He felt Candice bump into him from behind, felt the tension humming through her body as surely as he felt his own.

The reporter reached them, eyeing first Candice, then Austin. Just as Mrs. Merryweather had predicted, he seemed extremely interested in discovering Austin's role in Candice Vanausdale's world.

"Is this your new boyfriend, Mrs. Vanausdale? Are you—"

"Boyfriend!" Austin managed a high, trilling laugh, fluttering a hand at the reporter. "Believe me, honey, she's not my *type.*" He slowly looked the reporter over, arching an interested eyebrow. "But you might be. Are you single?" Behind him, he heard Candice smother a gasp.

For a comical moment the reporter was speechless. Finally, he stammered, "Are you—are you saying that you and Mrs. Vanausdale are just—"

"You mean Candy? Well, I guess nobody calls her that these days." Austin tittered again, lifting his voice several octaves above his normal range. "Candy and I go way back, honey. Back to high school, in fact." He leaned in to whisper, "She knew about me long before anyone else, if you know what I mean."

The reporter licked his lips, trying to appear subtle about moving away from Austin's grinning face. He grabbed the camera and lifted it to his eye.

Austin snatched it down, forcing another silly grin. "Oh, no, you don't want to take any pictures! If Jo Jo finds out I was talking to you, he'll—"

"Jo Jo?" the reporter gulped.

"Yes, Jo Jo." Austin feigned a pout. "He's my

boyfriend, but I'm thinking of leaving him. He's so *possessive*, if you know what I mean." He turned and wrapped an arm around a speechless Candice, pulling her in for a chummy hug. "Candy here has just about convinced me to dump him. She doesn't think he treats me right." He squeezed her shoulders and beamed at her. "Isn't that right, Candy girl?"

Before she could think of answering, Austin squinted beyond the reporter's shoulder, allowing his eyes to widen in fear. "Oh, no! I think I see his car. Candy, is that Jo Jo?" Frantically, he flapped his arms at the reporter. "You've got to leave before he sees us together!"

"But I'm not with—"

"Go, go! He'll tear you apart with his bare hands—just ask Candy! The last guy he caught me with couldn't talk for days after Jo Jo finished with him."

"C-Couldn't—" The terrified reporter stumbled back, his mouth agape. He turned and ran to the van, hopping inside and nearly knocking his head against the roof in his frenzy. The starter ground several times before it caught; black smoke billowed from the tailpipe as he gunned the engine.

Austin kept his arm around Candice as the news van sped out of the parking lot and disappeared onto the freeway. He felt like a big dumb fool, but also proud. Mrs. Merryweather wouldn't be chomping on *him* tonight, he thought smugly. And Candice could sleep without worrying about tomorrow's papers.

Candice stirred against his side. "You were wonder—"

"I'd really prefer to forget about it."

"Of course."

He detected the laughter in her voice and groaned. Turning her firmly into him, he covered her smiling lips with his own.

"What—what was *that* for?" she demanded—a little breathlessly, Austin noted with satisfaction.

"Just reestablishing my manhood," he growled softly, taking her arm and heading for the truck. "Now let's get Mrs. Merryweather's eggs and get you the hell home."

"Why don't you want her to know I'm your brother?"

Austin snorted his disbelief that Jack had to ask the question. "I'd think the reason is obvious. Who in their right mind would want anyone to know they were related to *you*?"

"Very funny."

"I'm not trying to be funny," Austin said, but his lips twitched at Jack's hurt expression. Quickly, he reminded himself that Jack hadn't paid his dues. Not yet. But he was about to.

"Other than the obvious, I don't want her to become suspicious about why I'm there." His mouth hardened into a flat line as he held out a hand, palm up. "Now give me the file."

Jack edged slowly away. "Do you have any idea how much trouble I could get into letting you see this file?"

Unperturbed, Austin reached around and snatched the folder from Jack's hand, which he had hidden ineffectively behind his back. "Do you have any idea how much trouble you're already *in*? Now go away like a good little sneaky, crazy brother."

Ten minutes earlier, Austin had surprised Jack in his office, then scared the hell out of him by closing and locking the door. Now, finally, Austin had the lovely widow's file in his hands.

Jack continued to sweat and plead. "You gotta give me a break, bro! Do you know how many bribes I've turned down over that file?"

With a casual flick of his wrist Austin opened the folder. "Yeah, I know," he said, without looking up. "I was here when that reporter offered you twenty grand. But this is different, and you damned well know it. I've got every right to know about the mother of my child, and it's all right here at my fingertips."

He couldn't resist taunting Jack. Hell, he

deserved it—and then some. No, he wasn't through with Jack. Payback was hell.

"How—how do I know you're not going to sell this information to the tabloids?" Jack demanded, still eyeing the folder as if he might snatch it back any moment.

Austin narrowed his eyes.

Jack flopped into his chair and put his head in his hands, moaning. "I could lose my job."

"Then you'd have no excuse not to go back to school and get your medical degree," Austin commented with a distinct lack of sympathy.

He'd hardly glanced at the first page, wishing Jack would go away so he could have some privacy. He wanted to read the file on Candice from cover to cover. Curiosity was eating him alive, and Candice wasn't satisfying it. Every time he tried to throw a casual reference to the baby at her, she got that suspicious, distrustful look in her damned cat's eyes.

Of course, that wasn't counting the times he'd missed opportunities to gather information because he'd actually forgotten about the baby when he was in her presence.

Hopefully, this would answer his burning questions.

"She could send me to prison for this."

Austin spared Jack a cutting glance, unwilling to relent just yet. "I could send you to

165

prison, too, little brother. And remember, you wouldn't be in this predicament in the first place if you hadn't been playing God. That was my . . . my *specimen*, dammit."

Jack kept his face in his hands, looking lost and hopeless. Austin had to strain to understand his mumbling.

"You've met her. How can you *not* understand why I couldn't tell her about her old man's useless sperm?"

"You think she'd rather hear about me?" Austin taunted. "This woman lives and breathes money, Jack. She sleeps on satin sheets and didn't have a clue how to eat pizza." *But she knew how to eat ribs in a way that made his bones dissolve.*

Jack lifted his head, his mouth slack with surprise. Austin groaned to himself, realizing he'd said more than he intended.

"How do you know all this? Are you saying . . . are you saying . . ." Jack rose from the chair and braced his hands on the desk, color returning to his face and hope lighting his eyes. "You've gotten to know her, haven't you?"

Austin growled and fixed his gaze on the folder, willing his brother to develop amnesia. It didn't work.

"By God, you *have!*" He slapped an open palm on the desk in his excitement, then winced from the sting. "I knew if you just got to know her, you'd like her, you'd see what a great person she is. Her personality is up there with the best of them, and she's gentle and sweet and—"

Austin held a palm in the air. "Spare me. I'll find out for myself, thank you." No way was he telling Jack that he'd found out plenty so far.

He then returned his attention to the folder in his hand. A very important folder, one that would, he hoped, lend him a little insight on the intriguing woman who now filled his dreams with lustful yearnings.

The future mother of his child.

He'd already discovered a mountain of things, such as her humorous personality and sensual nature. Then there was the way she blushed yet didn't shy away. Of course, he couldn't forget the softness of her lips and the honeyed warmth of her mouth or the fullness of her breasts. . . .

He glanced up to find Jack watching him with a gleam in his eye that Austin immediately recognized. And feared. He glared at him in warning. "I swear to you, Jack, if you attempt to interfere in *any way* with Candice and me, I'll kill you with my bare hands. *You* got me into this mess, but *I'm* getting me out, without your interference."

Jack was smart enough to wipe his expression clean, but he wasn't smart enough to keep his mouth shut. "You're not going to hurt her— I won't let you. She's been through more than most people, and she doesn't deserve to be mistreated."

"I'm not mistreating her, believe me." Austin smiled as Jack picked up on the insinuation and began to look alarmed. "All Candice needs is to learn how to live."

"By *your* standards?" Jack laughed in disbelief. "You should have gotten counseling when you were younger, bro. I thought *I* was scarred, but, man, you are really bad."

"She's—"

"*Not* our mother!" Jack shouted, momentarily forgetting that Austin could shake his teeth loose. "Having money doesn't necessarily make someone a bad person. I thought you were smarter than that. What are you trying to do to her, turn her into a bum like you?"

Austin squeezed his fist around the folder, unwilling to admit Jack's words held a smidgen of truth. "Why don't you go to lunch or something while I study this file? After I'm done, I'll get out of your hair, and you can put your precious records back under lock and key."

Jack, apparently realizing he was getting nowhere, let out an exasperated breath and stomped to the door.

"Wait!" Austin called out just as Jack grasped the doorknob. There was a question he didn't think he'd find answered in the file on Candice Vanausdale. "Why is Candice so dead-set against getting remarried?" For a moment, he didn't think Jack would answer. His mouth clamped shut in a gesture Austin knew well. When Jack got that look, nobody could change his mind.

Then, just when Austin was about to admit defeat, Jack sighed and shook his head. "I expect she's had her fill of dominating, bullying tyrants, which is why I'm surprised she likes *you*."

"What does—"

"It means, dear brother, that if Mrs. Vanausdale *did* decide to remarry, you would not be her type." Jack opened the door with a jerk, nearly unbalancing himself. "And, frankly, I don't think you deserve her."

The door slammed shut. Austin frowned at it, pondering Jack's parting shot. What the hell did he mean? And why had Jack brought Austin into the remarriage issue, anyway?

Candice wasn't *his* type either, and he certainly wasn't thinking about marrying her.

Was he?

Damn Jack.

Chapter Nine

Mrs. Merryweather took the news about Austin's moving in with surprising calm.

She didn't throw anything.

"He's *what*?"

Candice stood her ground, hoping her own control would shame the housekeeper into lowering her voice. "He's moving into the house with us. You said yourself that I didn't take those vultures seriously enough, and the incident upstairs proved it."

For a moment, the housekeeper's ample bottom was the only thing visible as she bent over, searching for something in the refrigerator. Finally, she straightened, balancing a honeydew melon in one hand and a bunch of red grapes in the other.

They were preparing a fruit salad to go with dinner. Candice glanced at the digital clock on the microwave for the hundredth time. Almost four, and no sign of Austin. Maybe he wasn't *coming* back. Maybe she had scared him away. Maybe after yesterday at Clyde's, he'd decided the job was too difficult.

Maybe he'd decided *she* was too difficult.

Mrs. Merryweather thrust the grapes into her hands. "Wash those good—God knows what kind of chemicals they're covered with." And then, with barely a pause for breath, she said, "What do we really know about Mr. Hyde? Other than the fact that he knows Dr. Jack?"

"And has known him practically all his life," Candice pointed out dryly. She rinsed the grapes carefully, then began pulling the red globes from the stems. Mrs. Merryweather was weakening, she thought. Time to move in for the kill. Keeping her head bowed over the fruit bowl, Candice told her in a subdued voice about the expensive watch Austin had found beneath the window and her suspicions about the owner.

"Well." Mrs. Merryweather positioned the melon on the cutting board and delivered a fatal blow with an evil-looking knife. Finally, she put down the knife and wiped her hands on her apron, sighing in defeat. "Sounds like your in-laws, all right. Maybe it wouldn't be such a bad idea to have someone staying in the house with us. I'd thought about suggesting a guard dog, but at least Mr. Hyde is housebroken."

Candice smiled at Mrs. Merryweather's doubtful tone. But her smile faded as she looked at the housekeeper, a loyal employee and, more than that, a friend. Mrs. Merryweather looked downright worried. "Would you feel better about this if I called Dr. Jack and asked a few questions about Mr. Hyde?"

"I'd feel better if you called the police or the FBI."

Shaking her head, Candice reminded her, "And have everyone knowing we've got a man living in the house? I'm not sure we can trust even law enforcement where the media is concerned. It's human nature for people to . . . gossip."

Grim-faced, Mrs. Merryweather agreed. "I'm afraid you're right again. The last thing we need is for folks to think you've got a live-in boyfriend—your in-laws in particular. We'll have to be careful."

"Yes." Candice tried not to think about that kiss in the parking lot. It was a risk they shouldn't have taken. Not that she'd had time to resist.

"And Mr. Hyde will have to learn to keep his mouth shut."

"Of course."

"Better call Dr. Jack, so we can both sleep soundly tonight."

Candice needed no further urging. Her face felt hot, flushed with guilt and embarrassment. She hastily wiped her hands and made for the phone in the den. The study was closer, but that was Howard's—*had* been Howard's—domain.

Once in the comfortable den, she propped herself on the sofa arm, pressing a cooling hand to her face as she dialed the phone. Why did she feel so guilty? Because of the other night, or because of this call? The embarrassment she could understand. When Mrs. Merryweather had mentioned Mr. Hyde in conjunction with the words *live-in boyfriend,* she'd gotten an instant, arousing image of them pressed tightly together. Blushing, she recalled the three times they had already been so. Once in the hall outside his bathroom. Once in her bedroom when he walked her home. And yesterday at Clyde's Rib Ranch, right in front of God and everybody.

Boyfriend? She had a sinking feeling that if

the media had witnessed her and Mr. Hyde any of those times, they would laugh at the term *boyfriend*. Nor would he be able to convince them that she wasn't his *type*, as he had yesterday's reporter.

Lovers. Yes, that would be their impression, however false.

Tingles rippled along her spine. Heat gathered between her thighs, and her breasts suddenly began to ache, so when Jack's voice came squeaking out of the receiver, Candice nearly shrieked in surprise.

She'd been lost in her memories, aroused at her own thoughts about Mr. Hyde. Yesterday had been almost magical. And definitely fun.

"Dr. Jack? Candice Vanausdale here." Oh, Lord, her voice. She cleared her throat and prayed the huskiness would disappear.

"Mrs. Vanausdale!"

Jack sounded startled to hear from her. And a little nervous? Candice frowned. "I'm calling about your friend, Mr. Hyde."

"Austin? What's he done? Look, I know he's a little rough around the edges, but you've got to give him a chance. He's like a big, harmless sheepdog, all bark and no bite. Keep him around, and in a week or two you'll wonder how you got along without him."

Candice bit her lip. Indeed. "Actually, I just wanted to ask you a few background questions before . . . well, we're thinking of letting him stay in the house, for protection, so can you understand our concern?" She heard the rustling of papers, then a long pause before Jack Cruise spoke again, sounding more agitated than before. Poor Dr. Jack, she thought, he must be having a rough day.

"Of course I understand. I understand perfectly."

"We thought of checking him out with the authorities, but—"

"No!"

Candice held the phone away from her ear and frowned harder. He'd actually shouted at her. "As I was about to say, we decided against it, because we don't dare risk letting the media find out."

"Smart thinking." An unmistakable sigh of relief, then, "What is it you want to know? When you asked if I knew of someone who might fit your requirements, my mind was a total blank. Then I remembered Austin, and bingo! I thought to myself, the big lug would be perfect! I knew he was in between jobs, and—"

"That was my first question. What, exactly, is Mr. Hyde's occupation?" Candice toyed with the phone cord, reminding herself that she wasn't doing anything wrong by asking these harmless questions. But, instinctively, she knew Mr. Hyde's opinion would differ. He

175

would be hurt to think she didn't trust him. Really, though, she was doing this for Mrs. Merryweather.

Okay, so she was also trying to satisfy her own curiosity, and she didn't have the guts to ask him herself. Curiosity was a very human emotion, wasn't it?

Jack's voice lowered an octave. "He's a painter, an artist. He's pretty good, but he hasn't had much luck so far. Meanwhile, he picks up odd jobs painting signs and such to tide him over until his big break."

"Has he ever been married?" Candice held her breath, her face growing hotter by the second. Dr. Jack would know the question had nothing to do with safety.

There was a stunned silence, more rustling paper. Then came Jack's hesitant answer. "No."

Candice waited, mentally willing him to volunteer more information. Did she dare ask why not? Would Jack know? Or would he tell her outright that it was none of her business?

"As far as I know, he hasn't found the right woman. Austin . . ." Jack trailed off into silence, as if he suddenly realized he was about to reveal more than she had asked for.

"You were saying?" She was amazed at her own persistence. It was so unlike her. Was it a sign of the new and improved Candice Vanausdale?

Jack sighed. "Look, if he's been sneaking women into his apartment, I'm sure you can just have a word with him about it."

Candice smothered a giggle with the back of her hand, recalling their stealthy meeting. "No, no, it's nothing like that. I was only curious. This might take a while, you know, before the court makes a decision, and I didn't want to take him away from his . . . for this to interfere with his personal life." What a lame excuse, and Dr. Jack would surely know it. She had never been a very good liar.

But Jack appeared to have a lot on his mind, for he didn't sound suspicious at all as he said, "No, no current girlfriend." He cleared his throat. "That I know of. As for moving him in, I'd give that some thought if I were you."

A thrill of alarm shot through her. She gripped the receiver. "Why?" If Dr. Jack didn't trust him . . .

"Well, he's messy, for one thing."

Candice dropped the receiver onto the sofa, then brought it to her ear again, her voice incredulous, "What?"

"Messy. A slob." He laughed nervously. "Believe me, I've lived with the guy."

Messy? She'd seen no evidence of slovenliness inside his apartment. Although his truck *had* looked as if he'd lived in it for weeks. Not that she had minded. On the contrary, she'd found it quirkily appealing. No, this was something else entirely. Dr. Jack was making excuses, silly ones at that. For some reason he didn't want Austin Hyde living in her house, and that only served to pique her curiosity.

"Can you be more specific?"

"Oh. Well, let me see. . . ."

Candice waited. And waited. She could hear the drumming of his fingers on something. Then more nervous rustling of papers. What *was* he doing with those papers? And why would he be nervous talking about a life-long friend—one he had recommended for the job?

"He sleepwalks."

This time, Candice laughed outright. "Dr. Jack, I hardly think sleepwalking is a danger, or an intolerable habit. Nor is messiness. Mrs. Merryweather will set him straight on the latter." *And I'll help with the sleepwalking.* The thought was delicious and wicked. Exciting. Just the possibility of tucking Mr. Hyde back into bed sent a breathless rush of pleasure coursing through her body.

What did he wear at night? His briefs? Pajamas? Nothing at all? Her guess would be a pair of his favorite faded pajama bottoms, the kind that tied in the front and rode low on his lean hips, leaving bare that sexy line of belly hair that disappeared into—

She slid from the arm of the sofa onto the

cushions and took a deep, shaky breath. This was insane. Totally reckless. Irresponsible. Highly unlike her.

And she knew telling herself these things would not make a difference. For years she'd lived like a porcelain doll, something for Howard to shine and buff to perfection or to ridicule and abuse when he took the notion. And then, for the past year, she'd been a recluse.

Maybe she still couldn't go out into the light, but she could bring a tiny spark inside. A spark that she suspected could start a forest fire without much provocation.

"Dr. Jack . . . he's harmless, isn't he?"

Jack's answer was filled with resignation. "Yeah, yeah, he's harmless. Austin wouldn't harm a flea."

"I oughta flush you down the toilet and tell Andre you got lost," Austin muttered, holding the furry animal by the scruff of its neck. Unafraid, the ferret stared back, twitching its whiskers and occasionally pedaling her feet uselessly in the air.

"It would serve him right for leaving you with me—and for leaving this mess." His voice softened. "But I guess it's not your fault, huh?"

According to the note Austin had found on the kitchen table, Andre had been accepted into an art program in London and didn't expect to return for at least six months. He'd packed and left in a hurry, leaving the apartment in shambles and leaving his pet ferret in Austin's trusted care.

He brought the animal closer, narrowing his eyes in question. "*Did* you make this mess?" The ferret squirmed and licked Austin's nose, not in the least intimidated by his growl. Ferrets were lovable creatures, but Austin knew from experience they could create havoc if left alone. Maybe the mess was the combined result of Andre's quick packing and Lucy's search for food. But why place all the blame on this helpless creature?

With a sigh, he placed the ferret against his chest and stroked her soft, musk-scented fur. She snuggled against him and began licking his neck as he crooned, "Lucy, Lucy, what am I going do with you?"

She nibbled his ear, inadvertently finding a ticklish spot.

"Stop that!" Austin laughed. "Ear-kissing won't work on me, girl. I can't take you with me." Lucy wasn't listening. She nosed through his hair and draped her long body on his shoulder, clearly intent on remaining there. Austin craned his neck to look at her. "Cuteness won't work, I tell you. You look too much like a weasel, or a rat. And you're a thief—Andre says so. Besides, Mrs. Merryweather—"

He halted his words, a dangerous smile curving his mouth. "Mrs. Merryweather would have a fit." And the mischievous pet might keep the old battle-ax busy, giving him more time alone with Candice.

Providing he could talk her into letting him bring Lucy inside. If he could gain Candice's sympathy, Mrs. Merryweather wouldn't have a choice. But did Candice like animals?

Good question. All children deserved a pet, didn't they? His mother had forbidden pets of any kind, even goldfish. They'd once managed to sneak a frog into the house, but when it was Jack's turn to keep it in his room, it had mysteriously died.

During those experimental childhood days, nothing living was safe around Jack.

Hell, nothing had changed.

Lucy nudged his cheek with her nose, commanding his attention. Austin absently stroked her, thinking, planning, and plotting. A lot depended on Candice and her views on pets. Austin knew there weren't any critters on the estate now. Maybe the late Mr. Vanausdale had hated animals, and Candice just hadn't gotten around to getting one.

He scratched Lucy's chin while she proceeded to lick every inch of his face with loving care. "It's a long shot, Lucy, but I guess we can give it a try. If Mrs. Dale doesn't approve, I suppose you can have my pad over the garage until we figure out what to do with you for the next six months."

Lucy finished bathing him to her satisfaction, then began to bathe her own face, apparently secure in the knowledge that *someone* would take care of her.

Austin grinned, watching her. "How could they resist you?" He'd grown fond of the lovable little animal in the two years he'd shared an apartment with Andre. "As long as you keep your sticky fingers to yourself, then we shouldn't have a problem. Oh, and no toe-biting." Lucy paused for a second to look at him, then calmly resumed her grooming.

Amazed at her intelligence, Austin placed her in the pet taxi for the ride back to the Vandausdale estate. Along the way, he'd stop at a convenience store and pick up a bag of her favorite cat food, cat litter, and a few squeaky toys. Maybe he'd buy her a new collar with a bell.

He whistled as he gathered his painting supplies and a few extra clothes for himself, stepping over the clutter on the floor.

If Lucy got lost in that museum of a house, it

might take Mrs. Merryweather days of serious searching to find her.

Even longer *without* the bell.

Two hours later, Austin rapped on the kitchen door of the Vanausdale mansion. In one hand, he carried the pet taxi; his other hand cradled an assortment of pet supplies. Lucy peered curiously through the bars of the cage door, sporting a brand-new hot-pink collar—with the warning bell safely stashed in his pocket.

Only Austin and Andre knew the ferret answered to a squeak toy. Andre was in London, and Austin wasn't talking.

The door opened, and Mrs. Merryweather stood on the threshold, staring first at Austin, then at the pet carrier. Finally, her neutral gaze landed on the pet supplies. A slight frown added a line or two to her face, but all in all, Austin thought it was a good reaction.

"A cat?" she asked dubiously.

He shook his head and forced a sad sigh. "No. A ferret. My roommate abandoned it, and I couldn't leave the little critter all alone." Her frown deepened. Uh-oh. Now she would demand that he take the "little critter" back where it came from.

"Well, don't just stand there. Bring the poor dear in. My younger son always had a thing for

183

exotic animals, and now he works at the zoo. Come to think of it, I believe he had one of these things when he was in college. They're a lot like cats, aren't they? I like cats, used to have a yard full of them."

Austin snapped his jaw shut and muted his expression of disbelief. Mrs. Merryweather was chatting with him as if he were an old friend, a drastic change from her earlier chill.

And she *liked* cats, her son had once owned a ferret, and now he worked at the zoo.

He couldn't believe his good luck. Now if only he could be so lucky with Candice.

Stepping inside, he set the cage on the floor and deposited the supplies on the table, hoping he'd find his voice before the housekeeper noticed his silence.

She stooped to look in the cage, chuckling as Lucy stretched her nose through the bars, attempting to catch the scent of this stranger, Mrs. Merryweather obliged by rubbing the little pointed nose with a gentle finger. "What's its name?"

Austin cleared his throat, wondering if he had walked into the wrong house. Mrs. Merryweather was being nice. Sweet. And she was making friendly clucking noises at Lucy, an animal that looked like a cross between a raccoon, a weasel, and a rat.

An animal that looked nothing like an ordinary domesticated house cat.

"It's a she, and her name is Lucy." His voice sounded strange, almost hoarse. What had changed Mrs. Merryweather's mind? Was it possible that Candice—Mrs. Dale—was responsible for this new-and-improved attitude? What had she told the housekeeper? His face grew warm as he considered the possibilities. She would never have mentioned the incident in the parking lot at Clyde's Rib Ranch, but for *some* reason Mrs. Merryweather had mellowed toward him.

Fascinated, he continued to watch as Mrs. Merryweather opened the cage and cradled a happy Lucy in her arms. True to character, Lucy took full advantage, snuggling contentedly against the housekeeper's ample bosom.

Austin rubbed his eyes and shook his head. "Does this mean it's okay if she stays?" He still couldn't believe it.

Mrs. Merryweather crooned to Lucy, who loved nothing better. "Of course it's okay for the little dear to stay." Suddenly, she fixed a stern eye on Austin. "As long as *you* clean up her messes. And speaking of messes, I'm not your maid, so you pick up after yourself, understand? I've got enough to do, and so does Mrs. Dale."

"Understood. How does Mrs. Dale feel about pets? I noticed she doesn't own any."

"That's because Mr. Howard didn't care for critters. Said they were filthy and too much trouble. Mrs. Dale likes them just fine."

"I like what just fine?" Candice asked from the doorway.

Austin swiveled to look at her, his hungry gaze taking in every delectable inch of her in the space of a few seconds. With Mrs. Merryweather ooking on, he could do little more. But his quick glance was enough to tell him she looked downright edible in a floaty sundress that bared her shoulders, arms, and a considerable amount of smooth legs. He recognized the dress as one she had purchased yesterday during their adventurous outing.

She wore her hair straight and shimmering. Loose.

The housekeeper held Lucy up for inspection, her eyes twinkling. "We've got a new houseguest—other than Mr. Hyde, that is."

So, Candice *had* cleared the way. Austin shifted, cocking his hip against a chair as he waited for her reaction to the ferret, wondering if Mrs. Merryweather knew Candice as well as she thought.

"Her name is Lucy," he volunteered.

Candice slowly approached the wriggling

186

animal, a hesitant smile on her lips. "But what *is* she?"

Mrs. Merryweather placed Lucy gently into Candice's arms. "She's a ferret, a domesticated version of the weasel family—am I right, Mr. Hyde?"

Austin nodded, his eyes on Candice and Lucy.

Lucy, who to Austin's knowledge had never met a stranger, scrambled against her until she could reach Candice's face. When she began licking earnestly at her chin, Candice laughed. "Oh, she's a sweetheart, isn't she?"

Her sparkling gaze met Austin's. He felt a warm shaft of contentment bury itself inside his heart. At the same time, a prickle of awareness jolted his pulse into overdrive.

She liked animals, and from the gleam in her eyes as she looked at him, she liked him, too.

Shifting again to ease the sudden tightness in his jeans, he saw her gaze dip low for an instant, and he caught a flicker of something hot and satisfied in her expression before she lowered the silky fan of her eyelashes.

"Are you hungry? We've eaten, but Mrs. Merryweather kept something warm for you."

Her voice was soft and a little husky. The sound tightened his gut to an almost painful degree. Oh, yes, he was *very* hungry—for her. He ached to bury himself inside her, to make her writhe and moan with hot, sexual need. She was Sleeping Beauty, and he, well, he was a randy prince just waiting for the opportunity to awaken the wild side of Candice Vanausdale.

But he'd promised.

What the *hell* had he been thinking when he made such a laughable promise?

". . . the matter, baby? You hungry, too?"

Her hushed, tender voice as she talked to Lucy thundered inside his head.

And he suddenly remembered what he'd been thinking about now when he'd made that promise. Baby, she'd said.

He'd been thinking about his baby, growing inside her.

Her reputation, too, of course. And the money, which seemed so important to her.

He opened his mouth to tell her that he'd already eaten, but at that moment, the doorbell sounded. Candice didn't look surprised. Calmly, she placed the ferret into his arms. As she leaned close, he caught a whiff of expensive, mind-blowing perfume.

"Expecting someone?" Was that *his* voice sounding so jealous and demanding? Hell, and now Mrs. Merryweather was looking at him strangely. He really needed to watch his mouth.

"Yes, I am. It's Luke. Luke McVey. My attorney." She flashed him a sunny smile. "He's right on time."

Austin swallowed a growl, watching her exit the room. And he had a nagging suspicion that she knew he was jealous of the fancy lawyer.

Was Luke the reason for today's sexy hair and alluring dress, or was she simply taking Austin's advice and finally learning to loosen up?

He started as Mrs. Merryweather's hand landed on his arm. He relaxed his taut muscles lest she suspect the reason behind his tension. Hell, after his reckless comment, she probably already knew.

"Would you mind taking out the trash, Mr. Hyde? And after that, I could use a hand with mopping the floors. My stamina's not what it used to be, I'll tell ya."

Austin slowly turned to look at her, bracing himself for the smug look he was certain to find on her face.

What he saw was far, far worse.

Sympathy . . . and a glimmer of warning.

Don't get stupid, her look seemed to say. He managed a passable careless shrug, but the smile he forced to his lips felt as stiff as beef jerky and as obvious as Madonna. "Of course I don't mind. It's my job, isn't it?"

Sensing his inner turmoil, Lucy stroked his rough chin with her tongue, trying to soothe the hurt.

It didn't help, dammit.

Chapter Ten

"I understand your need for a bodyguard," Luke McVey said. "Especially in light of what you told me." He sighed and flipped his suit jacket open, sticking his hands into his pants pockets.

Tall, distinguished, with thinning gray hair and hazel eyes, he looked every inch the successful lawyer. Candice had liked him the moment she'd met him, and their friendship had continued to grow over the years.

"But no matter how innocent the relationship between yourself and the . . . handyman, if anyone finds out he's here, you know what a big stink they'll make of it."

Candice shifted uneasily on the sofa as Luke

paced in front of her, knowing she'd be a fool to scoff at his well-meaning advice. And she didn't have to ask who he meant by *they*; her in-laws would indeed love to have something they could twist to their advantage.

She cleared her throat, hoping he wouldn't notice the heat in her cheeks as she voiced the question, "Wouldn't they have to prove that our relationship *wasn't* platonic?"

Luke stared at her for a long, considering moment, as if debating whether he should pry further. "All they really need is a tiny seed of doubt to sow. My advice to you is to be careful. Keep this Mr. Hyde out of sight as much as possible."

He stopped in front of her and took her hands in his, his eyes warm with genuine concern. "Candice, are you sure you can trust this guy?"

Candice didn't hesitate. "Yes, I'm sure. Dr. Jack recommended him." *Besides, he's fun, and he makes me feel wonderful and makes me laugh.*

Luke lifted a skeptical eyebrow at that but didn't comment. He resumed pacing. "You've got a lot at stake here," he reminded her. "Your future and your unborn baby's future depend upon your discretion. Just be careful, okay?"

"I will." Candice waited until she was certain the attorney had finished his speech before she changed the subject. "Luke, I was wondering if you knew anyone who might be interested in buying a few pieces of my jewelry."

He glanced at her sharply. "You need money? Why didn't you tell me? I'd be more than happy to make you a loan."

Firmly, Candice shook her head. "It's sweet of you, but I'd rather do this my own way. I no longer have any need for most of the jewelry Howard bought me." She didn't add that she hated the costly reminders of her subservience, nor did she try to explain that she and Howard had not shared the same taste in jewelry. Luke and Howard had been friends, and out of respect, she kept her opinion of her husband to herself.

"Is it that lousy deadbeat stepfather of yours?" Luke demanded, reminding Candice more of an outraged father than an attorney. "Is he sniffing around for money again?"

She smiled at the sight of his fierce frown, but her smile quickly faded as she thought of the last ugly scene with her stepfather more than three months ago. Nothing ever changed about Pete Clancy; he always looked unshaven, unkempt, and she couldn't remember a time when he didn't stink of whiskey. "I think I convinced Pete the last time that the well had gone dry."

Of course, that was *after* she'd given him her

garish pre-engagement ring to sell. Luke would never understand her intense satisfaction in knowing she'd seen the last of it. The ring had been nothing more than a symbol of ownership in Howard's eyes. If she'd thought she could get away with it, she might have disposed of her wedding band and diamond as well.

When it became obvious by her silence that she wasn't going to confess her reason for needing the money, Luke finally shrugged. "Get together what you want to sell, and give me a call. I know of a reputable jeweler who will give you a fair price."

"Thanks, Luke."

"Don't mention it. Being Howard's attorney has made me a rich man, and helping his lovely widow is the least I can do."

Candice flashed him a teasing smile. "And here I've been thinking it was *my* charm all along."

"That's part of it," Luke agreed, returning her smile. He moved to the door, his expression growing serious again. "Keep a sharp eye on your handyman, will you? You're in a vulnerable situation, Candice. I'd hate to see someone take advantage of you."

Candice remembered Luke's warning later that night when she discovered several pieces of jewelry missing from her dresser. She'd decided to do an inventory before going to bed, eager to get started on the nursery with the extra cash the pieces would bring.

"I can't imagine . . ." she muttered, crawling on her hands and knees to look beneath the bed and dresser. Nothing, not even a dust bunny. Of course, not finding a dust bunny shouldn't surprise her; Mrs. Merryweather was a fanatic about cleaning.

But not finding the jewelry *did* surprise her. She couldn't really believe someone had taken the pieces. And each time Mr. Hyde's name popped into her mind, she firmly shoved the ridiculous notion away.

Stumped, she sat back on her heels, thinking aloud. "Now, why would they take one diamond earring and my pearl necklace and leave the emerald brooch?" The brooch was worth far more than the pearls. Surely a professional thief would know that.

"Maybe they were hoping we wouldn't notice if they only took a little?"

Candice turned to find Mrs. Merryweather standing in the bedroom doorway looking very close to tears. She wore a cotton nightgown patterned with tiny pink roses, a matching robe, and fuzzy pink slippers on her feet.

"I can't find my mother's locket," she announced with a sniff, removing a handkerchief from her housecoat pocket and blowing noisily. "It's not worth a fig to anyone but me."

"If it doesn't have any monetary value, then why would someone take it?" Candice got to her feet and sat on the bed, deeply disturbed by the strange thefts. This time when an image of Mr. Hyde popped into her mind, she knew she couldn't ignore it.

He'd just moved into the house. But even if he *were* a thief, surely he wouldn't be so bold so quickly. It would be a dead give away. And why would he take one earring and leave the other? Then there was Mrs. Merryweather's locket. Candice remembered it well, for Mrs. Merryweather sometimes wore it on Sundays. It was pretty but obviously inexpensive.

It just didn't make sense.

Mrs. Merryweather joined her on the bed, her bosom heaving in a weary sigh. "I hate to think this, Mrs. Dale, but what if Mr. Hyde—"

"No."

"Beg your pardon?" Mrs. Merryweather slowly lowered the handkerchief from her red nose and looked at Candice through tear-blurred eyes. "How can you *not* consider him? If it isn't me, and it isn't you, that only leaves one other possibility."

Candice shook her head, ignoring the logic

that insisted she consider Mrs. Merryweather's theory for longer than two seconds. "It just doesn't make sense. If he's a professional, he would know better than to take something right away, and he would know your locket isn't worth stealing. Not that it isn't precious," she added hastily when Mrs. Merryweather began to sniffle again.

The housekeeper lowered her chin to her chest as if she were doing some serious thinking. "Maybe I misplaced the locket," she mumbled. She didn't sound convinced. "But there's still the matter of your missing jewelry. Mr. Hyde was in here a long time this evening, and then he said he had 'things' to wrap up in his apartment before he moved in. He had the perfect opportunity."

"He's agreed to help me with the nursery, remember? He was probably making plans." They just couldn't go around accusing someone without proof, Candice decided. She knew better than anyone what kind of havoc could be created by jumping to conclusions.

But what would it hurt to ask him a casual question or two? To appease Mrs. Merryweather, of course. It had nothing to do with the fact that she was eager to see him again.

As if to mock her flimsy excuse, her heart leaped joyfully at the thought.

"How about if I go talk to him? I'll just ask him if he happened to notice any jewelry lying around on the floor when he was in here earlier. Maybe I scattered it searching for something." Warming to her theory, Candice added, "Perhaps he found it and put it in the wrong place."

"Like his pocket?" Mrs. Merryweather muttered darkly.

Candice let her remark slide. "Tomorrow we'll do a thorough search of the house. It's not the first time we've lost something in this big ol' place, is it?"

Mrs. Merryweather let out a long, shaky sigh. "Maybe we'll find that little critter, too."

"Lucy's missing?"

"I'm afraid so. I let her have the run of the place, and she disappeared."

"Well, don't worry. I'm sure she'll come out when she gets hungry. Now, why don't you go on to bed?"

"Not a chance." Mrs. Merryweather lumbered to her feet, her battle armor in place once again. "I'll just go make myself a cup of hot tea, and if you're not back in thirty minutes, I'm calling the cops."

Candice suppressed an exasperated sigh as she pulled a terry-cloth wrapper from a hook on the bathroom door and threw it over her black silk pajamas. She belted it tight. "Mr. Hyde wouldn't harm a hair on my head. If he wanted to, he's had plenty of opportunities."

As Candice let herself out through the back door, she immediately noticed the blaze of lights coming from Austin's apartment. It looked as if every lamp in the house was on. Puzzled, she crossed the drive and crept silently up the steep steps.

The door stood ajar.

She stepped closer, listening for any sound from within. The eerie quiet made her flesh crawl. What if they had been burglarized, and the burglar ran into Austin, and . . . ?

Stifling the instinct urging her to turn tail and run, she reached out and pushed the door open wider, peering inside. She had to see for herself that he was okay.

Her breath lodged in her throat as she caught sight of him. He stood with his back to her, bare to the waist, his bronzed skin rippling with muscles as he lifted his arm. A rag splotched with paint hung from his back pocket as if he'd absently jammed it there.

He was painting.

"Aus—Mr. Hyde?" *That's right, girl, keep it formal.* Remember Luke's advice. After the hearing, well, then she would be free to do whatever her heart desired. . . .

A naughty shiver stole over her at the thought.

Austin swung around at the sound of her voice, his handsome face momentarily blank. Finally, his eyes focused on her. He smiled. On cue, her heart gave a foolish leap in response. It continued to pound as he slowly looked her over, leaving her entire body warm and trembling as if he'd stroked her with those big, wonderful hands.

Would the reality be as mind-blowing as the fantasy? she dared to wonder.

As if he read her wicked thoughts, he wiggled his golden brows suggestively. "Is it bedtime?"

She'd known it would be hard to remain aloof. How did a woman resist a man like Austin? *Mr. Hyde,* she reminded herself sternly.

"No, I—may I come in?" Now she wished she had taken the time to dress. Her pajamas, coupled with her robe, covered her entire body, but pajamas made her think of bed, and bed was something that that seemed to come easily to mind when she was around Austin.

He waved a brush in the air, carelessly slinging a streak of paint onto his jeans. "Of course. I was just finishing up."

Candice stepped into the room. She was determined to keep her distance, but the canvas drew her like a magnet. "May I look?"

"Little miss 'May I,'" Austin teased softly. "Don't you ever demand anything?"

She licked her lips and tried not to stare at his magnificent chest. There were plenty of things she would *like* to demand, but nothing she dared mention out loud.

Candice focused on the painting, immediately impressed. "You're good," she told him sincerely. It was a marvelous depiction of a woman cradling a baby in her arms. *Nursing* a baby, she realized on closer inspection. Evening shadows slanted across the woman's bowed head, and a tiny hand clutched the smooth curve of her exposed breast.

Looking at the woman's face again, a jolt of familiarity shot through her. She glanced sharply at Austin.

"I hope you don't mind," he said with an odd edge to his voice.

He sounded flustered, maybe a little . . . embarrassed?

So she was right. The woman looked familiar because—She swallowed hard. "That's me, isn't it?"

He nodded, smiling that boyish, endearing grin that made her pulse accelerate.

Recalling his previous inquiry about breast-feeding, Candice blurted out, "Did your mother breast-feed you?" She turned to study the painting again to hide her flush.

200

His snort sounded bitter. "I don't think silicone is safe for human consumption."

Another hint about his mother, just enough to make her want to know more. Candice braved another question. "You don't like your mother much, do you?"

"No."

She waited for him to go on. When he didn't, she asked softly, "Do you want to talk about it?"

His fingers closed over her chin, turning her face slowly in his direction until she had no choice but to look at him.

His eyes burned into hers. "Do *you* want to talk about your husband?"

"No." She had to choke the word out through the sudden constriction in her throat. And damn him for bringing it up. He couldn't know that she'd spent the last year trying *not* to think of Howard, could he?

"Good. Then we're even. It seems we both have painful memories we'd rather not talk about. Maybe some other time."

He let go of her chin, his smile returning with an ease that made her blink. The hard light she'd glimpsed in his eyes had vanished.

"Let's talk instead about why you're walking around late at night without your bodyguard."

Candice gave a start of surprise. She'd forgotten her reason for coming. But then, he had a way of distracting her. Trying to sound casual, she explained, "I seem to have misplaced a few pieces of jewelry, and I thought you might have noticed them lying around when you were in the nursery. . . ." She trailed off, realizing by the slow fading of his smile that she'd blundered despite her caution. "I'm not accusing you, Mr. Hyde. I—"

"Aren't you?"

"No. I simply thought I might have knocked them onto the floor and that you might have found them and put them somewhere." It was true. She had only considered the alternative for a few seconds.

"Like in my pocket?" he suggested softly, inadvertently echoing Mrs. Merryweather's words.

Candice could no more have stopped the flood of guilty color rushing to her face than she could have stopped the hurt from entering his. Feeling defensive for no good reason, she met his flinty gaze head-on. "I can't help what you believe, but I never thought that you took them. *Found* them, yes, but not stole them."

For a long, tense moment, Candice feared he'd go on believing the worst. Then he sighed and ran a hand through his sun-streaked hair. She let out a slow breath of relief, only to draw it in sharply again as he said, "I suggest you keep your pretty baubles in a safe. Glittering things are hard for her to resist."

"*Her?*" Candice gasped in outrage. "If you're implying that Mrs. Merryweather is a thief, then you are way out of line, Mr. Hyde."

"I thought I told you to call me Austin."

She was speechless in the face of his lazy grin. How dare he stand there so calmly while he accused poor Mrs. Merryweather of stealing! Coldly, she said, "For your information, *Mr. Hyde*, Mrs. Merryweather is missing her locket as well."

Austin nodded as if the news came as no surprise. "Is it gold, maybe? And shiny?"

Confusion momentarily distracted Candice from her growing anger. "Why, yes, it is. But how would *you* know?" His description rekindled a suspicion she could no longer ignore. There was only one explanation for his having such knowledge, wasn't there?

"Because Lucy likes things that are sparkly or shiny—gold, silver." He shrugged. "You get the picture."

Candice paused, then sucked in a furious breath. Oh, she got the picture all right. He had deliberately allowed her to believe—oh, the absolute orneriness of the man! She had never in her life met anyone so *exasperating*.

And now he was laughing.

Well, there was funny, and then there was *not* funny, and in her book Mr. Hyde had just crossed the line into not funny. Flashing him a look that should have ignited his paint-splattered jeans, she marched to the door.

"Wait! Don't you want your ice cream?"

Candice paused, her chest heaving. She should ignore him *and* his contrite tone. She should keep right on walking. Yes, that's exactly what she would do. His offer was probably just another sick joke.

"Double chocolate chip cookie dough."

Her mouth watered. How did *he* know she'd been craving chocolate chip cookie dough ice cream? Rich and smooth, with little nuggets of dark chocolate. Giving herself a mental kick, Candice reached for the doorknob with renewed determination. Mr. Hyde could take his ice cream and shove it.

"Topped with chocolate syrup. Consider it a peace offering."

Again she hesitated. If he were truly sorry, then wouldn't it be churlish of her to refuse? Not to mention biting off her nose to spite her face.

Behind her, she heard the sound of the freezer door opening and shutting. She jumped as he reached over her shoulder and placed a round tub of cold ice cream into her arms, balancing a bottle of syrup on top of the container. Still miffed, and with Luke's warning fresh in her mind, she kept her voice cool and distant— and didn't turn around. Looking at him would be a mistake. "Thank you. You'll find a pillow and some blankets on the sofa in the den."

"Don't mention it. If you'll give me a moment to turn out the lights, I'll walk over with you." He was standing too close, and the husky note in his voice wreaked havoc with her self-control.

Feeling an urgent need for fresh air, Candice mumbled, "I'll wait outside on the porch. It's—it's hot in here." She *did* feel overly warm, but then, she always did in his company.

"Hmm. I know what you mean," came his low-voiced agreement.

Candice hastily stepped outside into the cool, refreshing air before the heat from her body melted the coveted ice cream.

Chapter Eleven

The toddler was almost to the edge of the second-story veranda.

Another few steps and he would be over the edge.

Austin pumped his legs as hard as he could, but he remained in place, as if an invisible treadmill rolled beneath his pounding feet.

No matter how fast he ran, how hard he tried, he remained a steady, agonizing yard from the child.

Sweat stung his eyes, but he couldn't lift his hands to wipe it away and didn't want to take the time to try. He watched in horror as the baby reached the edge, toppled, then fell.

Austin screamed, and with a mighty effort that

*corded the muscles in his arms, he leaped at the
baby. His fingers closed around a tiny heel; then
he was propelled forward as if a giant hand had
pushed him. Over the edge he went after the
baby, falling, falling—*

He rolled from the couch and hit the floor
with a heavy thud that jarred his bones and rattled his brain into consciousness.

A dream.

It was just a dream. No, not an ordinary
dream, a nightmare.

Austin blew out an exhausted sigh of relief
and lay still, his nose buried in the carpet, his
body still shaking from the aftermath. He
much preferred erotic dreams about Candice,
which normally disturbed his slumber and had
for the past three weeks since he'd moved into
the house.

Right now, she slept peacefully in a guest
room upstairs, because the paint fumes from
the nursery adjoining her bedroom nause-
ated her. Just thinking about her lying in
bed, her cheeks flushed with sleep, her
white-gold hair spread out on the pillows,
was enough to make Austin groan. God, he
wanted her in the worst way. Badly. Terribly.
Achingly.

And every passing day spent in her company
strengthened that need. She felt it, too, he was
certain. Yet since Luke McVey's visit, she had

changed. Oh, she was nice and friendly, but it wasn't the same.

He feared she was back to the old Candice Vanausdale.

With the exception of her eyes. He often caught her looking at him, and he recognized the look. It was the same one he saw in the mirror. Hungry. Lonesome. Needful.

Whatever had changed between them, he suspected the attorney had something to do with it. The suspicion made him feel ill every time he thought about it.

So he wouldn't think about it.

Austin gathered the covers and rose from the floor, planting his sore body onto the couch—his bed. It wasn't quite morning yet, but that translucent time between night and day when the sky turned gray, then flushed pink, before uncovering the blue, blue sky. Austin knew he wouldn't go back to sleep, not after the nightmare. Besides, the sofa wasn't exactly a dream come true in the snooze department, especially after the grueling work he'd been doing for the past three weeks.

Candice had offered him a room upstairs—one next to the guest room she slept in now. He'd taken the room for a place to keep his clothes, shower, and change, but what would be the point of sleeping upstairs? He was here to protect, wasn't he? How could he do his job if he was upstairs? Although she wasn't sleeping in her room at the moment, her bedroom suite was downstairs. So he slept every night on the sofa in the den, shrugging off her objections.

Austin lifted his arms, wincing as he did, and cradled his head with his hands. He waited impatiently for daylight, wary of navigating the still unfamiliar room in the dark. A bruised shin and a stubbed toe had left him cautious.

His thoughts returned unerringly to the subject that occupied most of his waking hours and damned near all of his sleeping ones, too, when he wasn't dreaming about babies.

Candice Vanausdale.

The file he'd bullied Jack into showing him had been a disappointment, containing nothing pertinent about the mystery woman herself. He knew the client's doctors weren't certain why she had failed to become pregnant the normal way, and he knew she'd undergone several tests in that area. The date on the file confirmed that Jack hadn't been lying when he'd said Candice and her husband had planned this baby before his death.

Austin couldn't fathom why Jack had been so nervous about someone's seeing that file containing only a lot of medical mumbo jumbo. Oh, sure, he realized that the number listed for Howard's sperm count was a joke, but Jack had known that *he* knew anyway, and that nobody else did. So Jack's reluctance didn't make sense.

Just as Mrs. Dale's abrupt transition from eager pupil in Relaxing 101 to Miss Class Act didn't make sense.

An ache began to form between his eyes, so Austin shoved his puzzling thoughts aside. From his position on the sofa, he watched through the floor-to-ceiling windows as dawn made its majestic appearance. The room began to lighten; objects blurred into dark shapes, then became more detailed in the morning sun.

It was time to rise and shine, get to work—and he had plenty of that to do. With another groan, he shoved himself from the couch and padded to the kitchen in a pair of faded cotton boxers, knowing he would be the only one up at this ungodly hour.

He poured a tall glass of juice and took it upstairs with him as he prepared to shower and change, going over his mental list of things to do. Mrs. Merryweather would have her own list ready and waiting, but Austin had plans of his own.

Today, he was going to finish the pale yellow trim in the nursery and start draining the pool. Yesterday, he'd drawn plans for a dog kennel, trimmed the hedges, mowed the massive lawn, touched up the paint on a few rough places on the east side of the house, and worked on the nursery until late into the night.

As he stepped into the warm shower, he wondered if having a baby gave everyone such energy. It certainly stimulated his imagination.

Boy, would Candice be surprised when she discovered the real reason he was draining the pool. And he couldn't wait to see her face when she discovered how he planned to brighten up those boring, sterile white walls in the nursery.

He lathered his body, humming to himself. After he had finished *From Discovery to Delivery*, he'd quickly begun *From Zero Months to Five Years*. He had discovered that babies needed lots of color to stimulate their vision.

Not endless white walls. Color. Well, he was just the guy to fix the problem, and surely Candice would appreciate his artistic genius. And by the time she delivered *their* baby, wouldn't she be so attached to him she'd cry for joy to learn he was the *real* father?

Austin grumbled as he quickly dried off and slipped into his work clothes—baggy sweat pants and an old blue T-shirt, both paint-spotted but clean. Okay, so she might not be happy to find out the father wasn't her blue-blooded husband, but at least by then he might have proven what a good dad he was going to—

He halted at the door to his temporary bedroom, registering the shock of what he'd just thought. When had things gotten so turned around? He had come here to ascertain that *she* was going to be a good mother to his child—a child Jack had forced upon him.

In fact, he still hadn't decided whether he was even going to reveal the truth to Candice, right? If he did, she would lose her inheritance, and so would the baby.

His baby. Not Howard Vanausdale's, but his.

Well, hell. What if she *did* lose the money and this house and her security? She would make it just fine . . . wouldn't she? Of course she would. *He* had. But then, he had *chosen* not to touch his inheritance.

Candice might not have that choice.

Austin paused in the hall outside her door, tempted to look in on her, make sure she was okay. Then he remembered the coolness of her smile, the I'm-the-employer-and-you're-the-handyman/bodyguard look she had been presenting to him since McVey's visit.

No. He couldn't just turn the knob and take a reassuring peek without the risk of losing ground, and he'd lost too much of that already.

Frowning, he shook his head and continued downstairs. There was always a chance she would lose the money anyway, even if he decided not to reveal himself as the baby's father. Then what would she do? By her own admission, she had no relatives other than an estranged stepfather, and while Mrs. Merryweather would obviously lay down her life for Candice, she was an elderly woman, close to retirement, and hardly rolling in dough.

Steeped in his thoughts, Austin nearly missed Lucy's chortling plea as he passed the utility room just inside the kitchen on the right. When he paused to identify the noise, she scratched against her cage door frantically. He sighed and gave in, filling her feed bowl before opening the cage to let her out.

Lucy sniffed the air, twitched her whiskers as if saying thanks, then immediately began to munch on the dry cat food.

Austin watched her for a moment, finally deciding she would be all right until he returned from activating the drain on the pool. Still, he issued a whispered warning, "Don't leave this room. I'll be right back."

He let himself out through the back door and turned in the direction of the pool, absently noting the warm, still air. Not yet six o'clock, which meant it was going to be another scorcher. Fairly typical for a California May.

Too bad he was about to put the pool out of commission.

Coming to a halt at the edge, he eyed the inviting water with longing, casting a speculative glance at the closed, curtained patio doors to Candice's room. She had slept upstairs, he reminded himself, so she couldn't possibly hear him and investigate.

Mrs. Merryweather wouldn't be up for another hour, and Candice for another two.

Should he?

Dare he?

It would take several days to drain the water, and several more to complete his surprise. Meanwhile, he planned to keep the pool cover in place. If anyone asked any questions—if they even noticed—he would make the excuse that he was too busy to keep it clean, nobody used it, and leaves from the overhanging trees kept the filters clogged.

Simple, logical explanations, and if luck stayed with him, Candice would continue to use an upstairs guest room as long as he kept painting in the nursery. In fact, he intended to make the job last as long as he could.

But right now he wanted to plunge into the cool water and swim a few laps, work the soreness from his overused muscles.

Before he could change his mind, Austin shucked his clothes and slipped naked over the side into the water. He'd have to make it quick before Sleeping Beauty awoke—or the fire-breathing dragon.

Austin's strokes were smooth and efficient as he sliced through the cool water to the opposite end of the pool, hoping he wouldn't regret his weakness.

The last thing he needed was for Candice to catch him swimming.

Candice came awake with the first loving lick of Lucy's tongue. "What—! Oh, it's you." She sat up in surprise at the sight of the ferret perched on the bed beside her. "How did you get in here?" Brushing her hair from her eyes, Candice glanced at the cracked door, then at Lucy, trying to look forbidding. Lucy twitched her whiskers and stared at her with tiny eyes outlined with black raccoon circles.

Finally, the ferret dived beneath the covers and came out holding something shiny and gold between her sharp little teeth.

Mrs. Merryweather's locket! With a delighted laugh, Candice tugged the locket away from the reluctant ferret and wisely closed it into the drawer of the nightstand. She'd give it to Mrs. Merryweather later.

A thorough search of the house a few weeks ago had uncovered her missing jewelry, but not Mrs. Merryweather's locket. Where had the little animal hidden it? she wondered, throwing the covers aside. They had found her earring and her pearls beneath the sofa. Obviously Lucy had decided not to place all of her eggs in one basket.

"You should be ashamed of yourself," Candice scolded gently.

Chuckling over the animal's antics, Candice gathered her up and padded downstairs. She tiptoed past the den, knowing that Austin had worked long into the night on the nursery and that he must be exhausted. As she reached the kitchen, Lucy scrambled in her arms, obviously wanting down.

Puzzled, Candice set her on the floor and prepared to grab her if she decided to run for it. Lucy scurried to the back door and began to scratch in earnest.

"You want outside?" Candice frowned, glancing down at her oversized cream silk pajamas. Not exactly the right attire for a morning stroll, but then, it was early. Too early for newspaper reporters. In fact, the kitchen was silent and shadowed, a strong indication that even Mrs. Merryweather was still abed.

Lucy scratched impatiently, then turned to look at her.

Candice smiled and relented. "Okay, but don't think I'm going to chase you, little lady." She patted her slightly rounded stomach. "I'm not in any condition for running, you know."

Lucy chortled her impatient agreement and

waited. Candice sighed and opened the door, wondering if she were making a mistake. She couldn't remember Austin's taking the ferret outside; and she was almost certain Mrs. Merryweather didn't.

But why, then, did the critter appear to know exactly where she was going? Hurrying to catch up with Lucy, Candice broke into a trot. Her heart began to beat faster when she saw that the ferret was heading straight for the pool.

Did Lucy know how to swim? If something happened to the little animal, Austin would be crushed. *She* would be crushed, and Mrs. Merryweather would cry for days.

Candice increased her speed, fearing she wouldn't have time to catch up with the critter. The bizarreness of her situation flashed briefly through her mind. It was barely six o'clock, and she was outside in her pajamas chasing a ferret who seemed intent on going for a morning swim.

The media would love it, and her in-laws would declare her insane. Mrs. Merryweather would put her to bed for a week, and Austin would growl and threaten to drown Lucy with his bare hands.

A laugh hitched in her chest just as Lucy made a graceful dive over the side.

Candice didn't hesitate; she dove into the

water, pajamas and all. She swam furiously until she realized the ferret was swimming, not drowning. Lucy's tiny legs paddled the water like a pro as she headed for the opposite side of the pool. Smiling, Candice treaded water and watched, relieved now that she knew the ferret wasn't in danger. Perhaps Austin had been allowing the animal to go for a swim in the mornings, and that was why she seemed so intent on getting into the water.

A movement to the left startled out a gasp that might have been a scream if she hadn't gulped a mouthful of water. Choking, she whirled, pinning her alarmed gaze on the dark shape gliding beneath the water along the side of the pool.

Recovering from the shock, Candice glanced behind her, her gaze narrowing on the ladder that appeared to be the swimmer's destination. He thought to sneak by and actually get out of the water before she saw him?

Then the implications slammed into her, one by one.

Austin was swimming. Not a beginner's swim, but a full-throttled breath-holding underwater swim that a novice couldn't possibly learn in three weeks.

Austin was also swimming for his life, because he knew how furious she would be.

But the most mind-blowing, pulse-crashing,

nerve-rending realization was that he wasn't wearing a stitch of clothing. Candice took a deep breath and closed her eyes, then quickly opened them again. She glanced down at the transparency of her own attire. She might as well be naked herself, for she could see the outline of her nipples, and lower, the shadowy thatch of hair between her legs.

She jerked her gaze up as Lucy paddled by on her way to catch Austin, who had reached the ladder and was now climbing up it in all his majestic nudity.

Despite the warning in her head ordering her not to look, Candice looked. And forgot to breathe. Yes, she'd seen him nearly naked before. But never like this.

Water sluiced from his tanned, magnificent body. Broad shoulders and a heavily muscled back tapered down to tight buttocks, which were a shocking white compared to the rest of him. His thighs hardened as he braced himself on the ladder, the light layer of hair darkened and slicked to his skin from the moisture.

She knew the moment he realized she was watching him. His back stiffened; the muscles of his forearms above his hands gripping the ladder knotted. As if in prayer, he lifted his face to the sun, then shoved his hair from his eyes before turning slowly around.

The absolute absurdity of the last few

moments hit Candice hard. If she recapped this story to the media, they wouldn't believe her. In fact, she hardly believed it herself. Was she actually in her pajamas, in her pool, with a determined ferret and a naked handyman, at six o'clock in the morning?

She was.

Austin finished the turn.

No question about it, he was naked. Lord, was he naked. Candice edged back until she felt the pool wall behind her. He was amazingly naked. Disturbingly naked.

She averted her gaze, wondering if her breathing would ever return to normal. It was hard to remember that she was supposed to be angry at him. Very hard. She gulped, wishing she'd never crawled out of bed, wishing she had listened to the saner side of her brain that had told her not to look.

Lucy had made it up the ladder and now stood shaking herself dry, oblivious to the havoc she had created with one stroke of her tongue. Desperately, Candice focused her dazed gaze on the ferret. Instead, she saw the curve of Austin's calf inches from Lucy's nose.

Grasping the edge of the pool with one arm, Candice swept a wet strand of hair from her cheek and forced herself to meet Austin's gaze. She couldn't stay in the pool all day, and he couldn't stand on the ladder baring everything, even if he did do it well.

Candice gave herself a mental shake and licked her lips. "Why . . . why did you pretend you couldn't swim?" And speaking of pretending, would pretending she hadn't noticed his obvious nudity work?

The answer was no.

As if her words released him from a spell, he stepped down the ladder into the water, turning his body slightly to the side and giving Candice a whole new, breathtaking view. She wondered if he knew how ruggedly beautiful he was.

His voice was rough, edged with regret. "I was curious about you, and at the time I thought it was a good idea."

"It was a dirty trick," she said, unwilling to let it go. Maybe anger would help her keep her head above water.

He nodded, watching her with eyes that smoldered with something she didn't dare question.

"At least I'm honest."

Candice stiffened, then laughed at the blatant, softly voiced lie. "Honest? You call tricking me into believing you almost drowned honesty?" She bobbed on the surface of the water, welcoming the anger, daring him to argue, and desperately wishing she wasn't Mrs. Howard Vanausdale for just a day so that she could have what she really wanted. Him. Mr. Hyde. Austin.

His jaw tightened perceptibly. He began to edge around the pool, his burning gaze never leaving her face. "Yes, honesty. But you wouldn't know about that, would you, Mrs. Dale? You would never resort to trickery to get close to someone, because you would never admit needing to in the first place. Especially if it meant you might get caught."

Candice realized his intent too late. In one smooth lunge across the water, he was there. He placed his arms on either side of her and balanced himself in the water. She flattened her back against the pool wall, but there was no escape. With agonizing slowness, he pressed his body against hers from toe to chest.

The shock of it numbed her for an instant before a riptide of sensation rocked her world. He lowered himself an inch, then eased his body up again, and with each slow stroke his manhood—that magificent thrust of male glory she'd glimpsed earlier—slid across the aching junction of her thighs.

She gasped and closed her eyes, her voice a thready whisper. "Don't—don't make me—"

"What? Don't make you tell the truth? That this is what you want, have wanted since our first kiss?" With a husky growl, he reminded her, laying claim to her gasping mouth and sucking the resistance right out of her.

Not that she had any left. No, she had surrendered the moment she saw his naked body gliding through the water. If she were honest with herself, she had known then that something was going to happen between them, that it had been building over the past few weeks with each heated, hungry look, every burning, erotic thought.

Her tongue clashed with his, then shyly retreated, only to be grasped and tugged back into submission. His teeth grazed her bottom lip before he broke loose, continuing the up and down sliding motion that was driving her crazy.

With the sheer strength of his will, he forced her to look at him. The low, driving intensity of his voice made her shudder with reaction and need. "Thoughts of you, of doing this to you, keep me awake at night."

Every move, every torturous slide of his body grazed her ultrasensitive nipples against his chest and increased the ache between her thighs. She couldn't speak, couldn't think. The only things that mattered right now were what he was doing to her and the sound of his ragged voice telling her how much he wanted and needed her. She clutched his shoulders, begging him without words to take her further, deeper, harder.

"Slow down, baby. Slow down," he cautioned, trailing hot kisses along her neck and down to the outline of her breasts. Through the wet silk of her pajamas, he took a rigid nipple in his mouth and flicked his tongue back and forth across the sensitive nub, keeping rhythm with the strokes of his body against hers.

Candice moaned, thrusting upward and out and forcing him to increase the pressure of his mouth. Lord, she felt as if she might splinter in two. She didn't think she could stand the pleasure if it got any better.

And then Austin proved her wrong. He proved she could take it and then some. "I want you," he growled against her mouth as he lowered her pajama bottoms, caressing each sweet curve feverishly. "Touch me and see how much I want you."

Trembling, Candice released one hand and lowered it into the water, finding him and clasping her fingers around him. He throbbed against her palm, a sharp hiss whistling between his teeth at her shy touch. In retaliation, his hand nudged her legs apart, and his fingers teased her, circling the burgeoning nub of her womanhood until Candice squirmed and pressed against him.

She wanted. . . .

She needed. . . .

"Austin . . . I want . . ."

"Yes, baby, tell me what you want." As if to taunt her, he closed his hand over hers, and together they guided his hard shaft between her legs.

Then he stopped.

Candice whimpered, and when she heard the sound and realized it came from her own throat, she grasped his shoulders and tried to pull him closer. He resisted.

"Tell me. . . ." he half demanded, half pleaded.

"I want you inside me," she let out in a rush of aching desire. And she did. Now. All of him.

Chapter Twelve

She wanted him inside her. . . .

They were the sweetest words Austin could ever remember hearing.

He crushed his mouth to hers, kissing her with a soul-searing passion that swept away the last lingering doubts about what was right or wrong.

For Austin, there was no wrong. He wanted her, ached for her, and needed her with a fever that startled him in its intensity. He had to have her. Now.

Maybe forever.

Cautioning himself to slow down before he exploded, he remained poised at the entrance of Heaven, the water swirling around him, adding to the delicious feel of her quivering against him. She squeezed her thighs together, trying to draw him closer. He gave a husky laugh that betrayed his crumbling control, bending to rake his teeth lightly over her pebbled nipples. First one, then the other. Back and forth, reveling in her whimpers of pleasure, pushing slightly against her opening, teasing, teasing . . .

"Austin . . ."

Half warning, half plea, her voice was like wind to his forest fire. Austin groaned against her damp neck, clasping her waist and drawing her closer, then closer still.

"Are you sure?" It was just a moan, nothing more. In fact, he couldn't be certain she understood his question. He didn't know why he asked it, doubting he could even stop even if she wanted him to.

"Yes!"

She didn't want him to.

Thank God.

Releasing a shaky breath, she pulled his head away and stared at him, her cat's eyes heavy with desire and deadly serious. "Please make love to me."

Austin met her lips halfway, wallowing in the heat and sweetness of her mouth, his tongue thrusting with gentle strokes in forewarning of what he was about to do to her.

If he could hold out.

It was debatable, because as he eased his hot length into her, she tightened around him, nearly catapulting him over the edge with that single, wonderful movement. He'd never been this hot for a woman, this out of control.

She kicked her legs, and it wasn't until she wrapped them around him and thrust down, sheathing him more fully, that Austin realized the object brushing against his arm was her pajama bottoms floating on the water's surface.

Candice wasn't waiting for him; she began to move, challenging his control with every thrust of her hips. The wall at her back gave her leverage so that Austin was helpless to slow her wild pace. Her teeth grabbed his tongue, and Austin knew the meaning of sweet revenge as she began to draw his tongue into her mouth. Her nails raked his back as she clutched him tighter, urged him faster, harder.

Austin was beyond pacing himself. He thrust into her, and with every withdrawal the sensuous feel of water washed over him before he buried himself again. She met him thrust for thrust, kiss for kiss as they climbed into the sky together. Frantically, he suckled her nipples, kissed her neck, and tasted her skin wherever he could. He couldn't get enough of her and knew he couldn't last much longer.

Suddenly, her back arched, her mouth

opened in a soundless scream. She closed her eyes. Austin watched her, awed by the simple beauty of her release. When her glazed eyes flew open again and fastened on his tense, watchful face, her obvious astonishment sent him flying over the edge.

"Candice!" he ground out, thrusting as deep as he could go. He thought the pleasure would rip him apart. It crashed over him, into him, mingling with her own convulsing body until he thought they both might drown. "Baby, baby . . ."

She clutched his neck, trembling in the aftermath of what Austin suspected was her first taste of pleasure. Her astonishment had struck a primal cord inside him, triggering the most satisfying release he'd ever experienced. Later, he would have to think more on this, try to figure out why it was so—so *different* with this woman.

When his breathing finally edged back into a normal range, Austin swept the wet hair from her face and cupped her chin. With a worried frown, he took in her flushed cheeks, her kiss-swollen lips, and dazed expression. "Are you . . . I didn't hurt you, did I?" Oh, hell, he'd forgotten about the baby. *How* had he forgotten? It was the reason he was here, wasn't it?

Now, he wasn't so sure.

"No." Her whispered assurance came out on

a sigh of contentment. Suddenly, she broke from his hold on her chin and dipped her head shyly against his shoulder. "It was just a surprise."

He held her close, a decidedly mushy feeling settling in his chest. Stroking her back, he hesitated, then gave in to curiosity. "Was it . . . Is this the first time you've . . ." Well, hell, he didn't have a bashful bone in his body, yet he couldn't find the right words to say what he wanted to say. He didn't want to embarrass her.

"Saw the stars?" came her muffled reply.

He felt her chuckle—right before she licked his shoulder, then placed a pulse-rattling kiss in the hollow of his neck. Austin was so very, very glad for the support of the water because his bones had dissolved.

Softly, she continued to blow his mind and inflate his ego to the size of the Hindenburg. "Touched the moon? Rocketed into space? Exploded?"

"All that?" he teased, bringing her face up for a long, lingering kiss. When he opened his eyes, he saw Lucy at the edge of the pool behind Candice. She sat very still, watching them. "We've got a visitor," he mumbled against her mouth. He immediately regretted his words as she stiffened against him, her eyes going wide. Damn. She thought—

With a panicky little twist, she tried to turn, but Austin held her tight. He muttered roughly, "It's just Lucy."

"Oh." She sagged against him, avoiding his questioning gaze. "I'd—we'd better get out of the pool before Mrs. Merryweather finds us."

Mrs. Merryweather . . . or someone else? Austin wondered, then berated himself for his suspicions. A few moments ago, he was certain she wouldn't have cared if he had announced the Pope himself was standing by the pool.

Austin felt deflated as the real world crept back in, then tried to laugh at his silly thoughts. Of course they couldn't stay in the pool and make love all day, however tempting the thought. She was probably cold, too. A quick glance at her shirt front confirmed this.

He grabbed her floating bottoms and helped her put them on, hot and hard again by the time the task was finished. Ignoring his condition, he clasped her arms around his neck and pushed away from the pool wall with his feet, sending them straight to the ladder. "Up you go." He swallowed hard as she climbed out of the pool, the sun slanting through the trees and outlining her body through the transparent wet silk.

His gaze lingered on the slight mound of her stomach; he hoped it would distract him, but it didn't work. He was just as aroused by the thought of his baby inside her as he was at the memory of himself inside her.

She turned and held out her hand, her gaze fixed on his face and nothing else, as if she'd made up her mind to pretend he wasn't stark naked. Austin grinned at her determined expression, guessing the cause as he grasped the railing, then curled his fingers around hers as he climbed out.

"Candice, I—" he began.

"Mrs. Vanausdale!" A high, nervous voice, shouted across the length of the pool. "Is this your new lover? Or has he been your lover all along? Is he the *real* father of your baby?"

Incredulous, they automatically turned to see who had dared to encroach on their privacy. It was the same Sacramento Star reporter who had hounded her at the clinic, and he held a camera to his eye.

The click and whir of the lens moved Austin to action. He shoved a frozen Candice behind him, his damned clothes out of reach.

"What the hell do you think you're doing?" he growled furiously. "This is private property. Get the hell out of here!"

Apparently, the reporter knew that Austin couldn't get to his clothes without exposing a trembling, half-naked Candice. He continued to snap his pictures.

"I'll kill you for this, you little weasel," Austin promised.

"No, Mr. Hyde, let me do the honors." It was an angry, red-faced Mrs. Merryweather, trotting up the walk in their direction.

Behind him, Candice moaned and clutched his waist, burying her face against his back. Austin simply gaped in amazement at the sight of the pellet gun perched on the housekeeper's shoulder and aimed at the reporter.

"I've been wantin' to get my hands on this vulture for a long time." And with that, she started firing the harmless but stinging pellets, cocking and shooting with admirable speed. "Get gone! And don't come back, you blood-sucking rat!"

The reporter took off at a dead run. Austin lunged for his pants and scrambled into them, but the reporter had already made it to the safety of the surrounding woods.

Stunned in the aftermath, they stood in silence, listening to the gunning of a van motor, followed by the screech of tires. Austin turned and headed for his truck. "I'm going after him," he stated.

Candice grabbed him by the arm. "No. It's too late."

Austin flinched at her pale expression, hating the defeat in her voice. "Like hell it—"

"Mrs. Dale's right, Mr. Hyde. He's gone, and

233

there's nothing you can do about it but pray he drops his camera."

Austin ground his teeth, hating to give up. The pictures the reporter had surely gotten made his gut clench painfully. Hell, not only had he been stark naked, but Candice might as well have been, for all the covering her wet silk pajamas gave her.

"You can sue if he prints those photos," he snapped, feeling sick as he recalled the questions the reporter had flung at her.

Hope flashed briefly in her eyes. Then she sighed and shook her head. "I could, but they won't care. It's worth it to them. Besides, anything we do now will only feed the frenzy."

Mrs. Merryweather cradled the pellet rifle, reached down, and swooped Lucy into her arms. The ferret had frozen in place, just as they had. Austin could see the poor thing trembling, no doubt from all the noise. He knew loud voices frightened her, and the gun was icing on the cake.

The housekeeper glanced at them, her expression giving nothing away. "Why don't we go inside and get breakfast started? Mrs. Dale, you know you get queasy if you don't eat something first thing."

As Austin walked beside a subdued Candice, he wondered what the housekeeper was thinking. It would only be natural for her to question why they were in the pool, him naked and Candice in her pajamas, yet she didn't ask. His admiration for the older woman edged up a notch.

He glanced sideways at Candice, wishing he could ease her misery. Yet he hesitated to reach out. Was she blaming him? And why wouldn't she? He'd started this whole rotten mess by giving in to the urge for one last swim before he drained the pool. No, he couldn't blame her if she hated him, because if he hadn't been in the pool, Lucy wouldn't have come searching for him, and the incident with the reporter wouldn't have happened.

But he couldn't regret their lovemaking, no matter how hard he tried.

He hoped she didn't either, but damned if it didn't look as if she did.

Candice dripped a tiny point of glue onto the bottom of the miniature rocking chair before pressing the base together, slowly counting to thirty. She'd been working steadily for the past two hours, and her hands had begun to cramp, but she refused to stop.

Working calmed her, gave her time to think rational thoughts, something best accomplished when she was alone. A plate of sliced oranges sat untouched at the edge of her work-table, but the secret pile of M&M's in her lap was rapidly diminishing.

She'd pulled her hair into a careless knot on top of her head and had searched through her massive closet for the oldest, softest piece of clothing she could find. Finally, she'd snagged an old silk kimono that was several sizes too big.

Comfort food. Comfort clothes. Work.

And while the kimono was definitely too large, it was perfect for hiding chocolate candies from a shrewd, overprotective house-keeper. Candice paused and popped an M&M into her mouth, silently thanking Austin. He'd made the chocolate run and sneaked the candy to her when Mrs. Merryweather wasn't watching.

As she remembered the quick, unloverlike exchange, she bit her lip on a moan of regret.

It was a week since she'd gotten her first taste of Heaven. An entire week since the reporter had taken the pictures, yet there had been no outrageous headlines, no pictures of her clad in wet silk pajamas climbing out of a pool with a naked Austin right behind her. And, thank God, no pictures of Austin facing the camera baring his all.

Candice shook her head in disbelief. She should be ecstatic, but she wasn't. She couldn't be, because she knew that she could never be so lucky. The reporter hadn't dropped his camera, as Mrs. Merryweather had wished. And even if he had, he would have printed the story without the pictures.

So why hadn't he? Every day that passed, her nerves grew more taut. She hated the waiting and almost wished they would get it over with.

Almost.

She rubbed her temples. Poor Austin. It was *her* fault he was about to be literally exposed to the world on the front page of a newspaper. He would be named as her plaything, love slave, just as he had joked about. Only he might not find it so funny in reality.

Her fault, for thinking that for one erotic, mind-blowing moment she could be anyone but Mrs. Howard Vanausdale, the rich widow who dared override God and have her husband's baby despite the fact that Howard was dead.

Candice gave a guilty start at the sound of Mrs. Merryweather's whispered footsteps behind her. Quickly, she scooted her legs beneath the table and clamped her knees over the pile of M&M's on her lap.

The housekeeper slapped a newspaper down beside her. Candice glanced at it, then looked away. She didn't want to see, didn't want to know.

"Nothing today, either." Mrs. Merryweather hesitated before adding, "But they called."

Candice swiveled around, remembering the candies in the nick of time. She placed her hands in her lap to stop their headlong rush to the floor. Her gaze flew to Mrs. Merryweather's grim features. "What—what did they want?" As if she didn't know! A nice juicy story to go with the picture. Not in a million years.

"He wanted to talk to you. He said—he said he'd hold off on printing the pictures if you'd give him an exclusive interview."

There was more; Candice could see it in the housekeeper's face. "And?" she prompted.

"That's mostly it." Mrs. Merryweather turned the untouched plate of orange slices around in slow circles.

Candice watched the revealing movement with growing dread.

"The deal is, you give them an exclusive interview about your marriage to Mr. Howard and tell them the real reason you're having this baby."

With a dry, disbelieving laugh, Candice said, "The *real* reason? So they admit they've been telling vicious lies all this time?" She laughed again, but it lacked humor. "And after they've told these lies about me, they actually expect me to grant them an interview?"

"Well . . ."

"Mrs. Merryweather!" Candice was shocked that the housekeeper would even consider it. "You can't mean you think I should. What's there to tell, anyway? What do they want to know? There was no physical abuse." She swallowed hard. "Except for that one slap, and that wouldn't have happened if I hadn't forgotten which earrings to wear." The horror of what she was saying sank in, and she snapped her mouth closed, her eyes watering.

The housekeeper clasped her hands in front of her and looked Candice square in the eye, keeping her voice low and gentle. "Not physically, maybe, except for that one time, like you said." She lifted a stern eyebrow before adding, "Which wasn't your fault."

Candice nodded, unable to stay a wave of hot shame.

"But we both know there was a lot of mental abuse." Mrs. Merryweather reached out and tucked a strand of hair behind Candice's ear, patting her hot face. "Mr. Howard was a strange man, and I've got a feeling he's got a lot of making up to do right about now."

"He—he wasn't that bad." Candice tried to sound convincing, momentarily forgetting that the housekeeper knew better than she just how bad Howard had been. Better because, unlike Candice, Mrs. Merryweather didn't try to make excuses or take the blame herself.

"I'm sorry, Mrs. Dale, but maybe it's time you dealt with it. And maybe telling those jackasses the truth will help you get over it."

Candice swallowed a ball of misery, a glaze of tears causing the housekeeper's benevolent image to waver. "Suppose I agree. What will my baby think when he or she grows up and reads the story someday?"

"What will the baby think when he reads the garbage they're printing now—and the garbage they're going to keep printing until you set them straight?"

Though repelled by the probability, Candice still hesitated. She was torn between the desire to end the war with the media and possibly save Austin from humiliation, and the all-out terror she felt at the thought of baring the sordid details of her married life to the world.

"Will—will they give me time to think about it?"

Mrs. Merryweather's lips thinned to a determined line. "They will when I get through talking to them." She gave Candice one last pat on the cheek and turned away.

Candice grabbed her arm. "Wait. What will I tell them about . . . about the incident in the pool? How can I possibly explain that?"

The housekeeper's eyes twinkled down at her. "No need to. I've already set them straight."

Stunned, Candice squeaked out, "You did?"

"I did. I simply told them exactly how it was."

"You did?" Candice blinked, knowing she sounded like a parrot but unable to help herself. She had not revealed a whisper to Mrs. Merryweather of what had really happened in the pool that day, and the discreet housekeeper hadn't asked, so how—

"I told them about you having that dizzy spell and falling into the pool, and how our brave Mr. Hyde heard your splash from his apartment over the garage. He had just stepped out of the shower, and he rushed right out to save you."

Candice listened to the preposterous story, and she actually *did* feel faint. "You . . . you said all that?"

Mrs. Merryweather nodded, not showing a flicker of embarrassment for telling what she had to know was an outright fib.

"All Mr. Hyde could think about was getting to you before you drowned. If he had stopped to put on his pants, it might have been too late, you know."

"Yes . . ." Candice whispered, impressed with Mrs. Merryweather's imagination. Impulsively, she reached for the housekeeper, intending to give her a grateful hug.

The forgotten M&M's slid from her lap and

bounced onto the carpet, rolling in every direction.

Eyes wide, Mrs. Merryweather looked down at the scattered multicolored tidbits. "You had chocolate M&M's—"

"I can explain—"

"Shame on you."

Dismayed, Candice stammered, "I'm sorry—"

"For not sharing them with me," Mrs. Merryweather concluded with a chuckle. "I'll help you pick them up, but I'd better warn you, what I find is mine. And I wish you wouldn't keep secrets like this. If I had known you were craving chocolate, I would have added it to my shopping list."

Mouth open in shock, Candice watched as Mrs. Merryweather lifted her apron and dropped to her knees. She began to pluck the M&M's from the carpet, popping one into her mouth from time to time.

Candice roused herself, then joined in.

If Howard could see me now, she thought with a wicked smile as she dived for an M&M before Mrs. Merryweather could get her greedy hands on it.

Aha! Got it!

"It's ready," Austin told the housekeeper standing at his side. A hushed silence fell between them as they stared at the completed nursery.

Austin was nervous. What if Candice hated it? What if she ran screaming from the room or, worse, started crying? Or what if she hated it but was afraid to hurt his feelings?

Mrs. Merryweather seemed to read his mind. "She won't like it."

He stiffened, his mouth turning downward. After all, Mrs. Merryweather knew Candice best.

"She'll *love* it," she clarified, chuckling.

Austin wanted to wring her neck. He was still adjusting to this new Mrs. Merryweather, the one with the marvelous dry humor. Most of the time he loved her to pieces, but other times, like now, he could gladly clobber her. "That was a dirty trick," he growled, but he couldn't resist asking, "How can you be so sure?"

Mrs. Merryweather shot him a glance. "Because Mr. Howard would have hated it."

Well, that was clear as mud. Austin gave up. "Can you explain that?"

"Why don't you just ask *her*?"

Austin heaved a frustrated sigh, wishing he could confide in the housekeeper. But they weren't *that* close. "I don't think she likes talking about her late husband." In fact, he was certain she didn't.

"Well, she might as well get used to it."

The woman was driving him insane with all this mystery. "Get used to *what?*" Austin asked between gritted teeth. He'd been working nonstop on the nursery, the pool, and taking care of one thousand and one jobs the housekeeper asked him to do daily. Sleep deprivation was a mild definition of what he felt.

Unruffled, Mrs. Merryweather bent to scoop a ball of lint from the new grape-colored carpet. She stuffed it into her apron pocket. "Get used to talking about her marriage. When she does the interview for the paper, she's gonna have to talk about it."

"Interview?" He gaped at her. "She wouldn't willingly give an interview, would she?"

Mrs. Merryweather nodded. "Why else do you think they haven't nominated you for *Playgirl* centerfold of the year?"

Playgirl? The old battle-ax knew about *Playgirl?* And then the meaning of her shocking words sank in. He frowned. "Are you trying to say she's doing this—this interview so they won't print that picture of me bare-ass-naked?"

"I'm not *trying* to say anything. I *am* saying it. She is. So you can forget about all those phone calls from hungry females you were expecting."

Austin tried to sift facts. He planted his

hands on his hips, his jaw hardening. "I won't let her do that. After all, it's my fault it happened in the first place."

"How's that?"

"If I hadn't gone for a swim, Lucy wouldn't have been looking for me, and Candice wouldn't have been chasing Lucy, and she wouldn't have"—Austin hesitated—"fallen into the pool."

And they wouldn't have made love. Austin gave himself a mental shake. No matter how incredible making love with Candice had been, he should have known better than to take such a risk. Should have known a reporter might be lurking. With Candice, there was always that chance.

But he hadn't exactly been thinking with his brain at the time.

No excuse.

"Well, that's not exactly true," Mrs. Merryweather said, edging backward in the direction of the door.

Austin watched her, his gaze narrowing. She looked guilty about something. "What's not true?"

She reached the door and kept going, backing into Candice's room. The door to the hall loomed behind her. "Lucy wasn't lookin' for you. You see, I'd been takin' her out every morning to let her swim in the pool."

She disappeared through the open doorway before the last word left her mouth, leaving Austin staring into the empty space.

When he thought about how much sleep he'd lost, how many hours he'd spent agonizing and blaming himself, he nearly exploded. Lucy hadn't been looking for him in particular; she'd simply been intent on getting her morning swim in a little early.

Still, he *was* the one who'd let her out of her cage in the first place.

Hell.

And then his humor, which had been sadly lacking these past two weeks since the incident with the reporter, came to his rescue.

That guilty look on Mrs. Merryweather's face had been priceless.

He threw back his head and let the tension roll out of him in a burst of laughter that threatened to rattle the nursery's pretty bay windows.

Chapter Thirteen

At the sound of his rich, deep laughter, Candice halted in the doorway of her bedroom. She dropped a hand to her rounding stomach, inhaling sharply. Austin, laughing in the nursery. Her child, growing inside her.

The combination gave her thoughts she had no business thinking. Still, she couldn't help it.

It wasn't the first time in the past two weeks that she'd wished this child was Austin's.

How could she not? He would make a wonderful father, so funny and loving. So caring and giving. And although he wasn't the father, he had proved over and over that he cared about the baby.

Before Austin, she never would have believed

a man could take such an interest in someone else's child, the way Austin appeared to. In fact, since they'd made love in the pool, she had experienced several episodes of shameful jealousy. The first time it had happened was when he'd proudly shown her the new dog kennel.

For the baby's new puppy.

Then there was the hedge shaping, which he had finally confessed he'd done with the baby in mind.

And the old Oriental rugs he'd found in the attic. After spending hours beating the area rugs with a baseball bat he'd also found in the attic, he'd spaced them artfully throughout the house, over the wall-to-wall carpeting, casually explaining that the little tot's knees could use the extra padding when he or she began to crawl.

Even their long walks in the woods every evening—after he had thoroughly scoured the area for lurking photographers—had been for the baby's benefit. Exercise was important for the baby's health, he'd informed her. During those many walks, they'd talked a lot.

About the baby.

And she'd tried quizzing him about his late-night work in the nursery, which he'd kept locked until now.

"Close your eyes. I've got a surprise."

Candice came out of her daze with a guilty

start to find Austin watching her. Her cheeks flamed, and she had to remind herself that he couldn't know about her ridiculous jealousy. "I'm—I'm sorry, what did you say?"

She searched for a glimpse of heated passion, something—anything—that resembled what she'd missed the past two weeks when he had been so busy doing things for her baby.

Her heart sank when she found nothing to reassure her. His expression remained carefully blank, as if they had never made wild, passionate love in the pool at six o'clock in the morning.

Which meant he still blamed her and obviously regretted what had happened between them.

And in turn, she couldn't blame him for blaming her.

What man in his right mind would want her? She was a media magnet, pregnant, and possibly on the brink of poverty. Not that she believed money mattered to Austin. On the contrary, she sometimes detected a trace of scorn in his voice for the finer things in life.

"Candice? Are you all right?" He snapped his fingers in front of her face. "I've asked you three times to close your eyes."

His sudden concern warmed her.

"Is everything okay with the baby?"

Irritation swamped the warm feeling. "The

baby's fine," she snapped. "Now, what's the surprise?"

"You have to close your eyes," he repeated, dangerously oblivious to her sudden downswing of mood.

"Close my eyes? What if I trip and fall?" Why was she being so obnoxious? It wasn't like her, yet she couldn't seem to stop herself. She ached to see something else in his eyes other than this I'm-your-buddy crap.

"Don't worry, I won't let you trip."

"Of course," she responded acidly. "We wouldn't want to hurt the baby." When he gave her a puzzled look, she sighed and closed her eyes. "Okay, okay. My eyes are closed."

He led her slowly across the carpeted floor of her bedroom. Her sandal bumped the slight rise of a door sill, telling her they'd reached the nursery. Candice inhaled, surprised when she caught only a faint whiff of paint. She could have returned to her own bed long ago, it seemed. But each time she mentioned it, Austin had countered her attempts by reminding her of the paint fumes.

Yet there were none to speak of. Her curiosity stirred.

"Now I want you to lie down. No, don't open your eyes yet."

Candice obeyed, wishing his grip on her

forearm contained some of the old heat. Instead, his fingers felt cool and impersonal, his voice as gentle and caring as Mrs. Merryweather's and just as platonic.

She squeezed her eyes more tightly closed, not because he commanded it but because she didn't want the sudden tears springing to her eyes to fall.

He tugged her to the floor. The scent of new carpet joined the faint smell of paint, and intermingled with these smells Candice detected Austin's unique blend of man and light, woodsy aftershave.

Her nipples instantly hardened, and a now-familiar ache between her legs returned. How could he do this to her without even trying? He obviously no longer felt any desire for her, so why, then, did her body insist on humiliating her this way?

She jerked as his hand landed softly on her stomach. Biting her tongue was the only way she kept the hysterical scream inside as he moved his hand across the material of her blouse, outlining the noticeable rise of her belly.

What was he doing? The man was obsessed with her baby, and she was getting damned tired of it.

"You can open your eyes now."

Perversely, Candice didn't want to. Why should she? The *baby* couldn't see what Austin had done for it.

She was immediately ashamed of her thought. Opening her eyes, she stared at the ceiling, then shot straight up. "Oh, my God!"

With a firm hand, Austin pushed her down again. "To get the full effect, you have to be lying down, like he will be."

"He?" Candice closed her eyes for a moment, wondering if she was dreaming one of those silly dreams again. She'd been having a lot of those lately. Dreams that Austin was her baby's father.

Lord, if she thought he'd gone off the deep end now, what if he really *were* the father? He'd drive her insane!

But wonderfully so.

"He or she. It was just an expression. Open your eyes, Candice. You can't see through your lids."

She felt his arm press against hers and realized that he had joined her, lying flat on his back.

More slowly this time, to minimize the shock, Candice opened her eyes.

It was still there, which meant there was a good chance she wasn't dreaming. Her lips parted, and a small gasp of awe sneaked out.

The entire ceiling was a circus, complete

with ringmaster dressed in black breeches, a red coat with flowing tails, and black top hat. Graceful tigers pawed the air. Smiling elephants balanced their cumbersome bulk on tiny blocks. Gaily dressed men and women soared on trapezes and dared the high-wire. There were white horses with flowing manes and glittering halters, and clowns in every imaginable shape and color cavorted through the riotous, wondrous arena that would put the Barnum Brothers to shame.

"So? What do you think? I've read that babies need lots of colors and shapes to look at—it helps develop their vision."

Candice blinked her dazed eyes, then covered her face with her hands and burst into tears.

His worst nightmare had come true; she was crying.

A tiny muffled sob escaped, and the sound damned near split his heart. He came up onto his elbow, watching tears seep through her fingers at an alarming rate.

Damn.

"What's the matter, Candice?" He intended to ask softly, but his upset deepened his voice, making it sound all gruff and demanding. "Tell me why you're crying."

She gave no indication that she'd heard him.

He tried again. "If it's the ceiling, I can slap a few coats of white paint over it and you'll never know it's there." She didn't have to know it would take more than a *few* coats to cover the ultra-bright paint. "I just thought—"

She shook her head without dislodging her hands. The tears continued to run between her fingers.

"No? It's not the circus that's bothering you?" Austin bit his tongue in frustration. Watching her cry made him feel like a jerk, completely helpless.

Her head shook again.

Nonplussed, Austin looked around, trying to guess what had started the waterworks. Was it the paintings he'd hung on the clear, washable white walls to break their monotony? The ones of the dancing bears? He thought they were some of his best works, each bear uniquely different.

He continued to study the room, trying to be objective. He'd thought the furniture, white with gold trim, a little prissy, but he had only assembled that; Candice had ordered it.

He shifted, then glanced down at the carpet cushioning his elbow. Maybe the carpet had upset her? Maybe he shouldn't have picked such a vibrant color, but she just had to say the word and he'd rip it up and start over.

"Candice?" He reached for her, desperate to do something to stop her tears. With infinite tenderness, he pulled her into his arms and began rubbing her back. Hadn't he read that pregnant women loved massages?

She quieted almost immediately, her sobs lapsing into heartbreaking shudders and sighs. Austin continued the soothing motion. Then he felt her lips against his neck, and he instantly became hard. No, no, it was inadvertent, he told himself.

But then a hesitant, trembling hand found its way inside his shirt. She curled her fingers into his chest hair, then raked her nails down, down, her actions soon growing bolder, more assured. Only the heavy buckle of his belt stopped her.

Austin's stomach muscles clenched as her touch stoked the inner fire he'd barely held in check for the past two weeks. And when she raised her head so that her mouth found his, Austin's sanity snapped.

Her mouth was soft and wet, a little salty from the tears yet honey-sweet and hot. Austin couldn't imagine how he'd gone two weeks without the taste of her, the feel of her.

Could she possibly have missed him as much as he had missed her?

No way.

She tugged his belt buckle loose and slipped the button from the hole, all the while kissing him, her tongue teasing the tip of his own in a way that made him shudder. The featherlight brush of her fingers against the rigid planes of his belly as she continued to work her way down made his heart soar with anticipation.

Maybe.

His breath caught in his throat as she unzipped his jeans with agonizing slowness.

Okay, a big possibility.

She closed her fingers around him and squeezed.

Yes, definitely!

"The door," he moaned against her mouth, surging into her hand. She had fingers like silk, and a mouth that held more surprises than a master magician.

Her whispered, "Lock it," had Austin on his feet in an instant. He shut and locked the door, then released the drapes from their tassels to cover the windows.

Breathing harshly, he turned back to look at Candice. Gone was the cool, shy Mrs. Dale, and in her place was the woman he couldn't resist. And why should he? After all, she carried his baby.

He hesitated, asking not for himself but for her, "Mrs. Merryweather?"

"Gone to the market." With a come-hither look that curled his toes, she began to unbutton her blouse. Slowly.

Austin swallowed hard. Candice was seducing him, and doing a damned fine job.

Something hard and savage hit his gut and knocked more force into the pulsing thrust of his shaft. The scrape of his zipper was a shocking reminder of just what she could do to him.

With a look, a touch, a flash of her cat's eyes.

He took a step forward, then stopped. Where was this going? He couldn't imagine the great Mrs. Howard Vanausdale giving up this mansion and the money and the million luxuries it all could afford her—for him. The handyman. An artist down on his luck.

Down on his luck? Right now he'd like to get down on the floor and give Candice exactly what she wanted, what they both wanted. He wanted to forget how rich she was. He wanted to forget how rich he didn't want to be. He wanted to forget, just for a moment, about the tie that bound them, whether she knew it or not.

The baby. What if there hadn't been a baby? Would he be here, in this room with her? No. Nor would he have met her in the first place.

He took another step, watching her watch him. She had pulled her blouse open, revealing to his hot, eager gaze a sexy lace bra and creamy cleavage. His mouth went bone dry as he eyed the quick rise and fall of her breasts.

The plain, sobering fact was, if not for the baby, Austin would not have taken the time to get to know Candice Vanausdale and would not have discovered that there was far more to her than a pretty, perfect face and a love for money.

No, he wouldn't be here if not for the baby. Yet . . . yet it wasn't all about the baby. Not now.

Then why didn't he just tell her the truth? Go from there?

Austin clenched his fists, knowing the answer but hating to admit it. He was afraid. Afraid of her reaction, afraid that that bone-jarring look in her eyes right now would turn to one of horror and disgust. Before Candice, he'd never cared what people thought of him or his chosen lifestyle, the way he lived simply and honestly. But that was before. This was now.

And the lady wanted him.

And he wanted her.

First things first.

Austin shook his head, then dropped to his knees.

She reached for him.

He reached for her.

Soon they were both naked. Candice clutched his tight buttocks and brought him to her with a force that shocked him. Then he was lost to all thought but to satisfy this woman and the deep ache inside him.

Poised above her, he stared into her beautiful, glazed eyes and whispered harshly. "Do you want me?"

"I want you."

"How much?" Even as he spoke the husky words, he eased himself into her moist, tight sheath. He gritted his teeth, not from pain but from pleasure.

She grasped his bottom lip and bit gently, panting against his mouth. "All of you."

Austin pushed to the limit, then stilled. Holding his upper body away from her, he bent and grasped a rock-hard nipple with his teeth, tugging gently, then sucking.

She went wild, trying to buck her pinned body against him, attempting to force him to move and give her what she wanted. But he continued to tease, much to his own torture, anticipating what she would want next without knowing or understanding how he knew.

Incredibly, it was even better than the first time.

Unfortunately, Austin thought with a rueful smile that felt tight on his face, he wouldn't last much longer because of it.

In a vain attempt to draw the lovemaking out to its fullest, Austin tried to move slowly, tried to pull away, then slide cautiously back in.

Candice wouldn't let him. She smoothed her palms over his back and wrapped her legs around his waist, lifting herself from the floor.

He smiled at her determined expression and felt on top of the world at the eager anticipation in her eyes. He was loving her, stroking her, touching the deepest part of her. And she, well, she was climbing into his heart and making herself at home.

As he began to quicken the pace, he watched her eyes widen and knew the exact moment when she let go, marveling at how quickly she came. Good thing, too, because he joined her in a hot spasm of release that jarred his teeth and made him mutter the warning, "Candice, hold on."

She bit her bottom lip and moaned his name, holding him tightly against her.

Holding him incredibly inside her.

Austin listened to the crashing of his heart against her chest—or was it hers?—as the most intense sensations continued to wash over him in knee-weakening waves until, finally, the last wave echoed gently away.

He didn't feel empty or restless as he often did in the aftermath of sex. What he felt, curiously, was contentment.

Of course, Austin decided as he buried his face in her neck and inhaled her essence, what they'd had wasn't just good sex but a combination of fantastic sex and old-fashioned love-making.

At that precise moment, with their hearts thundering as one, Austin realized that he loved this woman who still quivered and convulsed against him and around him. He loved her fiercely, and it had nothing to do with the baby.

Damn Jack.

Austin rolled to his side, taking her with him and keeping her close. They lay together, their raspy breathing the only sound other than the distant chirping of birds outside the window.

Maybe he'd get lucky and she'd lose her fortune.

It might be his only chance.

"Why were you crying? Do you hate what I've done to the nursery?"

Candice had feared he would ask the question. She'd also been hoping he had forgotten in the heat of the moment, because she really didn't want to think about her silly outburst.

She couldn't possibly tell him the real reason. *She* didn't understand this absurd jealousy over the baby, so how could she expect Austin to understand?

Snuggled in the crook of his strong arms and feeling more secure and contented than she had ever felt in her life, she sighed quietly and said, "It's wonderful, what you've done with the nursery. I wasn't crying because I didn't like it. I love it, really."

When she hesitated, Austin kissed the top of her head. It was a gentle encouragement to continue, and so vastly different from Howard's cruel taunting that for a moment Candice simply basked in the disparity.

She finally settled for a half-truth. "You've been—you've been so distant lately that I thought—I thought you blamed me for what happened at the pool."

Austin tensed. "Our lovemaking?"

"No! The photographer. The . . . lovemaking was a mutual thing, but the photographer— why are you laughing?" And he was. A low, rumbling laugh that vibrated through her and sent her pulse dancing.

"Because I thought *you* were blaming me."

"Oh." Candice digested this, then chuckled. "I guess we're not very good at communicating, are we?"

He pressed against her lower body and drew in a ragged breath. "I'd say we communicate pretty well."

Laughing softly, Candice agreed. "Yes, but I'm referring to *talking*. We hardly know each other. I don't even know your middle name, or if your parents are dead or alive."

"You know more than you think."

"Well, I know that you hate cucumbers, and that you're a wonderful artist, and that you'd make a—" Candice bit the words off, heat washing her face as she realized she'd almost said *a wonderful daddy*. How bold could she be? He'd think she was hinting and probably set out at first light, leaving a Dear John note on the kitchen table.

And a gaping hole in her heart.

Thankfully, he didn't press her to finish the sentence.

"You're right, we need to talk about us."

This time it was Candice who tensed, because there was something in his voice. . . . Reluctance? Fear? Why would he be afraid to talk to her? Had he done something terrible that he was ashamed to tell her about? Spent time in prison? Robbed a bank? Killed someone?

Or was he about to tell her that he wasn't the marrying kind, and that he could never raise another man's child? Yet that didn't quite jell, because if he didn't care about her baby, why would he go to such extremes to make her think he did?

Candice shifted restlessly, chilled by her thoughts. She didn't want to know, not now, not while she felt this vulnerable and weak from their lovemaking. Slowly breaking free of his hold, she placed a kiss on his mouth and began to gather her clothes. "There's something I want to show you."

He seemed to sense her sudden agitation, for he remained quiet as they dressed. When they were both ready, she took his hand and led him upstairs to her workroom, pushing open the door and standing aside for him to enter.

When he caught sight of the dollhouse taking up a good portion of the table, he moved closer, then bent forward to peer inside.

Candice gripped the door facing until her fingers hurt. She chewed her bottom lip until it stung as she waited for his reaction.

He took his time, running a finger along the shingles, the chimney. Then he reached inside and removed the rocking chair she'd finished last week.

"This is incredible! Where did you get this stuff? It's handmade, isn't it? I know people who would pay a fortune for quality work like this." There was no mistaking the admiration in his voice.

Candice forced herself to breathe before she passed out. Was he only making fun of her?

"In fact, this rocking chair alone must have cost you—" He broke off, his azure eyes alight with excitement as he brought the chair to her and pointed to the rose pattern on its back. "Look at this design. Do you have any idea how long it probably took the guy to do this single carving?"

"Two weeks," Candice managed to whisper, staring at the chair so she wouldn't have to look at his face. Any moment now, she would hear his mocking laughter. She told herself that it wouldn't matter, that it was just a rocking chair, just a dollhouse filled with silly little furniture. Austin didn't have to like her work; it wasn't a requirement for being her friend.

Or her lover.

After a brief, confused silence, Austin repeated, "Two weeks. How do you . . . ?"

Candice couldn't bear the suspense any longer. She braced herself and looked at him, mentally cursing the silly tears that spilled over and ran down her cheeks in a warm flow. For Heaven's sake, she'd just finished crying a bucketful!

When she was certain she could speak without sobbing, she said, "It's mine. I made it." She reached out and ran the rough pads of her fingers over his knuckles, reminding him. "All of it."

Chapter Fourteen

For a moment, Austin stared at her face, wet with tears and shining with the most poignant gratitude he'd ever witnessed. Such naked emotion humbled him and made him feel ashamed for ever thinking this brilliant, wonderful woman was anything like his mother.

With a lump the size of an egg in his throat—though he *wasn't* on the verge of doing anything so unmanly as to cry, he told himself—he replaced the rocking chair, then returned to Candice. He gathered her in his arms and kissed the tears away.

Okay, so he wasn't crying, but damned if his eyes weren't watering.

"You were afraid to show me, weren't you?"

he asked softly, stroking her hair as she cried quietly on his shoulder. She nodded and sniffed.

"Can you tell me why?" He suspected he knew, but he hoped he was wrong. She lifted her head, and Austin framed her face with his hands, his touch gentle, his gaze coaxing. Tears spiked her lashes and shimmered in her gorgeous eyes. He kissed them away with tender care, his lips finally moving down to press softly, briefly, against hers. Finally, he drew back and waited. Loving Candice had turned him into a sap, he decided wryly.

"Howard—Howard was difficult sometimes," she began in a halting voice.

"Difficult?" Austin's gaze narrowed. "How difficult?"

Her smile was a sad, fleeting thing that tore at his heart.

"You really don't read the papers, do you?"

"No. I'm not following you. What does the newspaper have to do with Howard's being difficult?"

"There were several maids that Howard decided didn't quite suit him. After he fired them, they didn't see any reason to remain loyal."

She pulled away and began pacing the room as she talked. "Reporters called, asking Howard to confirm or deny the rumors, but

Howard would never talk to them. The more he refused, the hungrier they became."

"What kind of rumors?" Austin strove to keep his voice level.

"Rumors about Howard's treatment of me. He picked my friends, my clothes, my food, and if I did something wrong, something against his wishes, he'd ridicule me, loudly enough for anyone and everyone in this house to hear."

Austin hated himself for asking, but he had to know. "Why didn't you leave?" *Was it because of the money?* The silent question was there, needling him, although he felt in his heart that it wasn't true.

Candice stopped at the dollhouse and stared down at it as if in a trance. "Several times I tried, but he . . . talked me out of it. I think I felt sorry for him, for the way he was. In medical terms, I think it's called obsessive-compulsive disorder." She opened a tiny shutter on the house, then gently closed it. "Then there were our marriage vows, which I took seriously, and the promise I made that I would never leave him."

Abruptly, she turned to look full at Austin, seeming to read his mind. "I didn't stay with him because of the money. I stayed because he promised me a child and because I believed— convinced myself— a baby would change him."

Austin believed her, could even understand her desperate logic.

"We tried for a couple of years, and when I didn't get pregnant, we went to a fertility doctor. He could find no obvious reason I wasn't conceiving, but Howard got impatient and arranged for the in vitro. That was just before the accident."

Just before the accident. Austin thrummed with shock as he silently repeated her words. The file Jack had given him was dated six months before Howard's death, which meant that Howard had been to the clinic long before the in vitro was to take place. Either Candice was mistaken, or something very fishy was going on.

Closing his eyes, Austin gave his forehead a mental slap.

Jack. Of course. Jack had left out a few details as usual. Why would Howard pay Jack a visit *before* Candice was tested?

"Austin?"

He came out of his pondering at the sound of her anxious voice. "Huh?"

"There's someone at the door."

He hadn't heard the doorbell ring, but he could hear it now, and somehow Candice had managed to slip past him and head for the front of the house. Catching up with her in the hall, he said, "I'll get it."

"What if it's a reporter?"

Austin quirked an eyebrow. "What could they possibly see that they haven't already seen?" To his relief, her expression relaxed and a smile returned. Much, much better, he decided, reaching for the front doorknob.

It wasn't a reporter, or at least, the man didn't look like any reporter Austin had ever seen. He was an older man, maybe late fifties or early sixties, with a thick crop of iron-gray hair and matching eyebrows. Austin flicked a glance over the man's expensive suit, then frowned as he met his direct gaze.

The man thrust out his right hand, shocking Austin speechless as he said, "You must be Mr. Hyde. I'm Luke McVey, Mrs. Vanausdale's lawyer."

This was Luke McVey? Why, he looked old enough to be Candice's grandfather.

"How do you know who I am?" Austin demanded, blocking the door to protect Candice. He didn't care if the man was the President; he'd never met him before.

"I recognized you from the pictures."

"What?" Austin fairly shouted.

Calmly, Luke McVey held up a manila envelope and withdrew a stack of glossy black-and-white 8x10's and handed them to Austin. As Austin automatically closed his fingers around them, Luke McVey turned sideways and stepped around him.

"You look different with your clothes *on,* of course, but I recognized your face." The lawyer didn't sound amused. In fact, he sounded downright glum.

Austin shut the door, his gaze transfixed on the glossy of Candice in wet, transparent silk pajamas. It had been the reporter's lucky day, for the sunlight had been directly on Candice. There wasn't an inch of her that wasn't revealed in sharp detail, from the puckered outline of her nipples to the V of dark gold between her legs.

Realizing this wasn't an appropriate time to ogle photos of the woman he loved, he quickly leafed through the rest. There was one of his backside as he climbed from the pool, then several frontal shots in which a lowered hand had managed to cover him to some small degree.

Frozen, he stared down at an image of his angry face and got mad all over again. Muttering an oath, he thrust the pictures at Candice, his furious gaze on the lawyer. "Where did you get these?"

Candice gasped. "They agreed they wouldn't print these pictures. I promised them an interview."

Luke held up a hand. "I'll answer all your

questions, but first, Candice, I think you'd better sit down."

Austin didn't like the sound of that. And he didn't like the way the lawyer kept staring at him. But then, Austin supposed, after seeing those pictures, anyone might be curious. Still, the man wasn't getting paid to be curious about his client's personal life, right?

Unless, of course, he worked for the enemy.

The suspicion lodged in Austin's brain and brought his eyebrows together in a frown.

"This is rather personal, Candice," McVey said.

So? And who in hell gave him permission to call her Candice? Austin continued to glare at the lawyer, willing him to back down.

"It's okay, I trust Austin. Anything you have to say can be said in front of him."

Ha! Austin knew he looked smug and didn't give a damn. In fact, he was tempted to snag an arm around Candice and pull her in for a lusty kiss.

Candice led the way to the den. Luke sat in a comfortable recliner near the window while Austin perched on the arm of the sofa beside Candice. When they were all settled, Luke steepled his fingers in front of his face and trained his somber gaze their way.

"First, the pictures came from Albert Hayes." When Austin glanced at Candice, she explained, "Albert Hayes works for Raymond and Donald, Howard's sons. He's their lawyer."

Without thinking, Austin reached for her hand. She was tense and trembling, but he was proud of the way her chin rose a notch. *That's my girl,* he silently cheered. Whatever came their way, they would handle together. How bad could it be?

Luke nodded, and Austin noticed that he studiously avoided looking at their clasped hands.

"How did he get those pictures?" Candice asked. "I made a deal with the reporter!" She bit her lip, then answered her own question. "But the deal was that he wouldn't print the pictures in the newspapers. We didn't discuss other options."

Austin gave her hand an encouraging squeeze. Did the creeps think to blackmail Candice? Well, it wouldn't work. "I take it the enterprising reporter made a hefty profit?" he drawled with a sarcastic snarl. If only he had caught the little bastard.

"I'm sure he did." Luke sat forward. "The younger Vanausdales were getting desperate, and this was just the ammunition they needed."

"I—"

Austin stood, interrupting Candice. "A few pictures of Candice in her own pool, in her pajamas—you call *that* ammunition? What can they possibly do about it? She's a widow, for crying out loud! I don't think anyone expects her to become a nun."

"It's not that. They needed to sow seeds of doubt, and, thanks to the reporter, it worked."

"Speak English, will you? What seeds of doubt, and *what* worked?" Austin realized he was holding Candice's hand in a grip that should have brought her to her knees, and he quickly released it. Damned lawyer wasn't making a lick of sense.

"Now that the judge has seen these photographs . . ."

Candice drew in a sharp breath of dismay, and Austin looked from one to the other. He was missing something vital here, and it frustrated him no end.

"Photographs of Candice with another man," McVey continued, "he granted their request." Luke paused significantly. "For a paternity test when the baby is born."

The floor rocked beneath Austin's feet as the full impact of McVey's announcement hit him. "A paternity test?"

Candice let out a shaky, relieved breath—and Austin sucked it right into his rattled lungs. She had no idea. . . .

Because you're too afraid to tell her.

"Oh." Candice laughed, and Austin felt the incredible urge to weep. "Let them have their test. I've got nothing to worry about. They'll look like fools, and so will the judge."

Shock waves continued to roll over Austin, making his heart pound with enough force to hurt. When he hadn't known Candice, it was different; he might have merely winced at the knowledge of her impending humiliation. Now, though, everything had changed. Everything.

Now, he loved her and couldn't bear to see her hurt, couldn't stand the thought of her being unhappy. In the end, he'd gotten his wish; Candice would lose her fortune.

His victory tasted like the ashes of an old fire.

If he told her . . .

If he didn't tell her . . .

Chances were, she would lose her fortune either way when the paternity test proved Howard wasn't the father.

If he told her, she would likely hate him for the tiny, microscopic, biological part he'd played in the whole incredible scenario, however unwillingly.

If he didn't tell her, then she might turn to him when she lost her fortune. He would have the woman he loved *and* his baby, which, he realized, was exactly what he wanted. Except . . . except she would never know he was the biological father, and dammit, he was proud of the fact.

Austin couldn't believe he was even considering living such an outrageous lie anyway. It was a selfish, unforgivable fantasy, and he knew he couldn't do it the instant he thought it.

Which left him with only one choice; he would have to tell her.

Damn Jack.

After a night of sleepless soul-searching, Austin decided he should tell her soon.

But first he had to finish the pool.

One more stingray cruising on the bottom, he told himself, and it would be ready to fill.

So it took a little longer to finish than he'd first thought. He was only human, right?

On Sunday, after another sleepless night, he slammed his paintbrush down and strode into the house with every intention of blurting it all out. He could stand the suspense no longer. Yet before he could speak, Candice had grabbed his hand and pulled him with her to the attic, her happy face alight with excitement and twisting his heart into agonizing knots.

With sunbeams dancing on the dusty floor, she proudly showed him her discovery: a beautiful antique rocking chair that would make a perfect addition to the nursery. The incident reminded Austin all too painfully of his deception, and of how much Candice loved her home and her life of luxury.

Also in the attic was a discarded sofa, and before the inspection was over Austin lost himself there in the eager warmth of Candice's arms. They made love passionately and, on his part, desperately. Afterward, he was certain he couldn't sink any lower.

Yet on Monday, Tuesday, and well into the evening on Wednesday, he managed to do just that by inventing one excuse after the other. Perfectly logical excuses, too. She couldn't strip and varnish the rocking chair all by herself, now could she? She didn't need to be breathing toxic fumes.

How could he tell her when she was so obviously happy? What harm would it do to wait? She wouldn't *have* to know until the baby arrived. In the meantime, he carefully hoarded each memory, every touch, and recorded in his mind the sound of her soft, happy voice.

In the end, ironically, Jack was the one who forced him to think about the wisdom of his delay. When Candice told him Jack was on the phone, Austin took the call in the den, the nervous feeling in his gut escalating at the sound of Jack's anxious voice.

"Have you read the paper today? Why didn't you *call* me?"

For a moment, Austin's mind was blank. Then he realized what Jack must be talking about. So the Vanausdales had wasted no time sowing the seeds of doubt to the rest of the world, via the bloodthirsty and often thwarted media. His mouth twisted into a disgusted grimace as he recalled who had gotten him into this situation in the first place.

"Calm down, Jack. They won't know until after the baby is born, so you've got another four months before they lock you up and throw away the key."

"How can you be so calm?" Jack screeched. "Have you told her? Does she know?"

Austin winced, glancing over his shoulder at the thankfully empty doorway. "No, I haven't, and no, she doesn't. I'm going to when the time is right." Even to his own ears, the words sounded lame. Each and every day that passed in her company, it became harder to risk it all by telling Candice the truth.

"Austin, you can't sit on this! These guys had to have some suspicion or the judge wouldn't have granted their request for a paternity test. And *you* are involved, up to your ears."

"And whose fault is that?" Austin grated. Then he sighed his frustration. "Look, Jack, I'll tell her when I get good and damned ready, okay? Just think of it this way: it'll buy you some time before she hangs you out to dry." He didn't want to think about his own punishment, because every time he did, he wanted to howl like a wounded animal. When she found out, she would hate him. Pure and simple.

"When the time comes, I think we should tell her together."

"You're crazy." Austin gripped the receiver, lowering his voice. "And you always have been."

"If we told her together, maybe *together* we could make her understand why we—"

"Why *we*?"

"Why *I* did what I did. You could help—tell her that I did it for her. Make her understand."

His brother's desperate comment reminded Austin of his earlier suspicions about Howard Vanausdale. It was a shot in the dark but worth a spin. "Maybe if you'd tell her the whole truth, she wouldn't blame you as much."

There was dead silence on the other end.

"The—the whole truth? What whole truth?"

Austin could always tell when Jack was lying. The nervous quiver in his voice gave him away. And Austin would bet the boat that if he could see his brother's face right now, his right eye would be twitching.

Mustering as much conviction as he could, Austin said, "I know that Candice's hubby came to see you a long time before the first scheduled in vitro." He wasn't sure about anything, but Jack didn't have to know that.

279

"How—how do you know that?"

"I saw the date on the file."

"A file you weren't supposed to see in the first place!"

Bingo.

"Do you think it matters at this point?" With a dazed shake of his head, Austin wondered how complicated this whole bizarre situation was going to get before it finally exploded. He, for one, couldn't take much more. "Howard Vanausdale is dead, Jack. You don't have to protect his privacy any longer—at least where Candice and I are concerned. We're not likely to sell the information to the media." This last statement was saturated in sarcasm.

"He trusted me. . . ." Jack sighed. "I guess you're right. When are you planning to drop this bomb?"

Austin winced at Jack's all-too-accurate description. "Meet me at my apartment in two hours. We'll talk about the best way to handle this. There's a key above the door—let yourself in if you get there first. And maybe you can clean the place up a little."

Jack began to protest.

"A little housework won't kill you. Besides, you owe me big time, Dr. Jekyll. I'm the one she's going to hate the most when she finds out."

Jack muttered something about bulldozers, then crashed the phone down.

Austin replaced the receiver. Not only were his hands shaking, but his heart was clenched in a vise.

Hell. What they said about love was true: It *did* hurt.

Chapter Fifteen

"I'm the one she's going to hate the most when she finds out."

Heart pounding, Candice quickly backed away from the door and fled to her bedroom. She had only caught the tail end of the conversation, but it had been enough to raise a thousand questions in her mind. What had Austin meant? What horrible secret was he hiding? And how was Dr. Jack involved?

Why would she hate him at all?

She sank onto her bed, willing herself to calm down and think rationally. Should she ask him? Demand an explanation? She didn't fancy having to admit that she'd been eavesdropping, although she hadn't done it intentionally. She'd been on her way into the den to suggest that Austin invite Dr. Jack to dinner.

Tears pricked her eyes as she thought about the past few wonderful weeks. Was she a fool for daring to believe that Austin truly cared for her?

Obviously.

Candice bit her lip against the pain welling in her chest. Not only had she been foolish to accept him into her life without question, but she'd been careless as well. Careless, blind, and foolish.

Because there was only one explanation she could think of that would justify what she'd overheard, only one thing that would make her hate him.

Austin Hyde worked for the enemy—either the media or her in-laws. And apparently Dr. Jack knew.

She fell back onto the bed, squeezing her eyes tightly shut. Her throat burned with the effort it took to hold the anguished sobs inside.

"You're in love with her, aren't you?"

If the situation hadn't been so serious, Austin might have laughed at the sight of Jack clutching a bundle of dirty laundry and wearing an old faded bandanna around his head. Beneath the odd assortment of socks, shirts, towels, and jeans, Austin caught a glimpse of his old apron, which bore the faded red letters of CAUTION: COOK IN TRAINING. With Austin Hyde in the apron, it wasn't just a silly logo, it was a bona fide warning.

His brother looked like a weary housekeeper having a bad day.

"You are, aren't you?" Jack's expression wavered, as if he couldn't decide whether he should be delighted or dismayed at the prospect. When Austin didn't immediately answer, Jack stomped into the tiny bathroom and dumped the clothes into the bathtub.

He shot Austin a dark look when he emerged. "There wasn't any room left in your hamper. As for those"—he pointed a righteous finger at the offending dishes in the sink—"you might as well trash them; they'll never come clean."

Austin sighed and plopped onto the sofa. "I don't have time to worry about dirty dishes, Jack. I've got bigger problems."

"Well, you should worry. This place is a pigsty! What would your landlord think if he saw it? In fact, he probably has—the door wasn't even locked!" He snatched up a bowl of dusty antique popcorn left to molder on the coffee table.

"I said you could pick up a little. I don't remember asking your housecleaning advice."

Before Jack could open his mouth again, Austin added in a tone that stopped his younger brother cold, "And yes, I'm in love with Candice."

Jack slowly sat the bowl of popcorn back on the coffee table and sank into a chair. "I knew it."

"You didn't know shit," Austin growled, glaring at him.

"How—how does Mrs. Vanausdale feel?"

Good question, Austin mused, and one he couldn't answer with any conviction. He didn't have any doubt that she liked him, or even that she desired him. But love? Candice hadn't mentioned it. But then, neither had he.

He settled for evasiveness. "We've grown very close."

"You're lovers?"

Austin bristled. "You may be my brother, but I don't think the details of my love life are any of your business!"

For once, Jack ignored the warning signs. "It might not be my business, but if her in-laws get wind of this—" He broke off, sucking in a gasp of horror as if something unpleasant had just occurred to him. "*You're* the reason the judge granted the request for a paternity test! They know about you, and—"

"They don't know shit," Austin snapped

defensively. He felt the heat of guilt creep into his face and cursed it. "All they have are a few lousy pictures of me naked and—"

"Oh, my God!" Jack sprang to his feet, crashing into the coffee table, upending the bowl of moldy popcorn, and knocking it to the floor. For once in his life he ignored the mess. "This is worse than I thought! When you tell her, she's going to think—she's probably going to believe you set the whole thing up!"

Austin scowled. Leave it to Jack to add to his problems by suggesting a scenario he hadn't thought of. But Jack hadn't mentioned a motive. "Why in hell would I do that?"

"Because you have this stupid thing about money!" Jack glared at him. "I wouldn't put it past you to do something like this, Austin, especially since you're in love with her."

"Something like what? You're not making any sense." Getting caught by the reporter had been an accident. He couldn't possibly have known he'd be lurking near the pool that morning.

"Are you saying you haven't thought about how much easier it would be for you if she lost the case? Without all that wealth, she might be glad to learn that you're her baby's father."

"No, I *haven't* thought about it," Austin said between painfully gritted teeth. It was a lie, but Jack didn't have to know. He *had* thought about

286

it and had come to the dismal conclusion that Candice would be furious over his deception no matter the outcome.

The fact that he'd played a major part in wrecking her future would probably fuel her anger and keep her hatred of him alive and thriving for years and years to come.

Austin closed his eyes and tilted his head against the back of the couch. Time was his only hope. If Candice fell in love with him in the next four months, he might have a chance of gaining her forgiveness when he told her the truth.

"Of course, Candice will think you're in someone's pay—either the media or her in-laws. The evidence will look pretty damning. So, what are you going to do?"

Opening one eye, Austin watched as Jack grabbed a discarded jacket from the back of the sofa and headed for the hall closet. He groaned inwardly, remembering the stack of pizza boxes he'd hidden there the day the land-lord popped by for a surprise inspection. "Jack, be—"

His brother's bloodcurdling shriek came as no surprise, but the fearful, high-pitched demand—"Who the hell are *you?*"—that fol-lowed brought Austin to his feet and running into the hall.

To his amazement, he saw a man standing in the closet.

Jack leaped back as the stranger stepped out, crushing pizza boxes with his scuffed, dirty boots. *A reporter*, was Austin's first assumption. But he didn't look like a reporter, and Austin saw no sign of a camera. Dumbfounded, he took in the older man's unshaven face, bloodshot eyes, and crumpled, outdated clothing.

He didn't recognize him, and apparently neither did Jack.

"How did you get in here?" Austin growled menacingly. The intruder didn't *look* like a reporter, but then, most people were surprised to learn that *he* was an artist. If the guy *was* a reporter—Austin clenched his hands and took a step forward.

The man's eyes widened at the threatening move. Hastily, he introduced himself. "The name's Pete Clancy." When Austin and Jack exchanged a clueless look, he added, "I'm Candy's old man."

Candy's old man? Austin's frown deepened. "You mean Candice's stepfather?" She'd mentioned him once, briefly. And, if his memory served him right, without much emotion. Austin had gotten the impression there wasn't any love lost between them.

"Yeah, yeah. Stepfather." Clancy shrugged, his bloodshot gaze darting back and forth between the two men. "If you want to get technical about it. I raised her after her mother died."

Jack, who had been staring at Clancy as if he'd discovered the boogeyman in the closet, finally found his voice again. "What the hell are you doing hiding in Austin's coat closet?"

A question Austin had been ready to ask himself.

"All in good time, Mr. Cruise."

With a visible jerk of shock, Jack squeaked out, "You know who I am?"

Austin didn't care for the cunning look that flashed in Clancy's eyes. He shifted, ready to spring if the guy so much as twitched before he answered their questions.

"I know who you are, but I didn't know you were *his* brother." His watery blue eyes settled on Austin. "You gonna offer your girlfriend's old man a drink? It was a mite hot in that closet."

"No, I'm not going to offer you a drink. What do you want here?" Austin demanded rudely, in no mood to play the congenial host. He didn't like the way Clancy's eyes darted to and fro, and he damned sure didn't like the snide way he'd referred to Candice as his girlfriend.

In fact, he had a sneaking suspicion there wasn't anything he was *going* to like about Pete Clancy.

Clancy rolled his shoulders in another careless, irritating shrug. "I wanted to talk to you."

Austin took a threatening step forward. His voice rumbled in warning. "You could have knocked on the door."

No, Clancy wasn't here for a social call, Austin was dead certain. He was also pretty sure he wasn't going to like Clancy's topic of conversation when he *did* get around to explaining himself.

"The door was already open," Clancy said. "I was about to knock when I heard you two talking." That odd gleam flashed again. "When I realized my daughter was the topic of your conversation, I couldn't help myself."

Shock froze Austin's tongue as he belatedly remembered the conversation Clancy spoke of. His gaze collided with Jack's.

"Austin, he heard—"

"So he did," Austin agreed softly, dangerously close to punching the man's lights out. But he knew physical violence would accomplish nothing. When Clancy regained consciousness, he'd still know the truth—a truth that could destroy them all.

Question was, what was he planning to do with the information? Sell it to the media? Tell Candice's in-laws? Run to Candice? Was it possible Candice suspected something and had asked Clancy to follow him? No, Austin thought, dismissing the last two possibilities. The Candice Austin knew would never stoop so low; she would simply ask him. Secondly, Clancy would gain nothing by telling Candice, and it was becoming dreadfully clear Clancy intended to gain *something*.

"Jack, fix the man a drink." Austin kept a steady eye on Clancy.

Jack sputtered. "But, Austin, he's—"

"Just do it." They'd get to the bottom of this, Austin vowed, and somehow prevent a disaster. He owed it to Candice to do whatever it took. To Clancy, he said, "Let's have a seat, shall we?"

Before Clancy could respond, Austin grabbed his arm and led him to the couch. He shoved a pile of clothes to the floor with his free hand and pushed the man roughly onto the lumpy cushions. Austin then sat across from him in the chair Jack had vacated a few moments ago. He could hear Jack in the tiny kitchenette, cursing as he searched for a clean glass.

Clancy tapped his fingers nervously against his leg and stared at the floor.

Austin watched Clancy. The silence stretched.

Finally, Jack returned. He gave Clancy something in a paper cup, shrugging when Austin shot him a questioning look. "I found a bottle of open wine in the fridge," he explained, "but no clean glassware."

Trying to remember when he'd purchased wine last, Austin frowned. It came to him just as Clancy tipped the cup up and drained the liquid; he'd bought a bottle to go with a spaghetti dinner he'd attempted to cook for a date.

Six or seven months ago.

"Got any more?" Clancy held the cup out. Jack snatched it, stomping into the kitchen for a refill, muttering, "Do I look like a freakin' maid?"

Austin almost smiled. But his humor faded when he thought of Candice growing up with Clancy as her father. He suddenly remembered the reporter at the clinic asking her about her alcoholic stepfather. Not that he needed the reminder; Clancy's bloodshot eyes and the eager way he guzzled the stale wine said it all.

When Jack returned and perched on the edge of Austin's chair arm, Austin addressed Clancy. "You can start by telling us who you're working for." He wasn't fooled by Clancy's indignant look or the feigned outrage in his voice.

"I work for myself!"

Unperturbed and unconvinced, Austin's gaze bore into Clancy's. "All right. So you're a freelancer. Who are you planning to sell your information to?"

Instead of answering, Clancy tipped the cup to his mouth and tapped the bottom. He eyed Austin over the rim. With a barely perceptible shake of his head, Austin let him know their efforts at hospitality had come to an end. No more booze until they heard some answers. Then, if he still wanted to commit gastrointestinal suicide, Austin wouldn't stop him.

"That depends." Clancy paused, his feral gaze wavering from Austin to Jack, then back to Austin again. Apparently, two cups of wine had given him a sense of courage. "On who has the most to offer."

Jack jumped to his feet, his voice shrill with a mixture of bewilderment and disgust. "Why would you do something like this to your own daughter?" he demanded.

"Stepdaughter," Clancy corrected perversely. "She stopped helping me out when her husband kicked the bucket."

Pointing an accusing finger at him, Jack cried, "You said yourself that you raised her! Doesn't that mean anything to you?"

Austin silently applauded Jack's spirited questions. It didn't happen often, but when Jack felt strongly about something, he reminded Austin of a small yet lethal tornado.

"This is blackmail, Clancy! Pure and simple blackmail, and if you think for one minute that my brother is going to—"

"Enough, Jack." Austin didn't have to shout to get his brother's attention.

Jack stared at him as if he'd suddenly developed horns and a tail. "Surely you're not going to let this low-life snake blackmail you?" he squeaked in disbelief. "Austin, I know that in the past I've mocked you for being so damned righteous, but I've always admired that about you, too. You can't let this—this excuse for a man corrupt you."

Austin swallowed a burning ball of pride. Jack had picked the wrong time to develop a conscience, because Austin knew with a deep, gut-wrenching dread that he didn't have a choice in the matter. The information Clancy possessed was far too valuable for a desperate man like Clancy to keep to himself.

And Austin wasn't ready for the proverbial ax to fall.

Pinning his cold gaze on Clancy, he said, "Clancy, why don't you tell Jack what will happen if I don't make you an offer."

Clancy licked his lips, squirming beneath Austin's open hostility. "I'll offer the information to the media first. If they decline, then I'll go to Howard's sons." His voice took on an irritating whine as he added, "I need the money to make a fresh start."

A moment of thick silence followed. Jack clenched his fists and approached Clancy. In the face of his fury, Clancy shrank against the cushions. "I think we should just kill him," Jack snarled viciously. "The world would be a better place without this scum running around wrecking people's lives."

Any other time and place and Austin wouldn't have hesitated to remind Jack in great detail about his own life-wrecking talents, but not with Clancy present. "I agree, Jack, but I don't relish rotting in prison because of this *scum*, either." He paused a beat to ask softly, "Do you?"

Jack paled at the reminder. What he'd done by substituting Austin's sperm for Howard Vanausdale's amounted to fraud, plain and simple. When Candice found out, she could press charges and send Jack to prison. She could also sue the pants off him for malicious intent and pain and suffering.

And she just might be mad enough to do it, Austin thought. Not that he'd blame her. So what choice did he have but to give in to Clancy's demands and hope the drunkard took the money and ran very far away? Austin didn't want Candice hurt. He also didn't want to lose his only chance of winning her over. And no matter how angry he was at Jack for getting him into this incredible mess, he didn't want his little brother to go to prison.

Bribery, blackmail—it was all the same. Clancy might be blackmailing him, but wasn't *he* bribing Clancy into keeping his mouth shut? And wasn't the loss of integrity a small price to pay to protect Candice from unnecessary suffering? Not to mention the possibility of a lifetime of loving the woman of his dreams.

Raising their baby together.

"Name your price," Austin announced abruptly.

"Austin, you're not planning to finally use your—"

Austin shut Jack up with one tight, warning glare. The last thing he needed was for Clancy to find out about the considerable inheritance he'd always refused to touch—until now.

"Fifty thousand," Clancy dropped into the astounded silence.

"You're crazy!" Jack shrieked.

Wincing at the shrill sound of Jack's voice, Austin echoed his disbelief. "Insane, indeed. Try again."

Clancy remained stubborn. "The media would pay that, probably more. I *know* the Vanausdales would."

"How do I know you won't take my money

and theirs as well?" Austin demanded, forcing himself to keep his voice low when what he really wanted to do was make the thin walls of his apartment shake.

"You don't. You'll just have to trust me."

"And you're such a trustworthy kinda guy," Jack sneered.

Instead of answering, Clancy just shrugged, as if he could care less what Jack thought of him.

Austin passed a weary hand over the stubble on his jaw. He'd forgotten to shave this morning. Again. "It will take me a few days to get that kind of money together." Tomorrow he'd have to make a transfer from his savings to his checking account, then give it a day or two to clear.

Clancy rose from the couch, keeping a wary eye on Jack. "You've got until Friday. I'll get in touch with you, and if you don't have the money—"

"I'll have it," Austin growled, disgusted with himself and Pete Clancy. "Now get the hell out of my sight before I decide I like Jack's plan better."

Clancy left in a hurry. Jack followed him to the door like a terrier protecting his territory. Austin heard the door slam, then Jack came back into the room.

He stared at Austin for a full moment before

he said, "I hope you know what you're getting yourself into, big brother."

"Everything has a price, and in this instance, I'm buying time." Austin closed his eyes and thought back to the carefree days when he had nothing more pressing to do than decide what blend of colors he would use for a sunset. He suppressed a sigh.

"It's very likely he'll come back for more." Jack knelt and began scooping up popcorn with his hands. "Blackmailers are like vampires; they find their victims and bleed them until they're dry."

Austin opened one eye. "You watch too many movies. Besides, by the time he uses the fifty thousand and comes back, it won't matter any longer."

Jack paused in his clean-up to look at him. "What are you planning to do?"

"Try to win the lovely widow's heart."

"And if it doesn't work?"

"I think you know the answer to that," Austin said with a bitter little twist of his lips. "You'll lose your job and your freedom. I'll lose . . . something that has become more important to me than I ever imagined."

Damn Jack.

Chapter Sixteen

"The roses are beautiful, aren't they?" Mrs. Merryweather remarked as she rearranged them in an expensive crystal vase. When she was satisfied, she transferred them to the small table in the kitchen. She stood back and clasped her hands together. "I'll just leave them here so that we can enjoy them. We haven't used the dining room in months, so they'd only be wasted in there."

Candice nodded despondently, hardly glancing at the two dozen perfect red roses she'd found on the back doorstep this morning. She didn't have to look at the card to know that Austin had left them, and she didn't have to be a genius to interpret the sparkle in the house-keeper's eyes. But Candice strongly suspected Mrs. Merryweather had it all wrong, as painful as it was for her admit.

The roses were not a declaration of Austin's devotion but the result of a guilty conscience.

To be fair, she had considered that Austin might have come to care for her and was perhaps having reservations over what he'd done. She'd even tried to convince herself in the past two days that she might have misinterpreted his dire prediction to Jack Cruise on the phone, but on further reflection, she had failed to come up with an alternative.

Very little could make her hate the man she'd grown to love so fiercely, but that kind of betrayal would give her a good head start.

A knock at the door startled her out of her gloomy thoughts. Since they rarely had company, she assumed it would be Austin. With her heart fluttering in her chest, she went to answer it, reminding herself that she didn't have proof of anything.

Austin lounged in the doorway, wearing his customary worn, low-slung jeans and a faded cotton shirt left unbuttoned to reveal the dark golden hair on his chest. Candice licked her dry lips and hardened her heart against his powerful sexual appeal.

"Good morning." She forced a smile to take the chill from her tone. "Thanks for the roses."

"Don't thank me yet," Austin muttered without his usual knock 'em dead smile. He ran a hand through his tousled hair, looking harried and fed up about something. Without preamble, he launched into an explanation. "It's like this, I sent Jack to the animal shelter to pick out a dog, and—"

"A dog," Candice repeated, relief flooding her. For a moment there, she'd thought Austin was about to blurt out a confession. Mrs. Merryweather came to stand beside her, and together they waited expectantly.

"Yes, a dog." Austin sounded defensive, as if he expected her to disapprove before he had a chance to complete his explanation. "You see, I thought we should get one from the shelter because it seems inhuman to go out and buy a dog when there are so many needing homes."

"Why, I think that's a fine idea," Mrs. Merryweather said, beaming her approval.

Candice, slightly confused, merely nodded and waited. It was obvious that Austin was flustered about something. She tried not to stare at the light sheen of sweat beading his upper lip.

"Well, you might not think it's a fine idea when I finish telling you what that idiot bro—

friend of mine did. I gave him specific instructions. I said, 'Get a medium-size dog, a cocker spaniel or something.' You see, I thought it was a good idea to have a dog on the property."

Mrs. Merryweather came alive at his explanation, revealing a bloodthirsty side of her character Candice had glimpsed the day the reporter caught them at the pool. She shook a threatening fist in the air. "Yeah, but something big enough that it can take a chunk out of one of those sneaky reporters!" She turned to Candice and gave her a look that was almost accusing. "We should have gotten one sooner."

But Candice wasn't listening; Austin had disappeared from the doorway. A few seconds later he reappeared leading the biggest dog she'd ever seen. A Great Dane, she thought with a visible gulp. Instinctively, she took a step backward. Mrs. Merryweather did the same, clutching Candice's arm.

Austin looked from one doubtful face to the other and groaned. "Now you know the rest of the story. Unfortunately, that's not all of it."

"N-not all?" What more could there be? Candice wondered. She loved dogs, but *this*? Taking a deep breath for courage, she held out a hand for the dog to sniff. Cautiously the Great Dane inched forward and lowered its massive head to catch her scent.

"Uh, no. You see, there were a few things

about Tiny that Jack didn't know and the people at the shelter failed to mention."

Fear speared through Candice as a dozen possibilities ran through her mind, each bloodier than the last. She snatched her hand back and pressed it against her pounding heart. "Dr. Jack's okay, isn't he?"

"He's fine." Austin sounded disappointed. "Here, hold the leash for a second, will ya? I'll be back in a flash."

Not given a choice in the matter, Candice gingerly palmed the loop attached to the end of the leash. If Tiny decided to make a run for it, she knew there was no way she could stop her.

The Great Dane stood obediently still, regarding her with intelligent, soulful eyes. Little by little, Candice began to relax. Yes, the dog was big, but it seemed gentle and harmless.

Like Austin.

But, like Austin, could the huge canine have a hidden agenda? Candice blinked as Austin came into view again. This time he carried a wicker basket, and his face was curiously flushed.

"I told Jack you'd hate me for this," he muttered, throwing aside the blanket covering the basket. He lifted it so that she could see the contents. "Nine puppies. *Nine*. Jack didn't even realize she was pregnant."

"Aren't they darlings!" Candice crooned, moving reluctantly aside so that Mrs. Merryweather could get a closer look. Nine tiny puppies, and by the looks of them, very healthy. She glanced up to find Austin watching them. His expression was so bemused, Candice couldn't resist a smile, and then she remembered what he'd said a few moments ago. *"I told Jack you'd hate me for this."* Was *this* what he'd been talking to Jack about? It had to be, she decided, relieved beyond measure. Austin and Dr. Jack had been talking about a *dog*. A very big, pregnant dog.

"I can take her back to the shelter," Austin offered, misconstruing her silence.

"No." Candice took another peep at the puppies, her gaze straying to Tiny. She looked every inch the anxious mother, sticking her nose in the basket to ascertain that her puppies were unharmed, then gazing at Candice as if to plead her case.

Candice's heart surrendered without a fight. "We'll just have to find homes for some of them when they're old enough." Feeling considerably lighter of heart now that a logical explanation for Austin's mysterious statement had presented itself, she added dubiously, "The doghouse you built *is* big enough, isn't it?"

Austin looked relieved. He shrugged, his boyish smile returning. "If it isn't, I can build a bigger one."

When Mrs. Merryweather excused herself for a moment to check the oven, his gaze heated up as he looked at her. Softly, he said, "Thank you."

"For what?" And would he be thanking her if he knew what she'd been thinking about him? Somehow, Candice didn't think so. She'd learned that Austin could be very sensitive about some issues—such as trust.

"For being you," he answered simply.

With a tenderness that made her tremble straight down to her bare toes, he leaned forward and brushed his lips against hers. He whispered next to her ear, "Meet me in the kitchen for a midnight snack." When he drew back, there was a soft light in his eyes that Candice had never seen before. "I've got to find a pet store and hope they have a sale on dog food."

Candice smiled. "I imagine she'll get pretty hungry feeding that many babies."

His hot gaze moved over her, taking her breath. "Speaking of hunger . . ."

Mrs. Merryweather suddenly reappeared beside Candice. "Oh, are you hungry, Mr. Hyde? I've prepared a huge spinach lasagna for supper. You're always welcome to eat with us."

Smothering a giggle as Austin hastily retreated with Tiny and the basket of puppies in tow, Candice shut the door.

"Was it something I said?" Mrs. Merryweather asked, looking bewildered.

"No, no. I think he was in a hurry to get to the store before it closed." The fib didn't come easily, but Candice wasn't about to tell Mrs. Merryweather that Austin hadn't been talking about food.

"Oh." The housekeeper's frown cleared. She wiped her hands on her apron and reached behind her to untie it. "I'll just go upstairs and get his laundry, then. I've noticed it piling up."

Remembering Mrs. Merryweather's complaints about her aching knees, Candice said, "Let me get it. The exercise will be good for me."

"No, it'll be too heavy," Mrs. Merryweather began to argue.

"I'll make two trips." Candice folded her arms and let the housekeeper know that she wouldn't take no for an answer. It felt good to assert herself *and* help her dear friend in the process.

"Well, mind you watch your step, and don't lift more than an armful at a time."

"I promise."

"And check the pockets. I don't think his driver's license can stand another washing. The things that man collects. . . ." Mrs. Merryweather moved away, muttering beneath her breath.

She headed for the guest room where Austin kept a few of his personal belongings, showered and dressed. Since he'd moved in, she hadn't gone into the room; privacy was something she had learned to respect at an early age, and with Howard it had become almost a religion.

Those habits were hard to overcome, Candice discovered when she reached the bedroom. She hesitated in the hall, telling herself she wasn't snooping. Mrs. Merryweather wouldn't think twice about barging in and gathering his laundry.

Armed with this stout reminder, Candice pushed open the door and stepped inside. Her heart fluttered just thinking about Austin striding around in here in all his naked glory.

With a nervous laugh, she began scooping up his scattered clothing. She dutifully checked each pocket, smiling at the odd assortment of items she found: a key she recognized as belonging to the apartment over the garage, an old, tar-coated buffalo-head nickel, a few sticks of gum, two crumpled dollar bills. Mrs. Merryweather hadn't been exaggerating.

Stacking the items on top of the dresser, Candice sorted through a pile of his shirts, mostly faded cotton in stripes and solids. She found a folded receipt in one pocket and a checkbook in the other.

The sight of the checkbook gave her pause. Austin had gone to buy a ton of dog food; hopefully he carried cash. She should have given him the money, since he'd gotten the dog for her, she mused, mentally kicking herself for the oversight. He probably didn't have much money to speak of, and it certainly wasn't his place to feed her dog. Why, on the salary she paid him he could hardly afford to . . .

Candice bit her bottom lip, recalling the doghouse he'd built to surprise her. He'd obviously purchased the materials out of his own pocket, and he hadn't given her any receipts for reimbursement. And then there was the day they'd gone shopping and he'd bought her that garish pink sweat suit and the tennis shoes. He'd also paid for their lunch. Small purchases that could add up quickly for someone on a tight budget.

How thoughtless she'd been for not once considering that he might be low on funds. He was an aspiring artist, and everyone knew that artists were poor. Not that Austin seemed to mind. In fact, he would probably be insulted if she *did* mention it.

Candice tapped the checkbook thoughtfully against her cheek. It wouldn't be right for her to look, of course. Just the thought made her face flame. She'd be snooping, pure and simple.

But it might give her an idea of just how poor he was. *If* she looked and it was as bad as she imagined, she would definitely find a way to reimburse him for everything he'd done. And if it turned out he wasn't, then she wouldn't take the chance of hurting his pride by offering him money. He wouldn't have to know about her snooping either way.

Before she could reconsider, Candice flipped open the checkbook and skimmed down the column of hastily written accounts to the ending balance.

The amount at the bottom sent her staggering backward.

She dropped the checkbook as if it were on fire, staring at it in horror. The amount flashed before her eyes like a gaudy neon sign outside a motel. *Fifty-two thousand, four hundred and ten dollars.* She pressed a hand to her mouth. Why would Austin take a handyman job with *that* kind of money in the bank? Granted, it was a drop in the bucket compared to the Vanausdale estate, but it was nothing to sneeze at!

Unless . . . A horrible thought came to her, one that made her feel immediately ashamed. But not so ashamed that it stopped her from reaching down and retrieving the checkbook.

Her fingers trembled badly as she once again turned to the last entry and checked the date.

Yesterday. Yesterday Austin Hyde had become fifty thousand dollars richer.

And today he'd brought her roses and a dog, which reminded her of her earlier suspicions about a guilty conscience. She felt physically ill. If Austin had sold a painting, he would have told her. She couldn't imagine his keeping such wonderful news to himself. No, this time there was no denying it.

He'd been paid, either by the media or by her in-laws.

Candice came out of her stunned daze to the sound of footsteps approaching down the hall. She quickly pitched the checkbook onto the dresser among the pile of items she'd dug from his pockets. She didn't want Mrs. Merryweather to know, not yet. The poor housekeeper would be as heartbroken as she was.

Heartbroken, humiliated, devastated, betrayed. Candice didn't need a thesaurus to describe how she felt. She should have trusted her brain instead of her heart.

Now it was too late.

Forcing a bright smile to her lips, Candice turned to assure the housekeeper she was nearly finished. Her smile froze. It wasn't Mrs. Merryweather.

Mr. Hyde's Assets

It was Austin.

He seemed as surprised to find her in his room as she was to find him in the doorway. Oblivious to the frost warning in effect, he flashed her a boyish smile. "I came back for my checkbook." He slapped at his empty pockets. "No cash."

Candice hardened her heart against his endearing smile. She found it disgusting to realize that he still held the power to weaken her knees.

"Tell me, Austin," she began in a tone so icy it seemed to chill the air between them. "Are you planning to include my sexual preferences when you give the media the interview? Or perhaps it was my in-laws who made you fifty thousand dollars richer. My guess is you played the field until the price was right."

Despite the trembling that began to shake her entire body, she ignored his dumbfounded expression and raked him with a contemptuous glance. He was good. Oh, he was very good. If she had not seen evidence of his bank deposit with her own two eyes, she might be convinced he didn't have a clue what she was talking about. Bitterly, she continued, "If it was money you wanted, you should have come to me. I would have doubled what they offered to protect my baby's future." Thank God she hadn't gotten around to telling him that the money just didn't seem to matter anymore, that she loved him beyond belief.

Austin's puzzled expression faded. His jaw hardened, and the perpetual twinkle in his eyes dimmed into obscurity. "If you had questions, why didn't you just ask me, instead of snooping through my things?"

So he thought to put her on the defensive, did he? Candice wasn't falling for his tricks so easily anymore. "So you're admitting it?"

"Not on your life." He stepped into the room and shut the door behind him with an ominous click that made her heart beat faster. "I'd be admitting to a lie."

Candice didn't have to force a disbelieving laugh; it came quite naturally. "You expect me to believe you?"

"I expect you to trust me." He walked slowly toward her, holding her gaze, a blue flame burning in his eyes. "The money was left to me by my father. For reasons I don't care to mention at the moment, I haven't touched it until yesterday."

"Can you prove it?"

"Have I given you reason not to trust me?" he countered softly.

A few more steps and he would reach her, touch her. The wall was behind her. She had nowhere to go, and if he touched her, she feared her resolve would desert her. She searched his eyes for signs of guilt or deception, but the only thing she found was disappointment. Why would he be disappointed if he wasn't telling the truth? And he had a point; he'd given her no reason not to trust him. Still . . . "What—what made you decide to use it now?"

A faint smile tilted one corner of his mouth, but Candice saw something dark and violent flicker in his eyes.

"Does it matter?"

Did it? she asked herself. That is, *if* she believed him. If she did, then it really wasn't any of her business what he did with his own inheritance. Still, it hurt to know he didn't feel as if he could confide in her. Unless it meant he no longer wanted or needed the job. Then it would matter plenty.

"I would never sell you out."

His hands closed over her arms, and the anger slipped out of her just as she'd feared it would. Would she ever get used to how easily he could arouse her?

"I guess I owe you an apology," she whispered, her voice noticeably husky.

Austin slid his hands to her waist and pulled her tightly against him. His voice matched hers. "Apology accepted. Now, I have another surprise for you."

Candice nearly groaned at Austin's

announcement. "How big is this surprise?" After the Great Dane, she was almost afraid to ask.

He laughed at her wary expression. "Big. Very big. Come on."

He pulled her out of the room and downstairs at a speed that left her breathless by the time they stumbled into the kitchen. She laughed at Mrs. Merryweather's startled expression.

"Brace yourself," Candice told the housekeeper as Austin tugged her relentlessly in the direction of the back door. "He's got another surprise."

"Oh, my Lord!" Mrs. Merryweather exclaimed, throwing aside her apron and following them.

They didn't have to go far to see the surprise; it was parked in the driveway leading to the garage, and it was taking up a *lot* of space. Not an elephant, but as Candice eyed the ancient-looking silver motor home, she had the niggling feeling it was an apt description for it.

"Isn't she a beaut?" Austin asked, watching her expectantly. "Got it cheap, too. It has a fully functional kitchen, a bathroom—the works. Just like being at home." When Candice remained speechless, Austin prompted, "Well? What do you think?"

Candice licked her lips, searching for something neutral to say about his latest surprise. She had to admit, he'd definitely topped the two-hundred-pound dog. "It's a surprise, all right, but what do you plan to do with it?"

"I'm taking you camping. We've got this beauty for a whole week before she has to go back to the rental place."

Candice scrambled for an excuse. It wasn't that she didn't like the idea of spending time alone with Austin, but the RV didn't look very reliable. "We can't just leave Mrs. Merryweather, Austin."

"She can come with us."

"And what about Tiny and Lucy?"

Austin shrugged. "We can board them. If you don't want to do that, I'm sure Jack wouldn't mind house-sitting." He grunted. "I'd say Jack owes us."

"Well," Mrs. Merryweather announced without regret, "I can't go. I'm terribly allergic to poison ivy." Candice caught the calculating gleam in the housekeeper's eyes just seconds before she added, "But I think you should go with him, Mrs. Dale. The fresh air will be good for you."

"And for the baby," Austin added, unwittingly resurrecting in Candice that old, nearly forgotten flame of jealousy.

She stared at the monstrosity sitting in her driveway for a long, considering moment.

What the heck. If it wasn't for Austin and his rather wild ideas, she would never get out of the house.

Austin draped an arm over her shoulder, his voice persuasive. "Just think—fresh air, a cozy campfire, hot dogs, roasted marshmallows, and best of all, my company. You can have it all."

Relaxing in the circle of his arm, she tilted her head to look into his innocent-looking face. "Mosquitos?"

"Not where we're going."

"Snakes?"

"Not the poisonous kind."

Mrs. Merryweather decided to join the game. "What about bears?"

Austin remained serene. "They don't bother you if you don't bother them." He cocked an eyebrow in challenge. "Anything else?"

Warming to the game, Mrs. Merryweather waved a hand at the RV. "What if you break down?" Her dubious tone indicated she thought it a distinct possibility.

"I've repaired the engine in my truck more times than I care to remember."

When Candice cast him a questioning look about this revelation, he bent his head and whispered in her ear, "We don't usually get around to talking much when we're together." His low, teasing reminder made her blush. He was right. Their midnight meeting had ended in frenzied lovemaking that involved the kitchen counter and an ice cube.

The ice cube hadn't lasted long in the heat they'd generated.

"Well, if you're set on going camping, I'd better start packing the food." Mrs. Merryweather fixed a stern eye on Austin. "I won't have Mrs. Dale living on hot dogs and marshmallows for a week, so don't you even *think* it."

"I'll help you," Candice offered, following the housekeeper inside.

In the kitchen, Mrs. Merryweather began to pull a large assortment of Tupperware from the cabinets. "Where do you suppose he got the money to rent that motor home? They don't come cheap, I'm sure of that."

"This one must have," Candice muttered dryly, smiling when Mrs. Merryweather lifted a graying eyebrow in agreement. "As to where he got the money, he says he inherited it from his father. For reasons he didn't care to explain, he hasn't touched it until now."

The housekeeper nodded. "That would explain the article, then."

"What article?"

"This one." Mrs. Merryweather opened a drawer and pulled out a yellowed newspaper. She handed it to Candice, then tapped a blunt finger against the article on the front page.

"Drummond Hyde. From what I read, he's not the kind of father a boy could be proud of."

Candice lifted her startled gaze to the housekeeper's. "You think Drummond Hyde was Austin's father?"

Mrs. Merryweather shrugged, a troubled frown deepening the lines in her face. "I found a pile of newspapers in the back seat of the Cadillac, this one among them. Read the article and see for yourself."

Chapter Seventeen

Mrs. Merryweather prepared and packed enough food for an entire Boy Scout troop, which didn't seem to surprise Candice but boggled Austin.

The next morning, before the dew had time to disappear beneath a warm sun, he and Candice said their good-byes to the tearful housekeeper.

Or at least they attempted to.

Austin recognized Mrs. Merryweather's stalling techniques and tried to be patient. He took the time to look his fill at Candice while the two women talked.

Candice looked fresh and sexy in a pair of loose-fitting denim shorts and a plain cotton T-shirt. His gaze lingered appreciatively on her breasts, where the material stretched tight. He guessed she'd been caught off guard by her increasing bustline. Tearing his gaze from the delectable sight, he forced himself to tune in to the conversation.

Maybe he'd see an opportunity to cut it short.

"Austin says the RV is equipped with a cell phone," Candice reassured Mrs. Merryweather. "When we get to where we're going,' we'll call and let you know that we made it. Won't we, Austin?"

Austin nodded dutifully. He saw no need to mention the cell phone didn't work. After all, he hadn't exactly *lied*. It *was* equipped with one.

Mrs. Merryweather continued to fret. "What if those reporters are waiting? What if they follow you?"

"I'll lose them," Austin informed her in a tone he hoped would pacify the housekeeper. "If that doesn't work, I have a few friends on the police force who would be more than happy to intervene."

After another fifteen minutes of what seemed like senseless talk, Austin managed to tug Candice into the passenger seat of the RV. He closed the door and stepped around the hovering housekeeper.

Mrs. Merryweather followed him to the driver's side, relentless in her quest for reassurance. "You'll take good care of her?"

"Of course." He climbed behind the wheel and started to pull the door shut. Mrs. Merryweather caught the edge and stopped him. Austin was finding it hard to believe the housekeeper had been gung ho for the trip yesterday. He hated to admit it, but it irked his pride that she obviously didn't trust him.

"You promise to call the moment you're there safely?"

Austin hesitated. Surely they would be able to find a pay phone. "I promise." Finally, he was allowed to shut the door and start the engine. He carefully turned the RV around and headed for the gates.

"Do you think she'll be all right?" Candice asked anxiously as he maneuvered the cumbersome motor home onto the road.

"You're worried about the fire-breathing dragon? A woman who can make a grown man tremble in his boots?"

"She's not that bad!" Candice protested, but he saw her lips twitching.

"Don't worry." Austin was silent for a moment as he concentrated on coaxing the sluggish vehicle along the uphill ramp and onto the freeway. "She's got her pellet gun, and now she's got Tiny."

"But—"

"And I've asked Jack to check in on her every day."

"Oh, good. She trusts Dr. Jack."

"I can't imagine why," Austin mumbled beneath his breath.

"What?"

"Nothing." He checked his mirrors and glanced from side to side for suspicious-looking vehicles or news vans. When he was satisfied they weren't being followed, he finally relaxed, enjoying the warm wind gushing in through his open window.

He could hardly believe his luck. This was his chance to show Candice the time of her life, to prove to her just how much he cherished her, how much he *loved* her. Oh, he wasn't going to tell her, not yet, but he wasn't going to show her that there was much more between them than physical attraction. Instead of making love, they were going to talk, spend quality time finding out about each other.

Sliding a quick glance at her slim, curvy legs, Austin chuckled to himself. His decision to ban sex from the camping trip might just prove to be not only painful but impossible.

It would be worth the agony, however, if together they created timeless memories that later she would remember warmly—later being the time when she hated him for deceiving her.

Austin winced inwardly, recalling how close he had come to blowing it by leaving his checkbook lying around. Well, hell, he hadn't expected her to actually look inside and see he had deposited fifty thousand dollars. In fact, he had deliberately put the entire tasteless exchange from his mind after writing Pete Clancy his check.

He snuck a glance at Candice, smiling as she fought to keep her windblown hair out of her face. She was definitely worth it, and more, he mused. He would have paid Clancy whatever he asked to gain time to spend with Candice and to postpone the shock. At this stage of her pregnancy, he felt it best to avoid any and all forms of stress.

"Does this thing have air-conditioning?" Candice practically had to shout above the noisy wind.

Austin wondered if he imagined the slight irritation in her voice. He shrugged inwardly. So what if he preferred the wind and she preferred artificial cooling? Hadn't he heard that opposites attract?

Obliging her, he flipped on the AC and switched the fan to high. A blast of musty-smelling hot air rushed into his face, mingling with the cooler wind rushing in the window. After five minutes of the same, he shut it off. "I don't think it works."

"What?"

He repeated the statement, raising his voice
to be heard above the wind. She didn't comment. Austin didn't know if this was a good
sign or a bad one. Hell, he'd never been one for
second-guessing a woman. Sneaking a glance
at her, he saw her reach into her purse and pull
out one of those scrunchy things. With quick,
deft strokes she pulled her hair away from her
face and secured it with the pretty gold hair-
band.

They finally left the suburbs behind them.
Traffic thinned, and Austin coaxed a little more
speed from the motor home.

It was a mistake.

Candice suddenly sat forward in her cap-
tain's seat. "What's that noise?"

Austin heard it, too, and he felt it as well. The
engine had developed an ugly hiccup. A loud
backfire startled them both. Muttering a few
choice curses he reserved for contrary vehicles,
he flipped on his blinker and pulled the motor
home onto the shoulder of the road.

So much for avoiding stress, was his gloomy
thought as he engaged the parking brake and
stepped down from the RV.

She was hot all right, but it wasn't the weather;
it was the sight of Austin's muscled, tanned legs
below his shorts that made Candice long for a

blast of cold air to cool her feverish skin. That, and his open shirt that revealed a large expanse of his chest.

Only last night they had indulged in a wild bout of lovemaking, yet here she was about to burst into flames just watching him. None of the informative pamphlets at Dr. Robinson's office had mentioned anything about being oversexed during pregnancy.

Candice gave a shaky laugh, eyeing Austin through the windshield. She didn't care if they had to spend the entire week right here on the side of the road as long as she could be with him.

Did he feel the same way? she wondered. Did he feel happy, carefree, warm, and wonderful when he was with her the way she did when she was with him? She couldn't honestly guess, since Austin *always* seemed to be happy, except in the presence of nasty reporters or lawyers bearing bad tidings.

The reminder prompted a smile. *Then* he could be fierce, protective, and possessive. Oh, she hadn't mentioned it, but his jealousy of Luke McVey had been very obvious. And endearing. Her own reaction confused her. When Howard had exhibited those traits, they had nearly driven her insane. Why would she feel any differently with Austin?

Because Austin was . . . Austin.

She sobered as the man who occupied her thoughts returned to the cab and started the engine. It hummed to life without a hitch, the odd hiccuping noise gone. She tried not to smile at Austin's supremely male expression of smug satisfaction. "What was wrong?"

"A spark plug wire popped off." His slow, sexy grin returned. "You want something cold to drink before we get started?"

When Candice nodded, he moved to the back and returned within seconds, handing her a canned soft drink. Caffeine-free. And warm.

"The refrigerator doesn't work," he informed her, unsmiling. "George will hear about this."

"George?"

"Yeah, George. He's the guy who rented me this rig."

To prove to him that it didn't matter, Candice popped the top and took a deep swig. It was awful, but she gamely kept a straight face. "It's not so bad. When I was a kid, I used to prefer my sodas hot." That part, at least, was true, but judging by the skeptical look Austin gave her, he didn't believe a word of it.

"Thank you for being such a good sport."

It was on the tip of Candice's tongue to ask him why he hadn't rented something more reliable, since she now knew he could afford it. With fifty thousand dollars in the bank . . .

"I know what you're probably thinking," Austin said, startling her with his uncanny perception. "You're asking yourself why I didn't rent something a little more upscale."

Well, since he mentioned it. "Yes," Candice admitted bluntly. "I was thinking exactly that."

Austin checked both mirrors in preparation for pulling onto the road, but Candice suspected he was avoiding her questioning gaze. After reading that old article about Drummond Hyde, many things about Austin had become clearer. She now understood his flippant attitude about wealth and luxuries, and his fierce dislike of reporters. But she still didn't understand why he'd suddenly decided to use the money he'd obviously ignored for many years.

She hoped he hadn't compromised his ethics just to impress her.

"The truth is, I owed that money to someone. Otherwise I wouldn't have touched it."

Candice felt relieved to discover she wasn't the cause but unexplainably chilled by something in his tone. "You—you aren't in trouble, are you?"

He flashed her a rueful smile as he pulled into the traffic and gained speed. "First a thief, then a spy. Now I'm a criminal." Still smiling, he shook his head. "Baby, if I was that suspicious of someone, I don't think I'd go off camp-

ing with them. How do you know I'm not planning to broaden my résumé *and* increase my
bank account by kidnapping you?"

Candice flushed at his mocking tone but rallied defensively. "I never thought you took my
jewels, and anyone would wonder why someone would take a job like yours if he had fifty
thousand dollars in the bank. The work you do
is—"

"For you and the baby—not for the money."
Austin looked straight ahead at the road, his
lips pressed tightly together as if he regretted
his words.

She stared at his rigid profile, wishing he'd
talk to her, trust her. Well, she had five days to
show him that she could be a trusted friend as
well as an employer and lover.

Five days.

Alone with Austin.

They stopped for lunch at a busy truck stop
shortly before noon, not only because they
were hungry but because the gas gauge had
made a rapid descent into the red in the last
half hour. Austin grumbled to himself as he
climbed down and hurried around to help
Candice. At this rate, he would be out of cash
before they reached their destination.

George would be sorry he'd ever thought to

swindle Austin Hyde—if they made it back. At least Candice seemed to be taking it all in stride, smiling at him in a way that made his throat go dry. Hell, he wished she'd turn the heat down until after the camping trip!

Inside the noisy restaurant, they both agreed on greasy hamburgers, greasy fries, and tall, fattening milk shakes. But as they made their way to a booth by the window, Austin caught sight of Candice's guilty expression and laughed.

"Don't worry. I won't tell if you won't tell," he teased.

Candice feigned innocence. "Tell whom? I don't know what you're talking about." To prove it, the moment her bottom hit the plastic chair, she grabbed her burger and took a huge bite, following it with a french fry.

Austin poured ketchup on his fries, then added an unhealthy amount of salt to his burger. He arched an eyebrow in her direction as he lifted the burger to his mouth, enjoying the food, the atmosphere—and Candice. "Are you saying you would have ordered this junk food if the dragon were with us?"

"Let's change the subject."

She dabbed at her mouth with a napkin, drawing his attention to her pink, moist lips. Austin nearly choked on his burger, trying to swallow before he chewed the food properly. Damn, the woman was dangerous. And she didn't even know it!

Deciding to give her a break from his teasing, he asked, "So, have you figured out where we're going?"

"Let me see." Candice dipped a fry in his ketchup and popped it into her mouth. She closed her eyes, a blissful smile curving her mouth as she chewed. "Mmm. These are delicious."

Austin forgot about his food. He stared at her, his groin tightening at the rapturous look on her face. He'd seen that look before, each time they reached the peak in their lovemaking. Fighting a ridiculous urge to snatch the fries and pitch them into the trash, Austin grabbed his shake and took a drink.

"Well, the air is getting cooler, we're heading east—my guess would be Lake Tahoe." She shot him a provocative look from beneath her eyelashes, a totally *un*Candicelike look that shocked him to his toes.

Austin bit the inside of his cheek. Hell, if he didn't know better, he'd think she knew about his no-sex plan! He'd been relying on her shy nature to help him resist, and here she was, turning into a sex kitten right before his very eyes.

"Of course, the signs advertising Lake Tahoe

helped," Candice added, laughing at his disgruntled expression.

Her laughter rippled over him like a blanket of warm honey. He deliberately kept the conversation bland. And long, he hoped. Hell, she left him no choice. As it was, he'd have to wait a while before he could rise without embarrassing himself. "Have you been to Lake Tahoe before?" He could have kicked himself when her smile faded and that old haunted look returned to shadow her gorgeous cat's eyes.

"Once, but it was a long time ago." She braced her elbows on the table—something else Austin didn't think she would have done two months ago. "It was before my mother died." She smiled faintly, her gaze drifting to the window. Outside at the pumps, truck drivers filled their tanks and stretched their legs.

"How old were you?" Austin prompted softly. He hated to see her sad, but he wanted to know everything about her, the bad *and* the good. In return, he would tell her about his life until their were no secrets left between them.

Well, except one very big one.

"When I came to Lake Tahoe? Or when my mother died?"

"When your mother died." Austin navigated the french fries and the hamburgers and caught her hand. He squeezed gently. "Both, if you'll share them with me."

331

She looked at him, her expression pensive, wary, yet hopeful. "And you? Will you share with me?"

Austin nodded. "We'll take turns. Deal?"

"Deal." She returned her gaze to the window, and it was a moment before she spoke again. "We came here right after my mother married Pete Clancy. It was their honeymoon, but there wasn't anyone else for me to stay with, so they had to take me with them. I was eight years old." She let the sigh out slowly, but Austin saw it, and his heart ached. "We didn't like each other from the start."

"You and Clancy?"

"Yes. But we didn't let on, because we both loved Mom. We were supposed to stay a week at Lake Tahoe, but Pete decided to cut the honeymoon short after two days and go back to Sacramento."

"Because of you?" Austin winced at the husky sound of his voice; he knew she wouldn't appreciate his pity.

Candice shrugged, but the hurt was still there, deep and painful. "He didn't say, at least not until later. But I knew. He claimed he remembered some business he'd forgotten to take care of, but every time he looked at me, I knew it was because of me. Mom died two months later."

Austin didn't realize his fingers had tightened around hers until she flinched. He forced himself to ease his hold. A visual image of Candice as a little girl, left alone with a man she not only didn't know but didn't like, just about broke his heart.

"Mom made me promise to take care of him," Candice said matter-of-factly. "So I did." She pulled free of his grip and reached for her shake. "It's all water under the bridge now. My obligations to him were over a long time ago."

Austin thought about Pete Clancy and the fat check he held in his greedy little hands. He also recalled Clancy's remark about how Candice had helped him out, and he suspected Candice was too ashamed to admit that she'd carried out her promise far longer than she'd had to. Obligations, it seemed, had caused Candice a lot of unnecessary heartache. And thanks to Jack, the heartache wasn't over. Austin closed his eyes, dreading the moment she found out.

"What's wrong?"

His eyes popped open. "Nothing," he croaked. "Let's get out of here."

"But it's your—"

"Turn," Austin finished. "I know, and I'm not trying to get out of it, but we need to be on the road if we're going to get there by dark. We'll talk later, I promise." He threw a tip on the table and slid from the booth, his heart pounding with dread.

Soon, she would know. Soon, she would hate him.

Knowing this, he couldn't find it in his heart to regret one single moment he'd spent in her company the last two months.

Slowly, he held out a hand to help her from the booth.

With the innocent trust of a child, she took it.

Something was wrong.

Candice felt the tension in Austin's hand, saw it in his face. The tight look remained long after he'd finished filling the tank on the motor home, purchasing several coolers and filling them with ice, and transferring the perishables from the malfunctioning fridge. Soon they were on their way again.

Was the possibility of talking to her that horrible, she wondered. Had she said something to cause his frown? She racked her brain, trying to recall the conversation word by word.

Nothing. She had done most of the talking, but about herself, so she didn't think she could have offended him with something she said. She leaned her head against the seat rest and closed her eyes. The heavy food had made her drowsy, and she hadn't gotten much sleep the night before, thanks to her midnight tryst with Austin in the kitchen. Not that she'd minded.

"We're almost there."

Candice jerked awake at the sound of Austin's voice, realizing she must have dozed off. Rubbing her eyes, she looked around her, then did a double take. She glanced at her watch and saw that she'd been asleep for two hours.

The scenery had changed dramatically in those two hours. Bumper-to-bumper traffic, miles of concrete, and high-rise buildings had given way to forests and mountains interspersed with large country homes and open fields. The temperature had dropped as well, at least fifteen degrees from the balmy eighty-five they had left behind in Sacramento.

Her memories of her last trip to Lake Tahoe were vague at best, but she didn't recall everything being so lush and green. A child of eight, she supposed, wouldn't notice or appreciate such things.

The motor home chugged up a steep hill, seeming to grunt with the effort. As they topped the rise, Candice caught a glimpse of silver in the far distance. Lake Tahoe, located on the border of California and Nevada, was well known for the clarity of its water and the beauty of its location. Rising above the forest surrounding them on both sides, majestic, snowcapped mountains provided excellent skiing.

Awed by the scenery she'd long forgotten, Candice whispered, "It's beautiful."

"Yes, it is."

Candice jerked her gaze around at the husky note in his voice. He wasn't looking at the scenery but directly at her. She blushed. Apparently he'd gotten over whatever it was that had been bothering him. *This* was the Austin she knew and loved, and she was glad to have him back. "Shouldn't you keep your eyes on the road?" she asked tartly.

"I'd rather look at you."

A car horn blared, and Austin hastily fixed his gaze on the road. Up ahead, a sign announced RV CAMPING. Austin pulled into the parking lot across from the office and cut the engine.

"I'll go sign us in," he told her, his gaze lingering on her face.

Candice was left alone to anticipate the coming night.

And she did.

Chapter Eighteen

By nightfall Austin had proven himself to be an expert camper. He built a blazing campfire inside the safety ring and fed Candice roasted hot dogs and marshmallows until she laughingly cried uncle. The temperature had dropped with the sun, but she didn't feel the chill; the warmth of the fire and Austin's denim jacket kept her toasty.

Trying to remember when she'd last felt so happy and peaceful, Candice watched him from her comfortable position in a chaise lounge as he fed the fire from a pile of dead branches they had gathered before dark. "Mrs. Merryweather knew where we were going, didn't she?"

He glanced up from his task, the fire high-lighting the masculine lines of his face. His teeth flashed in a smile. "She insisted. How did you guess?"

Candice shrugged, hugging her arms across her chest. "Extra blankets, warm clothing that *I* didn't pack, and she didn't sound the least bit surprised when I talked to her on the phone."

"You should have been a detective," Austin drawled, dusting his hands on his jeans. He snapped open a lawn chair and sat across from her, propping one ankle on his knee.

The twinkling of lights from their camping neighbors were distant enough for Candice to ignore. What she could *not* ignore was the man facing her. He'd changed into a hunter-green sweater in a ribbed material that emphasized the breadth of his shoulders and made his jeans appear tighter by comparison.

Or maybe it was her wicked imagination.

Dragging her gaze away with some effort, she stared into the fire and marveled at her raging libido. She didn't know whether to be embarrassed or exhilarated.

"Would you like a cup of hot cocoa?" Austin asked.

She nodded, her gaze following him as he disappeared into the motor home. A few moments later she heard a muffled curse, followed by a clanging noise she feared would prompt a ranger into investigating.

Austin emerged from the camper wearing a fierce scowl. Candice bit her lip to keep from grinning. "Let me guess—the stove doesn't work?"

"No, the stove doesn't work," he growled. He ran a hand over his bristly chin. "I need to shave, too."

"Does the plumbing—"

"Probably not." With a disgruntled sigh, he returned to his seat. "I guess we can rough it for one night. I noticed the public bathrooms have shower facilities."

"No problem." Candice snuggled into the oversized jacket. Was she imagining it, or did Austin seem to be avoiding physical contact? Other than a casual touch of his hand helping her in and out of the motor home, he hadn't attempted to kiss her or pull her close.

It was dark. They were relatively secluded, alone with the stars above, the mountains around them, and the campfire between them. A night made for cuddling, for romance, for love. Was he perhaps waiting for her to make the first move? Candice mulled over the possibility. What if she did, and it *wasn't* what he wanted?

She reached a hand inside her jacket and

placed it on the growing mound of her stomach, forcing herself to consider that her advanc-
ing pregnancy could be the answer to his
sudden aversion to touching her. Oh, he still
looked at her with enough fire in his eyes to
scorch her skin, and he was still the same atten-
tive Austin he'd always been. Except he hadn't
touched her all day. Yet just last night . . .

"I guess you're waiting," Austin said, interrupting her troubled thoughts.

"What?" Candice blinked at him, uncertain
of his meaning. Could he somehow know what
she'd been thinking?

"The promise I made? You share with me
and I'll share with you?" he clarified.

"Oh." She hoped it was dark enough to hide
her fiery face, because she'd been thinking
something entirely different! "Yes, that. Well,
whenever you're ready. We've got all night."

Obviously he wasn't in a hurry to go to bed.

"You already know that my father left me
some money," Austin began. "And I told you
that I haven't touched it for reasons I didn't
care to mention. The biggest reason is because
my father didn't come by his fortune honestly."

"Drugs?"

He glanced sharply at her. "How did you
know?"

"I'm psychic?" Candice smiled impishly, hoping to put him at ease. Talking about his father

was clearly a painful subject. "Actually, Mrs. Merryweather found an old newspaper in the Cadillac. There was an article about Drummond Hyde that caught her attention." She shrugged to show that it made no difference to her who his father was. And it didn't. "Together we figured it out."

The sharp planes and angles of his face softened visibly. He even managed a faint smile. "Nancy Drew in the flesh. So now you also know why I've preferred to make my own way instead of using my inheritance."

Candice nodded. "Were you very young when he died?"

"Young enough not to remember him. My mother remarried six months later."

"So you grew up with a stepfather, too," Candice observed. Something else they had in common. "What was he like?"

Austin snorted, turning his gaze to the fire and away from her searching eyes. "I wouldn't know. My mother hired a score of nannies to ease her guilty conscience, and when I was old enough, I was shipped off to boarding school."

Candice leaned forward. "Was it so horrible? Boarding school, I mean? I've already considered—"

"No!"

She jerked back at his vehemence.

He continued in a hard-edged tone she'd

341

never heard him use before. "Promise me you will never send you—your baby to a boarding school!"

He'd nearly said *our* baby, Candice noted, her entire body suffusing with warmth at the slip. How different her life would be if it were true!

It could still happen, a tiny voice of hope whispered. Austin wasn't her baby's biological father, but if they were married, she knew with certainty that he would make a wonderful stepfather.

She clasped her hands together to still their silly trembling. "If it's as bad as you say, then of course I won't consider it. I only want what's best for my child."

Austin sighed. "Some boarding schools are okay. I guess it was worse for us because—"

"Us?"

"Me and my brother." He squinted into the fire, his voice devoid of self-pity but laced with an underlying bitterness that made Candice wince on his behalf. "It was worse for us because we knew we'd been abandoned. Mother was too busy spending her new husband's money to bother with her children."

She hadn't known Austin had a brother. Good grief, she was sleeping with the man and she hadn't known he had a brother! "Is your mother still alive?" she asked gently.

"Yes. She lives in Italy with her fifth husband."

The fire flared as another branch caught. Through the flames, she saw his mouth twist, but she didn't think he was smiling.

"We don't see much of her."

He didn't sound as if he cared, but Candice instinctively sensed that he did. Just as she cared that Pete Clancy had always resented her, even after her mother died. Childhood wounds left scars that took a long time to fade.

She hesitated over her next question, wondering how far she should go. "Is your mother the reason you've never married?" When he lifted a questioning eyebrow, she flushed. "Dr. Jack said as much."

His answer was abrupt, yet his eyes traveled over her in that all-consuming way that made her forget his tone. "I never married because I never found the right woman."

"Oh." Candice didn't know what to say, but she knew what she wanted *him* to say.

She wanted him to say *until you*.

"I'm glad we've had an opportunity to talk," Austin said.

Candice suppressed a sigh. Not exactly the words she longed to hear. "I'm glad, too." She

343

hastily covered her mouth as she yawned. The long trip, the food, and the warmth of the fire were all catching up with her.

"Sleepy?" Before she could answer, he leaped to his feet. "I'll go make our beds. Mrs. Merryweather will have my head if I bring you back exhausted."

Beds. As the word sank in, Candice wanted to shriek her frustration. She had been looking forward all day to falling asleep in his arms, and he was making their *beds*! Apparently her growing suspicions about his waning desire were true.

Then why, she asked herself, did he still look at her as if he desired her?

Candice got angrily to her feet, exasperated and confused by his conflicting signals. She would go inside and make her own damned bed, show him that she wasn't helpless. If Austin harbored some crazy notion that she would beg him to make love to her, then he was sadly mistaken.

She begged no one.

By the third night, Austin decided he'd rather do without air to breathe, water to drink, and food to eat, because doing without any of those necessities couldn't possibly make him as miserable as he was when he wasn't touching Candice.

And it wasn't just the great sex, either, he concluded as he stared at the RV's ceiling sometime after midnight and listened to the steady patter of rain. He missed the softness of her skin, the eager way she hugged him when he held her, and the absolute joy of kissing her very kissable mouth. If he thought he could trust himself, he'd leap over into her bunk right now and pull her close. Hold her all night long. Kiss her neck and whisper sweet nothings in her ear.

Even more frustrating was the fact that Candice didn't seem to notice or care that he wasn't his usual affectionate self. She smiled and laughed, proving to be a great conversationalist and a fun companion. He'd known she would be, of course.

Secretly, though, he had been hoping she would protest the separate bunks. But to his chagrin, she had yawned in his face, wished him good night, and crawled beneath the covers without a hint of reluctance. Moments later, he'd heard her snoring softly while he lay awake, his body aching, his mind torturing him with erotic fantasies.

They had talked about everything under the sun. Not surprisingly, Austin discovered that many of their values and beliefs about life in general were similar.

He took her fishing on the second day, and

today they had sailed around the lake until the clouds rolled in and forced them to come ashore. Once inside the motor home, they had eaten cold ham sandwiches and played a long, competitive game of gin rummy. Candice had beaten him soundly, gloating over her victory until Austin had teasingly threatened to lock her out in the rain.

She had tossed her head and dared him to try.

With a groan, Austin turned onto his side. It was different when they were fishing, or sailing, or simply huddling around the campfire outdoors. Now, with the rain keeping them in the close confines of the camper, he didn't know if he could resist making love to her. Hell, they could hardly *pass* each other without inadvertently touching.

Finally, lulled by the rhythmic sound of the rain, Austin felt himself relaxing.

He awoke the next morning to the sound of Candice humming lightly. He lay still for a moment, holding his breath, listening for another sound that he dreaded to hear.

And there it was: rain. A natural element that was quickly becoming synonymous with agony. With a muttered curse, Austin rolled from his bunk and landed on his feet. And froze.

Candice stood before the small hotplate he'd

purchased at a bait shop after failing to get results from the small camper stove. She wore an oversized sleep shirt that left a tantalizing amount of thigh exposed. Her feet were bare, her face was scrubbed free of makeup, and she'd tucked her hair into a lopsided bun on top of her head. The careless style left long tendrils of soft blond hair lying against her neck.

She looked not only happy but incredibly sexy.

Desire weakened Austin's knees. Gritting his teeth, he reached out and gripped the bar holding the folding dining table in place against the wall. "What the hell are you doing?" he demanded hoarsely.

She gasped and jerked around, clutching a spoon to her chest. "Oh, you startled me. I'm scrambling eggs." Her sunny smile mocked the gloomy weather. "Aren't you hungry?"

Was he hungry? Hungrier than a bear after a long winter. A male bear, that is, one more interested in finding a mate than in finding food. As he stood there, struggling against the urge to snatch her up and carry her to bed, she dropped her spoon.

Watching her bend over was almost as agonizing as the rain. She didn't squat but bent from the waist, giving him a full view of her long slim legs and her perky bottom encased in white cotton panties.

Austin's throat felt terribly dry. It sounded it, too, when he commanded her to turn off the burner.

She looked surprised. "Why would I do that? The eggs aren't finished yet."

"Because they'll burn," he croaked.

Her brow furrowed with concern. "Austin, are you sick?"

"You could say that." Addiction was a sickness, wasn't it? And he was definitely addicted to her.

Her concern deepened. She turned off the burner and laid the spoon in the skillet. "Is there anything I can do? Are you running a fever?"

Slowly, Austin let go of the bar and steadied himself. His gaze burned into hers as he said softly, "Maybe you should come here and check."

He was going to break his temporary vow of abstinence and spend the whole rainy day making love to her over and over. They'd talked enough, hadn't they?

She padded over to him, standing very close. So close, in fact, that Austin was certain she could feel his arousal against her belly.

That was his first clue that she knew the exact nature of his problem.

Her eyes were soft and glowing as she pressed a cool hand against his forehead. She quirked an eyebrow. "No, you're not warm there." She moved her hand to his bare chest, curling her fingers in his hair.

Austin sucked in a scorching breath and held it. The minx.

She shook her head, her lips twitching. "Not here, either."

Her hand dropped lower. Slowly, her fingers closed around his throbbing length. "Now, *this* is hot," she murmured, sounding very satisfied.

With a primitive growl Austin swooped her up and carried her to his bunk. She laughed and wound her arms around his neck, kissing his throat, his chin, and finally his mouth.

The rain continued well into the evening, and Austin didn't care.

Later, as he and Candice lay snuggled, spoon fashion, on the bunk after a prolonged bout of lovemaking, he stroked her damp hair from her brow and tried not to think about the uncertain future. He wished like hell he could just blurt out the truth and get it behind them.

But fear of rejection stilled his tongue.

Candice moved his hand to cover her belly, then covered his hand with her own. "When you didn't touch me," she said softly, "I thought *this* was the cause."

Austin sat up abruptly. He turned her onto her back so that he could look at her face. It never occurred to him that Candice would think such a thing. "You have to know that's not true!" he exclaimed. The irony of it struck him. "You become more desirable to me every day." Which was true.

When she didn't look convinced, he bent forward and pressed his lips to her belly, then turned his cheek so that it lay against her soft skin. What more could he say without making her suspicious? And he couldn't tell her, not now.

He wanted—no, he needed—this time alone with Candice. Here in the park, miles from the city and reporters and his crazy brother, he could almost pretend everything was perfect. And he could almost hope she would fall hopelessly, eternally in love.

The sun was high in the sky, the rain long gone by the time they stumbled out of the motor home the next morning and headed for the showers.

Austin left Candice on the threshold of the women's rest room after a sweet, lingering kiss before making his happy way to an empty shower stall in the men's section. Armed with soap, shampoo, deodorant, clean clothes, and a towel, he whistled as he scrubbed himself beneath the tepid spray.

He was forcing himself to think optimistically. Maybe Candice did love him enough to forgive him. When she was in his arms, he could believe it; it was the harsh light of day that brought on the doubts. He lathered his hair with shampoo, closing his eyes tightly as he stuck his head beneath the spray to rinse off. If he could just convince her that he hadn't meant to hurt her—

"Here's a washcloth," a familiar voice said, shocking him into opening his eyes.

What the hell—? Soapy lather rushed in before he could get them closed again. He groped around until his hand closed over the proffered washcloth, pressing it against his aching eyeballs.

"Sorry. Didn't mean to scare you."

Austin dared to open one burning eye as if his brain refused to believe what his vision had not yet verified.

Jack's apprehensive face peered back at him around the shower curtain.

So he wasn't hallucinating. Jack was here. Right here with him in a park rest room hundreds of miles from home. A bad feeling settled in his gut—which wasn't unusual when Jack was around—only this time it was worse. For Jack to travel so far could only mean bad news.

He quickly finished rinsing his hair and snatched the towel from Jack's fingers. As he dried himself, he began to fire questions at his half brother. "How did you find us?"

351

"Wasn't easy. I got here yesterday afternoon but didn't find your camper until late." He shook his head. "I have to admit, bro, you could have done better than that piece of tin."

Jack didn't know the half of it, Austin thought sourly. "Go on." If ever there came a time when Jack had *good* news to tell him, he would kiss his feet. He felt pretty confident he would never have to.

"As I was saying, I found you late last night, but I decided to get a hotel room and come back this morning." He paused before adding solemnly, "I thought it would be best if Mrs. Vanausdale didn't see me."

Austin finished toweling off and stepped out of the shower stall, glad to find they were alone. He plucked his clean shirt from the pile of clothes neatly folded on the bench—compliments of his compulsively neat brother. Funny, how Jack didn't practice what he preached regarding his own appearance. "How did you know I'd come here?"

"I didn't. I parked at the empty site next to yours and waited until you came out of the camper. When I saw where you were heading, I followed you, keeping a safe distance so as not to encounter Mrs. Vanausdale." He stuck his hands in the pockets of his wrinkled pants and looked around him at the damp, grayish walls of the shower area. "I hope Mrs. Vanausdale uses an antibacterial soap," he muttered.

"If she's had you coaching her, I'm sure she does." Austin ground his teeth as he yanked his jeans over his hips and fastened the metal button. He loved Jack, but he resented this intrusion. "Are you going to get around to telling me why you've come all the way from Sacramento? And let me warn you, Jack, it had better be good. Damned good."

"That's not exactly the word I would use, because the news is grim."

Austin shot him a look before sitting on the bench to slip his sandals over his bare feet. "Are you sure you're not being overly dramatic?" he asked hopefully.

Jack wore a tragic expression as he said, "Someone broke into my office, Austin."

"Who was it?" Austin came to his feet, resisting the familiar urge to shake the information from Jack.

But then he remembered how unrevealing Candice's file was.

Relief turned his bones to butter, forcing him to resume his seat. "There was nothing in Candice's file, Jack, that would implicate you *or* me. Seems you came all this way for nothing." Not to mention scaring the shit out of him.

"I wish that were true."

Hell. Double hell. Austin stared at Jack, blood rushing to his head. In a low, furious voice, he asked, "Exactly what are you saying?"

Jack put a comfortable distance between them, his face pale and strained. "I kept some personal files locked in my desk, notes and things on various transactions."

"Such as?"

"A list"—Jack swallowed visibly, then finished in a rush—"of possible donors. Your name was circled, with Mrs. Vanausdale's name written beside it."

Austin gripped the bench—hard—to keep from hitting Jack. "How could you be so careless?" he managed between clenched teeth.

"I never thought someone would break in!" He lifted his slim shoulders in a helpless shrug. "I hate throwing things away. I always need them later."

"Shh! Keep your voice down, you idiot!" Austin rose braced his hands against the clammy wall, and took several deep breaths. It didn't help.

"Maybe they won't use—" Jack's words ended abruptly as Austin snapped his head up to face him.

"They will, and you know it. Whoever broke into your office didn't risk going to jail just to satisfy idle curiosity."

"Austin?"

Both men froze at the sound of Candice's muffled voice on the other side of the door.

Finally, Austin found his tongue. "I'll be right out!" he shouted. To Jack, he instructed in a low voice, "Make sure you're home tomorrow night around eight o'clock. I'm going to bring Candice straight to your house, and we're going to tell her everything before she hears it from someone else."

"Gotcha."

"I'll see you back in Sacramento." With a heavy heart, Austin gathered his toiletries and strode to the door. When he reached it, he turned to glance back at Jack. The sight of his little brother standing in the dim light, looking lost and guilt-ridden, did what it always did; it softened his heart and allowed a smidgen of forgiveness to creep in.

"Thanks for warning me, Jack. Drive safely, and don't worry." Austin managed a wry smile. "Things can't get any worse."

Jack groaned.

Chapter Nineteen

Slouched in the passenger seat of the motor home, Candice pulled the bill of Austin's baseball cap low over her brow so that Austin wouldn't see the tears she tried to stem.

She didn't want to leave.

Did Austin feel the same? She slanted a glance at him as he drove the clumsy vehicle with an ease she admired. The past week had been incredible, almost dreamlike. They had nearly exhausted every topic under the sun, and she couldn't remember a single awkward silence between them. When they weren't talking or making love, they simply enjoyed each other's company.

She had fallen even more deeply in love with

Austin, a realization that filled her with an odd mixture of elation and apprehension. He'd not mentioned love to her, not once, yet each tender gesture, each hot, possessive look, told her how much he cared. But did he believe their lives too different to allow for a more permanent relationship? she wondered. Was that the reason he didn't mention love or talk about the future?

God, she couldn't imagine a future without this funny, loving, sexy man. Austin Hyde had helped her realize that she shouldn't dwell in the past but instead look forward to a future *she* could control. Absently, she stroked the silky material of his football jersey. It was Austin who had insisted she disguise herself for the trip back to Sacramento. Not quite understanding his almost desperate concern, she had finally relented, digging into her suitcase for the football jersey she had packed to give back to him. She had stuffed her hair beneath a proffered cap bearing the logo SUPPORT YOUR LOCAL ARTISTS, and beneath his jersey she wore a pair of brand-new maternity jeans.

Eyeing the grim set of his jaw and the bunched muscles in his arms, Candice frowned. As they'd cleaned the campsite before their departure, he'd been a little somber, but then, so had she. She had assumed their reasons were similar; they both hated to leave and return to the chaotic life of intrusive reporters and nasty in-laws.

But as an hour stretched into two, she began to wonder if there was a more sinister reason for his withdrawal. *Uptight* might better describe how he looked. At first, she tried to dismiss the notion, but it kept creeping back for another insistent nudge.

Finally she could stand the suspense no longer. She closed the outdated magazine she'd found beneath the seat and took a deep breath, waiting until he finished a skilled maneuver between lanes before asking, "Is something wrong?"

The camper swerved slightly as he shot her a startled look. "No."

Candice sat straighter. For an instant, she saw a flash of fear in his eyes before he returned his gaze to the road. Once before—in the nursery—she had sensed the same fear but had shied from wanting to know the cause.

But that was before she realized how much she loved Austin Hyde, painter and handyman, whose favorite color was *every* color. She loved his gentleness, his caring nature, his wonderful outlook on life, his strength . . . she loved *everything* about him. He could take her for a rocket ride to the moon with his zealous loving or soothe her nerves with the gentle reassurance of his voice or a touch of his hand.

He could make her feel reckless and happy, safe and secure, wanted and needed. How could she *not* love him? And if he still kept secrets from her because he feared she'd reject him, then she wanted him to know that nothing he could tell her would stop her from loving him.

Candice sighed wistfully, not for the first time wishing she was plain ol' Candice instead of Mrs. Howard Vanausdale. But most of all, she wished she'd never married Howard, and that Austin was the father of her baby. It was an incredible fantasy, and a dangerous one to entertain, yet she couldn't stop thinking about how simple, how wonderfully simple her life would be right now if she'd met Austin instead of Howard on that hot, tired day in July at the Burger Barn.

If she had . . .

Candice closed her eyes, bringing forth a hazy image of a white frame house complete with a picket fence, children, and a brown-and-white collie. She grinned, thinking she should at least try to be original.

"A penny for your thoughts."

The low timbre of his voice snapped her eyes open, dispelling the fantasy. Her laugh was a little shaky. "They're not worth repeating," she lied, then wondered why she didn't just blurt out the truth. Because he might laugh? Or because he might squirm like a fish on a hook?

It was the thought of him squirming that sealed her lips. She didn't think she was ready to find out that Austin was having second thoughts about their relationship. Instead, she said the first thing that popped to mind. "Actually, I was wondering why you insisted on this disguise." She tucked a strand of windswept hair under the cap and adjusted the bill again so that she could see his face more clearly.

"Do you want someone to recognize you?"

"You didn't seem to be concerned when we left, or during the trip down," she pointed out.

His lips tightened. "Your disappearance has probably caused a stir, don't you think? They'll be frothing at the mouth and hiding around every corner waiting for your return."

Candice couldn't argue with his logic, so she remained silent. He was probably right, she thought gloomily. She might as well face the fact that her idyllic vacation was truly over.

They made three more stops during the eight-hour drive, and each time Austin stuck to her like flypaper. He followed her to the rest rooms and waited for her to come out. He waited until she was safely inside the RV before he filled the tank, and, much to her exasperation, he wouldn't let her buy a newspaper during one of her trips to the bathroom at a convenience store.

"No," Austin said, steering her away from the newstands and out into the parking lot so fast that she had to run to keep up with him.

"Austin! What has gotten into you?" She tugged her arm from his hand and stopped in the middle of the lot, refusing to budge another inch until he gave her a reasonable explanation. He had taken this far beyond normal caution!

He turned, his face set, his eyes expressionless. "Reading while riding will make you carsick."

Candice shook her head. She wasn't buying it. No, something was wrong, and Austin didn't want to tell her. "You saw me flipping through a magazine earlier and didn't complain."

"If you want a magazine, I'll get you one." He started back in the direction of the store, but Candice caught his arm.

"You don't want me to see a newspaper." When he simply stared at her, she knew she'd hit on the truth. "I'm right, aren't I? You know something I don't, and you're trying to protect me." She was close enough to see a muscle ticking in his jaw.

"I need for you to trust me on this," he said, reaching up to cup her face. His expression softened; the familiar glow he seemed to

361

reserve just for her returned to his eyes. "I don't want you hurt any more than you have to be."

Candice braced herself, finding strength where once upon a time there had been only resignation. "I'm not going to break, Austin. Whatever it is, believe me, I can handle it." Gazing steadily into his eyes, she grasped his hands and lowered them from her face. "I'm going to get a newspaper."

"Candice . . ."

She began walking toward the store, resisting the urge to turn around and forget it, to let Austin continue to shield and protect her. But that was the old Candice. The new Candice was strong; she could meet any challenge life threw her way. She would prove to Austin that she wasn't as fragile as he believed.

An hour later, she refolded the newspaper and laid it aside. To her relief—and confusion—she'd found nothing in it that would justify Austin's sudden paranoia. "Would you like for me to drive so that you can read the paper?" she asked. When he began to shake his head, the devil in her prompted, "Or maybe you think a delicate creature like me couldn't handle this tugboat."

Her taunt hit a nerve.

Flipping the right blinker, Austin pulled the camper to the side of the road and got out. Candice silently cursed her wayward tongue as she climbed into the driver's seat. She'd never driven anything so big before. As she waited for Austin to buckle up, she looked over the controls. Everything seemed familiar, and it was an automatic. What could be so difficult about it?

Trying to appear casual, she shifted the gear lever and checked her mirrors. She joined the flow of traffic so smoothly, she couldn't help smiling. A piece of cake, she decided, relaxing and enjoying the drive. From the corner of her eye, she noted that Austin wasn't watching her but flipping through the paper.

"You're not nervous with me driving?" she asked, darting a glance at him.

He shrugged, keeping his gaze on the paper. "Should I be?"

Unconvinced, she deliberately swerved.

He didn't even blink.

Several moments ticked by before she relented. "All right, so maybe you're not a sexist."

"Apology accepted." Now he did look at her, his eyes brimming with laughter. "But I really think you should pull over."

"Why?"

"Because that cop behind us thinks you're ignoring him."

Candice gasped and checked her side mirror, then gasped again when she saw the flashing lights. Oh, Lord, it really was a cop! She glared at Austin as she directed the RV to the side of the road. "Stop laughing. It isn't funny!"

Austin burst into fresh laughter.

Ignoring him, she found her purse and fished out her driver's license. A tapping at her window startled her. Seeing the uniform, she quickly rolled the window down. "Hello, officer." She tried smiling at him.

The state trooper remained stone-faced. "Can I see your license, ma'am?" His gaze narrowed in suspicion, he glanced beyond her to where Austin sat laughing and wiping his eyes.

"Certainly." Vowing to maim Austin the moment they were alone again, Candice handed the trooper her license.

He studied the card a moment, then looked at her long enough to bring a guilty flush to her checks. "I noticed you swerving, ma'am. Have you been drinking?"

For a moment, Candice was speechless. Austin hooted. She silenced him with a killing look before replying indignantly, "No, I have not been drinking."

"Would you step out of the vehicle, please?"

"You're joking, right?" Candice let out a shaky, disbelieving laugh. "Officer, I assure you that I have *not* been drinking. I'm going to have a baby!"

The trooper pointed her driver's license at Austin. "How about your husband, ma'am? Has he been drinking and driving?"

"No." Although she could certainly understand why he thought so! How could anyone breathe laughing so hard? As for the trooper assuming Austin was her husband, what else was he to think? Not only did they look like a happy couple on vacation, she had just declared she was pregnant. Imagine his shock if she blurted out, *"He's not my husband, he's my handyman and my lover."*

"You see, he wasn't watching me, he was actually reading the newspaper, so I . . ." She faltered, realizing just how silly her explanation sounded. The trooper looked as if he thought so, too. With a sinking heart, she watched as he flipped open the ticket book. She'd never gotten a ticket in her life!

"I'm going to give you a warning this time, ma'am."

Candice let out a breath of relief. "Oh, thank you, officer."

"But I'd advise you to save the fun and games until you're in the safety and *privacy* of your home."

"G-games?" Her jaw fell. Austin snickered.

"You do know it's against the law to expose yourself in public?"

Mortified, Candice began to shake her head vehemently. "You've got it all wrong, officer! I didn't mean—"

The trooper shoved the written warning into her hands and tipped his hat. "Drive carefully, ma'am."

She sat frozen in the seat, her face burning with embarrassment. To give Austin credit, his laughter had died to a ripple of chuckles interspersed with mirthful sighs. It wasn't his fault anyway, and she knew it. But did he have to laugh so damned hard?

It took a moment for her embarrassment to ease so that she could see the situation as he saw it. The trooper had actually believed she'd been flashing Austin, and all because of her stupid notion that Austin didn't think she was capable of driving the camper.

"Come here, woman."

Candice listened to the sound of his ludicrously deep drawl, her chagrin fading. A reluctant smile tugged at her lips. Wouldn't she have laughed if their roles had been reversed? Yes, she would have. She would have laughed until she cried, just as Austin had done.

She unfastened her seat belt and moved into his arms willingly, accepting his deep kiss and returning it with a fervor and desperation that matched his own. Finally, they came up for air.

Austin's gaze wandered over her face, all

traces of amusement gone. In fact, he looked so serious, Candice felt her heart skip a beat.

"No matter what happens, I want you to remember this moment, okay? And all the others we've shared."

"Austin—"

He put a finger to her lips, then replaced it with a tiny, tender kiss that melted her bones. "Promise me that you'll remember how good it is between us."

He wasn't talking about making love, Candice realized. He was talking about the closeness they felt, the funny moments they shared, and everything in between.

An icy shiver trailed down her spine as she stared into his somber eyes.

She saw pain and regret, and it frightened her as nothing ever had.

Candice let Austin drive the rest of the way to Sacramento. The incident with the trooper, followed by Austin's mysterious appeal, had left her drained and shaky. Austin had turned so fiercely solemn, where only moments before he'd been laughing, a seesawing of emotions that not only confused her but concerned her as well.

More than ever, she suspected that he was hiding something from her. Candice sighed and looked out her window, suddenly realizing Austin had taken a turn she didn't recognize.

She sat straighter as she asked, "Aren't we going home?" It was getting late; Mrs. Merryweather would be worried if they didn't arrive on schedule.

Austin gave his brief answer without taking his eyes from the road. "We've got one stop to make."

Slightly piqued that he didn't consult her about the detour, Candice reminded him, "Mrs. Merryweather is expecting us."

"We won't be too late."

As dusk fell subtly around them, he turned the camper left onto a residential street with the unlikely name of Jelly Bean Hill. Small, neat houses lined both sides of the streets. It was a middle-class neighborhood where children played and dogs barked and lawns were mowed every Saturday without fail.

Intrigued, Candice leaned forward as Austin turned into a narrow driveway and parked in front of a closed garage. Light filtered through curtains in the windows of the house. Austin sat still, drumming his fingers on the steering wheel until Candice grew impatient.

"Aren't you going in?"

"I want you to come with me."

He opened the door and came around to help her down before she had time to agree or disagree. With growing apprehension, she tried to catch his eye as he pulled her along the sidewalk to the front door.

"Austin, what—" She was interrupted as the door was suddenly yanked open.

To her amazement, Dr. Jack stood on the threshold. His gaze bounced off her. *He doesn't recognize me*, she thought, mildly pleased with the effectiveness of her disguise.

"Nice bone structure but a lousy dresser. Where's Mrs. Vanausdale? Say, isn't that your old football jersey she's wearing?"

"Jack, this—"

"And your favorite cap? Good grief, doesn't she have any hair? Is she clean? How many times have I warned you not to pick up hitch-hikers?"

"Jack—"

Jack's scornful gaze raked Candice from her worn sneakers to her capped head. "Honey, you'll have to find something to do while big brother and I talk. We've got a situation on our hands here."

Candice gaped at Dr. Jack, her gaze darting between the two men. Austin Hyde, with his shaggy blond hair and beautifully muscled body; Jack Cruise, a dark-haired little man who looked forever crumpled but always wore dress slacks, shirt, and a tie.

"You guys are *brothers?*" she breathed in disbelief.

Jack recognized her voice instantly. He paled, doing a double take. "Mrs. Vanausdale?"

Austin muttered a curse and guided her inside, forcing Jack to back away. Candice stood in the center of the living room, too stunned to move. Austin and Jack were brothers? But why hadn't Austin told her? Why say they were just friends? Could this be the reason he looked so worried? He thought she'd be angry because he hadn't told her? He'd mentioned a brother, but not that it was Jack!

Confused, Candice stared at Austin's tight expression. "What's going on?"

"Jack is my brother. My half brother. Same lousy mother, different lousy fathers."

Jack protested, "Hey, *mine* wasn't so lousy. At least he didn't—"

"Shut up. She's already heard the sordid details about my father."

This much was true, at least. "Austin, why didn't you tell me about Dr. Jack?"

"It's Dr. Jekyll," Austin corrected, still unsmiling. "I think you'll agree with me when you hear what he has to tell you."

Slowly, she turned to Dr. Jack, who looked about as bad as Austin. Same fearful gaze, same tight jaw. Yes, there was some resemblance, but one that urged her to run for her life.

"What is it you have to tell me, Dr. Jack? Is it—" Her breath caught. "Is it something about my baby?"

"Sit down, Mrs. Vanausdale."

"I don't want to sit down. I'm perfectly fine."

"I think you'd better sit—"

"Dammit, Jack, just tell her and get it over with!"

The raw agony in Austin's shout had Candice spinning around to face him. She locked her gaze onto his and said, "No, Austin. If there's some bad news about my baby, I want *you* to tell me." He'd had the last five days to tell her. Why hadn't he?

For a long moment, neither moved, and Jack was temporarily forgotten.

"Austin?" It was a whisper of hope. Until that moment, she hadn't been completely aware of how much she depended on him to keep the darkness at bay. How much she trusted him, loved him, and feared losing him.

Austin stuck his hands into his pockets, his voice unsteady as he said, "Howard was . . . sterile."

"*What?*" Candice stumbled back a step, fighting a sudden bout of dizziness. Surely she hadn't heard him right. "What did you say?"

Jack rose quickly and led her to a chair. Candice let him, feeling numb. When Jack started away, she grabbed his hand and forced him to look at her. "Is he telling the truth?" she demanded.

He nodded. "Howard came to me about six months before he died."

"Six months . . ." Candice shook her head, trying to absorb the shock of Austin's announcement and make sense of it all.

"He knew he was sterile, you see. Some kind of accident he had a few years before he met you."

"So what . . . how . . . why did he come to you?" Oh, she was afraid she knew but prayed she was wrong. Howard wouldn't do this to her, would he? She could see Austin standing very still, and she wondered how long he'd known. He looked as stunned as she, which didn't make sense.

Jack straightened and stepped away as if he feared she might explode. He hesitated, then said, "He gave me a list of requirements for a donor."

"Donor." Candice whispered the word. "Go on."

"He did this for you, because he'd promised you a baby, and he didn't want the media finding out that he couldn't father children." Jack shrugged and slid his gaze away. "He never meant for you to find out."

"Then why . . ." Of course. The paternity test. Dr. Jack had known what a shock it would be for her to find out from a stranger. How compassionate of him. If she could just forget his part in this deception, she might even manage to be grateful. But it had been wrong of

Howard not to trust her, and wrong of Dr. Jack to go along with Howard.

And terribly painful to realize that Austin, of all people, had known and had not told her.

"There's more."

She jerked her head up. "More?"

Jack began to pace. When she looked at Austin, she saw that he still hadn't moved. The only sign of life was the burning intensity of his gaze and the tiny flickering of a muscle in his jaw.

The sight of that guilty tic chilled her more than the sight of Jack pacing swiftly to and fro.

"The qualifications Howard demanded of the donor were nearly impossible to match." Jack waved a frustrated hand in the air in remembrance. "He wanted intelligence, an excellent physique, blond hair, athletic traits, artistic talent." He paused for breath. "There aren't many donors who meet the high standards of Mr. Vanausdale, I'll tell you."

But Candice was no longer listening to Jack's complaints about Howard's unreasonable demands, because she realized he had just described someone awfully familiar to her.

Someone she loved and trusted with her very heart.

Austin Hyde.

Chapter Twenty

Hope is a fragile emotion, a wisp of nothingness that can be squashed in a flash or lifted in a heartbeat, Austin thought as he watched Candice sway in her chair.

And for him, all hope was lost.

"Jack, leave us alone for a while."

Jack stopped pacing, glancing at Austin in surprise. "But I haven't told her the—"

"Get lost," Austin said in a carefully controlled voice. He felt on the edge of violence, like a storm about to unleash its fury. If Jack wasn't careful, he would get caught in the deluge.

"Austin, don't you want me to tell—"

"She knows."

"But I haven't told her—"

"I said, she knows. *Now get lost!*"

Finally, his words got through to Jack, who turned to look at Candice, his eyes widening on her pale face. With a wince and a grimace, he hurried out of the room.

Austin approached Candice and knelt before her. He wanted to touch her, but he didn't dare. She looked brittle enough to shatter.

Accordingly, he kept his voice soft and level. "Are you okay?"

The tiny laugh that escaped her taut lips was harsh and quick. She arched a brow above eyes curiously bright. "Why wouldn't I be? I just found out that my husband didn't trust me, and that instead of telling me the truth, he went behind my back and *ordered* a perfect baby. As in everything else, Howard never considered my feelings."

It was true, all of it, so what could he say?

"How long have you known?"

He wasn't ready for the question. He didn't think he would ever be. "Jack told me the day we first met outside the clinic." After a slight hesitation, Austin continued. "At first I was upset, but once I knew you, I forgot about being mad and started thinking about the baby, about *us*."

She locked her fingers together in her lap, obviously trying to hold the tears inside. Austin started to reach out, but she shook her head in warning. "No. Don't touch me. Everything is a lie, isn't it? Your kindness, and—" She choked but managed to recover. "Everything you did was because of the baby, wasn't it? You didn't want your baby raised by someone like your mother, so you were making sure that I fit your requirements. I guess you and Howard have a lot in common."

Austin flinched. It was a low blow, but he deserved every damned bit of it. He should have come clean, should have told her the truth at the beginning.

He didn't know what to say.

"And making love to me was another test, wasn't it Mr. Hyde? You wanted to see if there was any warmth in me, despite my alleged blue blood, right?" Her voice lowered to a whisper, but she might as well have shouted. "Well? Did I pass?"

Austin searched for moisture in his mouth and finally swallowed dry. "If it had been a test, you'd have passed with flying colors. But I made love to you because I *wanted* to. Because I couldn't resist you. It had nothing to do with the baby." When she looked incredulous that he should utter such a lie, he gripped her shoulders and held her still as his gaze burned into hers. "I love you. Don't you know that?"

With a surprisingly strong jerk, she broke

free. "I told you not to touch me. No, I don't know, because I don't believe you. How can I? You've lied to me, tricked me, and manipulated me. Really, Austin, you didn't have to go to such extremes."

Oh, why wouldn't she listen? "I admit that I tricked you into trusting me, but that was before I got to know you. It wasn't long before I realized that I liked you, and not long after before I knew it was more than that. I love you, Candice, and it doesn't have a damned thing to do with the baby!" One glance at her stony expression and Austin knew she wasn't listening. He ran a frustrated hand through his hair and stood. "Maybe you're just looking for an excuse."

She reeled as if he'd slapped her. "An excuse? An excuse for what? An excuse for trusting you? An excuse for believing in you? No, it's you, Austin, who's found an excuse. Why don't you just admit that it's the baby you want, not me?"

"And what good will wanting you do me?" Austin asked, losing his temper. "I'm just a painter, someone beneath your lofty class." He almost regretted his words when she paled another shade, but he couldn't stop until he'd purged his own fears. "One of the reasons I didn't tell you is because I was afraid of losing you. Having a fling with the handyman is one thing; having a *future* with him is another, isn't it?"

Candice rallied, color returning to her face in a heated rush. She jumped to her feet. "Who's the real snob here, Austin? Sounds like you're the one who judges people by how much money they have." Finally, the tears drifted over her bottom lashes and rolled down her cheeks.

Austin turned, his gaze following her stiff walk to the door. Still in her disguise, she reminded him of a teenager with an attitude. God, he loved her. For richer or for poorer, for better or worse . . . Somehow, he would have to convince her of his love, but right now he suspected she was too stunned by both Jack's news and his own apparent deception.

At the door she paused and ripped the cap from her head, sending her hair cascading around her shoulders. Despite her fury, she was breathtakingly beautiful.

"Money is not the most important asset a person can have, Austin. Love is. I learned that lesson the hard way."

With those words, she sent his cap sailing through the air. He caught it, wishing he could erase her haunted expression.

"I'll be in the camper," she said, "while you talk to your *brother*."

"Candice, I—"

The slamming of the door left him talking to the air. And left his heart in shambles.

The story broke with a vengeance, and the reporter Candice had promised an interview to took full advantage of the hype by printing his own story, complete with photographs of Candice and Austin by the pool.

Candice simply didn't care anymore—about the publicity, the scandal, or the Vanausdale money. She wasn't even curious about how the media came by the information.

During the following week, she tried to forget Austin. She tried, but she couldn't. Everywhere she turned, she was reminded of him. The hedges shaped in the form of animals, the Oriental rugs, Tiny and her puppies, the doghouse, the rocking chair he'd retouched for the nursery—and the nursery itself. The nursery was the very essence of Austin.

She thought about redoing the room, to erase her poignant memories, but as she surveyed its kaleidoscope of colors, its unique decor, the bear paintings on the walls, she knew she wouldn't change a thing.

Austin Hyde might have ripped a hole in her heart, but *he* had taken up permanent residence there. She couldn't bring herself to destroy a single brush stroke.

With a sigh, she sat in the rocker by the window and examined the framed paintings. There were eight in all, each dancing bear dressed in a different costume, from the mismatched clothing of a hobo to the formal attire of a tuxedo. Her favorite was the bear wearing faded jeans and a worn cotton shirt open to the waist. His engaging grin and casual outfit reminded her of Austin.

Austin. She missed him terribly, and with each passing day, the hollow feeling in her chest grew bigger.

When she'd realized that Austin was the father of her baby, her first reaction was swift and irrefutable. She had been elated, delirious. After all, it was exactly what she had been wishing for. Yet, almost immediately, ugly doubts had stolen in and crushed her joy. Doubts about why he had befriended her, then later, made love to her. Maybe Austin himself didn't realize that everything he'd done had been for the sole sake of the baby.

Oh, sure, she'd believed him when he confessed he'd been upset with Jack for doing what he did. And she could understand why he'd changed his mind about the baby after he'd had time to adjust to the idea.

And while it would make her the happiest woman in the world to believe that he loved her, she feared it was an illusion, maybe one he believed in himself.

Mrs. Merryweather came into the room as the natural light began to dim, throwing shadows onto the nursery floor. "So there you are. I've been looking all over the place for you."

Candice glanced at her, then returned her gaze to the paintings on the wall. She pushed the rocking chair with one foot, finding a small measure of comfort in the soothing motion.

"Our Mr. Hyde's got talent, doesn't he?" Mrs. Merryweather said, following the line of Candice's vision. "A bear from every walk of life." She craned her neck at the ceiling. "And that circus—it's unbelievable."

Candice agreed without much spirit. "He's a very good artist. The baby will love this room."

The housekeeper frowned. "He didn't do this just for the baby, Mrs. Dale. He did it for you."

Candice felt a spark of energy stir to life. She swung her gaze to Mrs. Merryweather. "How can you say that? He knew he was the father all along. I should have suspected something, the way he knocked himself out doing things for the baby. And the camping trip? Just another manipulative plan to win me over and to soften the blow."

"Hmm." The housekeeper moved to the chest of drawers and turned the lamp on. "The way I see it, he did it all for you because he knew how much you wanted this baby. I don't know how you can blame the man for being confused, considering how things happened. Don't forget, he was just as surprised as you were, only a bit sooner."

Candice had told the housekeeper everything, leaving out only the most intimate details; there was just so much humilation she was willing to share. "He should have told me sooner."

"Would you have believed him?" She didn't give Candice time to answer. "I don't think so. And if you *had* believed him, you didn't know him, and you would have been shocked to find out your baby's father was a total stranger. Instead, he waited until you two got to know each, didn't he?"

Candice stopped rocking. "How do you know he would have told me at all if that reporter hadn't taken those pictures and Raymond and Donald hadn't demanded a paternity test?"

Mrs. Merryweather clucked her tongue. "You know Mr. Hyde better than that. I think he was bursting to tell you, but he was afraid."

Austin had tried to say as much.

"I came to find you because there's something I think you should see, but give me a moment to fetch Lucy. She's missed her morning swim since Mr. Hyde started working on the pool."

Still pondering Mrs. Merryweather's insights, Candice waited for the housekeeper to return with the ferret before following her onto the patio. Lucy scrambled down, heading as fast as her little legs could scurry to the pool.

The ferret didn't jump in as Candice expected her to. Instead, she hovered on the edge, then whirled and came running back in their direction. Mrs. Merryweather laughed and scooped her up.

"They're not real, sweetheart."

Bewildered, Candice stared at the housekeeper. "What's not real? Why didn't she jump in?"

"Come see for yourself. It was another one of Mr. Hyde's surprises, and I hate it that he's not here to see your face."

Me, too, Candice thought, wondering when the ache would lessen. She sighed. Not as long as she was constantly reminded of Austin and his crazy way of surprising her. She followed the housekeeper to the edge of the pool and looked down into the clear blue water.

Wonder rounded her eyes. Illuminated by the underground pool lights, dolphins, Manta rays, whales, and a school of brilliantly striped fish appeared to be moving beneath the gently lapping water.

It took a moment for Candice to realize the gorgeous creatures had been painted onto the walls and floor of the pool.

"They look real," she breathed finally, not

knowing whether to laugh or cry. "No wonder Lucy wouldn't jump in."

Mrs. Merryweather chuckled. "Poor man wore himself out to get this done before you got suspicious. He may not be good with words, and he might be clumsy at showing you how he feels, but he sure can express himself with a paintbrush."

"Yes, he can." To Candice's dismay, she felt silly tears sting her eyes.

Mrs. Merryweather patted her shoulder, and Lucy tried to reach her face with her tongue from the safety of the housekeeper's arms. Candice laughed, but the sound emerged as a sob. "I can't seem to stop crying these days."

"It's normal. When I was pregnant, everything used to make me cry. Good and bad. Jim walked around feeling guilty all the time for no reason."

Suddenly, a shadow fell across the water to her left. It wasn't Mrs. Merryweather, because she stood on her right.

Candice turned, her breath hitching at the sight of Austin standing behind her. Big and silent, disturbing and wonderful.

"Well, I'd better get Lucy inside and feed her a little supper," the housekeeper said briskly, seeming not at all surprised by their unexpected visitor. The next moment, she'd disappeared through the patio doors, leaving Candice alone with Austin.

A week. An entire week had passed, and Candice soaked up the sight of him, not caring if he knew she stared or if he could see the hunger in her eyes.

He spoke first. "I'm glad you like the pool."

"I—I do. I mean, it's unusual, but then—" She stopped before she added *it's just like you*, realizing he might be offended by her comment. There had been so much misunderstanding between them already.

"I've missed you." He took a step forward, closing in. His voice was rough as he repeated, "I've missed you like hell."

Candice swallowed, tingling with anticipation. Another step and they would be touching. "I've missed you, too." Without thinking, she took the final step that brought them together. Her pulse leaped at his harsh intake of breath when her nipples, already hard and thrusting, grazed his chest.

How could she have been so blind? His reactions to her had been too spontaneous, too heartfelt, to be faked. No, what sizzled between them had nothing to do with the baby.

And everything to do with love.

Their lips met in a welcoming, yearning kiss that quickly deepened to burning desire.

Candice trembled from the force of her need, and when she slipped her palms to his chest, she found that he, too, trembled.

Brazenly, she began to back him in the direction of the patio doors and her room. She wanted—*needed*—the reassurance of his love.

Austin caught her shoulders, breathing harshly, caressing her face with hot, glazed eyes. "What about reporters?" As he asked the question, he searched the area behind her.

Candice smiled, running a teasing tongue across her bottom lip. Her smile widened as he groaned. "Does it matter? Besides, there isn't much they don't already know." She grabbed his hands and moved them to cover her breasts, closing her eyes at the burning contact.

With a soft growl that weakened her knees, he took her nipples between his fingers and squeezed gently. Candice began to walk them backward again, reaching around him to slide the doors open. Austin lifted her into his arms and carried her to the bed, then returned to close the doors and dim the lights.

Candice watched him, stunned by the urgency she felt to have him inside her. When he returned to the bed, she wasted no time removing his clothes, while he did the same to her.

"I want to make love to you all night," he

whispered huskily, sliding his mouth along her belly as he rolled her shorts over her hips and thighs.

"No." The denial startled Candice, coming from her own lips as it did. "We've got the rest of our lives to make love slowly. I want you *now*."

Austin didn't argue. He stripped the rest of her clothes off in a frenzy, then finished discarding his own. As hot flesh melded with cool satin, he cupped her face and looked into her eyes.

Candice held her breath, awed by the powerful love she saw shimmering in his gaze.

"I love you, Candice. I want to marry you and have many, many babies—the old-fashioned way. I want to wake up beside you every morning, make love to you night and day, and grow old with you."

She smiled. "I love you, Austin Hyde, and I want to do all of those things, too. But right now . . ." She lifted her hips in a silent plea and pulled his mouth to hers.

Austin eased inside her, filling her so completely, she feared she would burst. Instinctively, he set a frantic pace that exploded into a starburst of pleasure.

They managed to stifle their mingled cries in a sealing kiss as they drifted back to earth, shaken and exhilarated.

* * *

For the first time in his life, Austin was having benevolent thoughts about Jack. If not for Jack, he wouldn't have met Candice and fallen in love. If not for Jack, he wouldn't be feeling so sated and content with Candice, he hoped, feeling the same as she lay in his arms. If not for Jack, there would be no baby—this special baby.

Austin's joy faded a little as he thought of something he had failed to mention to Candice. Tightening his arms around her, he said, "There's something I need to tell you." He felt her stiffen and couldn't resist a chuckle. "It's not *that* bad."

She lifted her head from his chest and looked at him apprehensively. "Tell me."

There was no easy way to say it, Austin thought, so he just blurted it out. "I paid Pete Clancy fifty thousand dollars to keep his mouth shut."

"My stepfather?" Astonished, Candice sat up. "But how did he know?"

"He was hiding in the closet at my apartment, and he heard me and Jack talking."

"So he blackmailed you." Her lips twisted slightly. "It doesn't surprise me. But I *am* surprised you paid him."

"I didn't want you hearing the news from anyone but me."

She relaxed against him again, feathering her fingers across his chest in a way that made it hard to concentrate on anything else. "So you gave away your inheritance for me."

"Uh, not exactly all of it." Austin prepared himself for one more confession. He had no idea how she would react when he told her. "I've got a few million left."

"A few million?" she squeaked out.

"Ten, to be exact. Minus fifty thousand. It's been sitting in the bank for twenty-two years." When she didn't respond, he squeezed her. "What are you thinking?"

"I'm trying to figure out how much interest ten million dollars would draw in twenty-two years."

As Austin struggled against disappointment and tried to understand, he felt her shoulders begin to shake.

No doubt about it; she was laughing!

"What?" he growled, flipping her onto her back and looming over her. "What's so funny?"

"You!" she gasped between guffaws. "You thought I was serious, didn't you?"

Austin slowly pinned her arms above her head. It was hard to stay focused with Candice squirming beneath him. "Do you have any ideas about what to do with ten million dollars?"

Candice was silent for a moment, her face

already flushed with anticipation of what he was about to do to her. Suddenly her eyes flared wide. "Why don't you open a drug rehabilitation clinic for those who can't afford to pay? That way you'd be helping to reverse some of the damage your father did."

His last lingering, shameful doubt about Candice melted away, leaving Austin whole and secure. He slowly lowered his body onto hers, his voice unsteady as his mouth drew closer to hers. "That's a hell of a good idea."

"I've got another one," she mumbled, her eyelids drifting down.

"What's that?"

Her lashes flew upward, revealing passion and a hint of mischief. "How about a swim?"

Austin smiled, remembering their last encounter in the pool. "Think you can handle the sea creatures?"

"Absolutely."

"Find your swimsuit. I'm afraid my briefs will have to do."

Moments later, they were ready. Grabbing her hand, Austin opened the sliding patio doors and started to pull her through.

The reporter standing on the other side shrieked in surprise.

Candice let out a startled scream, and Austin growled, recognizing the familiar face. Then all hell broke loose. The reporter stumbled backward, trying to run while keeping his terrified gaze on a bellowing Austin.

He forgot about the pool.

There was a mighty splash, quickly followed by a piercing scream as the reporter caught sight of the sea animals that seemed to be moving all around him. He scrambled to the side and leaped out of the pool, slipping and sliding in his attempt to run for his life. His ruined camera hindered his progress, popping him in the chin. By the time he reached the woods, he was sobbing.

"Should I let Tiny go?" Austin asked, restrained laughter rumbling from his chest.

Candice shook her head, her lips twitching. "I think he's suffered enough."

Their gazes locked. They collapsed against each other, tears of laughter streaming down their faces. Finally, Austin recovered enough to grab her and tumble them into the water.

They came together, hip to hip, mouth to mouth.

"I love you," Austin gasped.

"And I love you."

Locked in a lover's kiss, they sank slowly to the bottom.

Epilogue

"So you see, Your Honor, Howard Vanausdale was the mastermind behind this unusual scheme to give his wife the child she so desperately wanted, and Mrs. Vanausdale, his wife, was completely innocent and unaware of his plans to acquire an anonymous donor. It was an act of unselfish love on Howard Vanausdale's part and surely proves that we should honor his last will and testament, which clearly states that after a generous bequest to each of his sons, the remainder of his wealth goes to Candice Vanausdale."

Bravo, Austin inwardly applauded, deciding he liked Luke McVey after all. And Mrs. McVey.

What a nice woman she was, a perfect wife for the distinguished lawyer. He glanced at Candice, his eyes softening as he took in the breathtaking sight of his wife and daughter. No matter how much time he spent watching them, he could never get enough.

At six weeks, little Jacklyn Suzanne Hyde already showed signs of taking after her mother. She had the ability to bring Austin to his knees with merely a look, a smile, a gurgling coo.

Candice glanced up and caught her husband watching them, as she often did. Right now he was staring at Jacklyn, his expression one of total absorption. When he finally lifted his gaze to hers, his eyes instantly darkened with love, edged with an unmistakable hunger.

It was a mutual feeling.

Sitting behind them, Jack leaned forward and patted Candice on the shoulder. "Well, congratulations!"

She was only aware of Jack's words as Austin's gaze held hers, reminding her of past heated moments, of urgent lovemaking. It had been well over six weeks since . . .

Without taking his gaze from the promise in hers, Austin asked Jack, "What happened?"

Jack looked from one to the other, releasing an exasperated breath. "Well, if you two guys would pay attention, you'd know. Candice won. She's rich again." He squeezed Austin's shoulder. "And you, big brother, are a sap."

Austin smiled, and Candice's heart did a funny flip-flop.

"Yes, I am."

"Yeah, well, if you guys need a baby-sitter—"

"No!" they both said hastily.

Jack affected a hurt look. "She's my niece! My namesake! What do you think I'd do to her? I'm learning a lot back in medical school. No way would I need to experiment on my little Jacklyn."

People were exiting the courtroom, Candice realized, finally tearing her gaze from Austin's. She placed Jacklyn into his willing arms, then pulled something out of her purse. Together, they stood and joined the flow of people moving down the aisle.

When they drew even with Raymond and Donald Vanausdale, Candice held out the diamond-studded watch Austin had found beneath her window many months ago. "I believe this belongs to one of you?"

Raymond glowered at her and snatched the watch from her hand, his mouth open to snarl something nasty. He clamped it shut as Austin's shadow fell over him.

But Austin wasn't watching Raymond. He was watching the enticing swing of Candice's fanny in the short hunter-green skirt that hugged her waist and outlined her hips.

"Ooooaahhh," Jacklyn cooed softly.

Startled, Austin glanced down at his equally gorgeous daughter. He grinned. "Oooaahhh is right, sweetheart. How about a nice long visit with Nanny Merryweather tonight?"

"Bllllaaah."

"Great. I'm glad you don't mind, because Mommy and I have to . . . talk. Yeah, we need to talk about your future. You don't want to be an only child, do you?"

Candice cleared her throat. Austin jerked his head up with a guilty start, grinning sheepishly at her narrow-eyed, amused expression. He had one pure thought among the erotic fantasies filling his mind: *Thank you, Jack.*

THE LOVE POTION
SANDRA HILL

Get Ready . . . For the Time of Your Life!

A love potion in a jelly bean? Fame and fortune are surely only a swallow away when Dr. Sylvie Fontaine discovers a chemical formula guaranteed to attract the opposite sex. Though her own love life is purely hypothetical, the shy chemist's professional future is assured . . . as soon as she can find a human guinea pig. The only problem is the wrong man has swallowed Sylvie's love potion. Bad boy Lucien LeDeux is more than she can handle even before he's dosed with the Jelly Bean Fix. The wildly virile lawyer is the last person she'd choose to subject to the scientific method. When the dust settles, Sylvie and Luc have the answers to some burning questions—Can a man die of testosterone overload? Can a straight-laced female lose every single one of her inhibitions?—and they learn that old-fashioned romance is still the best catalyst for love.

___52349-3 $5.99 US/$6.99 CAN

Dorchester Publishing Co., Inc.
P.O. Box 6640
Wayne, PA 19087-8640

Please add $1.75 for shipping and handling for the first book and $.50 for each book thereafter. NY, NYC, and PA residents, please add appropriate sales tax. No cash, stamps, or C.O.D.s. All orders shipped within 6 weeks via postal service book rate. Canadian orders require $2.00 extra postage and must be paid in U.S. dollars through a U.S. banking facility.

Name_____
Address_____
City_____ State_____ Zip_____
I have enclosed $_____ in payment for the checked book(s).
Payment <u>must</u> accompany all orders. ❏ Please send a free catalog.
CHECK OUT OUR WEBSITE! www.dorchesterpub.com

Masquerade

Katherine Deauxville, Elaine Fox, Linda Jones, & Sharon Pisacreta

In the whirling decadence of Carnival, all forms of desire are unveiled. Amidst the crush of those attending the balls, filling the waterways, and traveling in the gondolas of post-Napoleonic Venice, nothing is unavailable—should one know where to look. Amongst the throngs are artists and seducers, nobles and thieves, and not all of them are what they appear. But in that frantic congress of people lurks something more than animal passion, something more than a paradise of the flesh. Love, should one seek it out, can be found within this shadowy communion of people—and as four beauties learn, all one need do is unmask it.

___4577-X $5.99 US/$6.99 CAN

Romeo & Julia
Annie Kimberlin

Liz Hadley is a cat person, and since she doesn't currently own a kitten, there is nothing that she wants more. The stray that was found in the snowy library parking lot is perfect; she can't wait to go home and cuddle. Still, the arms that hold the cat aren't so bad, either. The man her co-workers call Romeo apparently also has a soft spot for all things furry, though it appears to be the only soft spot on his entire body. The man has the build of a Greek god and his eyes are something altogether more heavenly. And in the poetry of his kisses, the lovely librarian finds something more profound than she's ever read and something sweeter than she's ever known.

___52341-8 $5.50 US/$6.50 CAN

Dorchester Publishing Co., Inc.
P.O. Box 6640
Wayne, PA 19087-8640

SECOND OPINION
EVELYN ROGERS

Lousy in bed, was she? What Dr. Charlotte Hamilton needs is a second opinion. Her ex-husband hurled the insult at her the moment their divorce was final, and the blow to the attractive doctor's self-esteem left her wanting to prove him wrong. Drowning her sorrows in a margarita, she finds herself flirting with a sandy-haired hunk at the bar. She isn't the one-night-stand type, but suddenly they are in a hotel room, where with his expert touch and stunningly sexy body, he proves her anything but lousy. But what she writes off as a one-night stand, Sam Blake sees as the beginning of something wonderful. In that one night, the handsome sportswriter is smitten. Sam will do anything to make the stubborn doctor his—even deny his own urges until she agrees to an old-fashioned date. And he is determined to give her the second opinion she really needs—not of sex, but of true love.

___52332-9 $5.99 US/$6.99 CAN